Praise for

A CONSPIRACY
OF FRIENDS

and the Corduroy Mansions series

"This third volume of Chekhovian soap opera is every bit as addictive as the first two." —*Kirkus Reviews*

"You cannot beat McCall Smith for subtle musings shot through with insight and wit. His deft characterization enlivens the inner workings of everyday characters. His work offers a heartening view of [the] world." —*The Daily Telegraph* (London)

"[Full] of warmth and wisdom and easy, accomplished writing that begs for a comfy chair." —*The Times* (London)

"Whimsical. . . . McCall Smith specializes in subplots that punctuate the book like polka dots, relying on his considerable literary skills to link them into a merry pattern of human events." —*The Washington Times*

"Quirky and original. . . . Told with warmth, wit and intelligence, and McCall Smith's cast of characters are beautifully observed." —*Daily Express*

Alexander McCall Smith

A CONSPIRACY
OF FRIENDS

Alexander McCall Smith is the author of the international phenomenon The No. 1 Ladies' Detective Agency series, the Isabel Dalhousie series, the Portuguese Irregular Verbs series, the 44 Scotland Street series, and the Corduroy Mansions series. He is professor emeritus of medical law at the University of Edinburgh in Scotland and has served on many national and international organizations concerned with bioethics.

www.alexandermccallsmith.com

BOOKS BY ALEXANDER MCCALL SMITH

A CONSPIRACY
OF FRIENDS

ALEXANDER McCALL SMITH

A CONSPIRACY OF FRIENDS

ANCHOR BOOKS

A DIVISION OF RANDOM HOUSE, INC.

NEW YORK

FIRST ANCHOR BOOKS EDITION, MAY 2013

The Library of Congress has cataloged the Pantheon edition as follows:
McCall Smith, Alexander.
A conspiracy of friends : a Corduroy Mansions novel / Alexander McCall Smith.
p. cm.
1. Neighborhoods—England—London—Fiction. 2. City and town life—
England—London—Fiction. 3. Pimlico (London, England)—Social life and
customs—Fiction. 4. Terriers—Fiction. I. Title.
PR6063.C326C665 2012
823'.914—dc23
2011051041

Anchor ISBN: 978-0-307-94800-7

Book design by Virginia Tan

www.anchorbooks.com

Printed in the United States of America
10 9 8 7 6 5 4 3 2 1

This book is for
Neville and Judy Moir
in gratitude

A CONSPIRACY
OF FRIENDS

1. The Only Unpleasant Liberal Democrat

OEDIPUS SNARK HAD a number of distinctions in this life. The first of these—and perhaps the most remarkable—was that he was, by common consent, the only truly nasty Liberal Democrat Member of Parliament. This was not just an accolade bestowed upon him by journalists in search of an amusing soubriquet; it was a judgement agreed upon by all those who knew him, including, most notably, his mother. Berthea Snark, a well-known psychoanalyst who lived in a small, undistinguished mews house behind Corduroy Mansions, had tried very hard to love her son, but had eventually given up, thus joining that minuscule group—mothers who cannot abide their sons. So rare is the phenomenon, and so willing are most mothers to forgive their sons any shortcoming, that this demographic—that is to say, in English, *these people*—is completely ignored by marketeers. And that, as we all know, is the real test of significance. If marketeers ignore you, you are not worth bothering about; you are nothing; you are—to put it brutally—a *non-demographic.*

So intense was Berthea's distaste for her son that she had once seriously contemplated arranging a DNA test to see whether there was any chance that Oedipus had been mixed up with her real infant in hospital and given to the wrong mother. She knew that this was clutching at straws, but she had read about such errors in a popular psychology magazine and concluded that there was a chance, just a chance, that it had happened to her. The author of the article had for years researched the psychological profile of those who had

3

lived a large part of their life under a false belief as to the identity of their father and had only later discovered the mistake. In the course of discussing this not entirely uncommon problem, the author had casually mentioned two cases of a rather different error, where the woman thought to be mother was discovered not to be mother after all.

One of these cases had been of a boy who had been given by his mother to her sister in an act of generosity. The donor, who had six children already, had decided that her childless sister's need for a baby was greater than her own and had generously—and not without some relief—donated this seventh child. It had worked to the satisfaction of all, and when the truth slipped out—as the truth sometimes does in spite of our best efforts to conceal it—the reaction of the boy, now a young man of eighteen, had been admirable. There had been no recriminations, or sense of betrayal: he had gone straight to the florist, purchased a large bouquet of flowers and handed it to the woman who he had assumed all those years was his real mother. *Love*, he had written on the accompanying card, *is thicker than blood.*

Berthea could not imagine Oedipus doing such a thing. In fact, she found it difficult to remember when her son had last given her a present; not that she held it against him, even if she had noted it as a point that she might at least touch upon in a suitable chapter of the unauthorised biography of him that she was currently writing. And here was the second of his distinctions: there are few, if any, examples of hostile biographies written by mothers. Berthea, though, was well advanced in her plans, and the manuscript of the work provisionally entitled *My Son Oedipus* was already two hundred and ten typewritten pages long.

Those pages took us only as far as the end of Oedipus's schooldays. He had been sent to boarding school when he was ten, spending a short time at a very dubious prep school in the West Country before winning a scholarship to Uppingham. The prep school, now closed down by the authorities, was found to be a money-laundering scheme dreamed up by an Irish racehorse owner; and while the boys were for the most part entirely happy (not surprisingly, given that the headmaster took them to the racetrack three times a week), their education left a great deal to be desired. Oedipus, though, had thrived, and had won the Uppingham scholarship by arranging for another boy at the school, an intellectual prodigy, to impersonate him in the scholarship examination. This had the desired result and brought, rather to the surprise of his mother, an offer of a full scholarship, covering the cost of tuition and boarding.

"I know I'm failing as a mother," Berthea confessed to a friend at the time. "I'm perfectly aware of that. But, quite frankly, much as I love my son, I'm always relieved when Oedipus goes off to school. I know I shouldn't feel this, but it's as if a great load is lifted from my shoulders each time I see him off. I feel somehow liberated."

"I'm not surprised," said the friend. "And you mustn't reproach yourself. Your son is a particularly unpleasant child—I've always thought so."

This verdict on Oedipus was shared by almost all his contemporaries at school. When Berthea had advertised in the school association magazine for "recollections—no matter how frank—of the schooldays of Oedipus Snark, MP," she had been astonished by the unanimity of opinion.

"I remember Oedipus Snark quite well," wrote one of her informants. "He was the one we all disliked intensely. I'm sorry to have to tell you this, as I gather that you're his mother, but we really couldn't stand the sight of him. What on earth possessed you to have him?"

And there was this from another: "Can you give me his current address? I promise I won't pass it on to anybody. I just want to know—for my own purposes."

Of course, Berthea did not pass on her son's address to that particular correspondent. She did not want Oedipus to meet any physical misfortune; she wanted him simply to be exposed, to be made to confront his shortcomings, to *accept responsibility*. And was there anything wrong with that? she wondered. Does it make me any the less of a mother for wanting to see justice done?

She had thought long and hard about what it was to be a mother. And from that, inspired by the article she read about disproof of maternity, the idea came to her that there had been a fairly long pause between the point at which Oedipus was taken from her in the maternity ward and the moment he was returned to her bedside. It was, she remembered, at least an hour, and during that time, as a nurse informed her, another three babies had been born.

"We've been worked off our feet, Mrs. Snark," said the nurse. "Four babies in two hours! All of them boys. A population explosion, that's what it is."

Berthea now thought: four boys, all lying in those tiny cots they put newborn babies in; physically indistinguishable, at that age, one from the other; identified only by a little plastic bracelet which could so easily slip off, be picked up and put on the wrong baby. Surely it could happen. Or was that just wishful thinking?

2. Nothing Can Be Everything; Everything Can Be Nothing

BERTHEA HAD NOT been surprised when she heard that Oedipus was going into politics, as she had come to know enough about politicians to understand that her son had all the qualities needed for that calling. Her psychotherapeutic practice in Pimlico was conveniently close to a large complex of flats—Dolphin Square—in which a number of politicians lived during the parliamentary term. This had proved to be a godsend when she had first set up, as it was simplicity itself for tired MPs, returning from the Commons, to slip unseen through Berthea's unmarked doorway and spend an hour unravelling the skeins of memory. Some of them went away much better, or at least relieved of some private angst or uncertainty; others found that the famous talking cure merely induced dependence on the therapist. On occasion this had put Berthea in an awkward position, as highly placed politicians—sometimes senior members of the government—would ask her to make decisions for them. It was not widely known, for instance, that at least one previous Chancellor of the Exchequer had asked her to help him with a difficult choice in the making of the budget. This minister, who arrived for therapy in a plain black government car, had slipped into the habit of calling Berthea *Mother*, a practice that she had tried unsuccessfully to stop.

"It's very difficult, Mother," he said. "I have to maximise tax receipts without giving the impression that I'm picking on anybody. What do I do?"

"Do you really need to gather tax?" she asked.

He had not hesitated in answering. "I do. And to tell the truth I enjoy it. I like to see the figures accumulating. I want to hold on to the money."

"And not give it away again?"

This had been followed by a short silence. Berthea waited. She had sometimes waited forty minutes for an answer and it was almost always worth it. Even when nothing is being said, she remembered learning in her analysis training, it's all being said. Nothing can be everything, she reminded herself; and everything can be nothing.

Eventually the chancellor spoke. "No, I do not like to give it away again." He lowered his voice. Now it was as if he were talking to himself; engaged in some private soliloquy. "It's mine, you see, Mother. Mine."

That unguarded revelation, like many of the little remarks that can give so much away, told her all she needed to know about her patient. She would have to move him gently, she decided; she would have to nudge him away from the retentive phase into the sunny uplands of the next stage, when retentive impulses would fade and he could give more freely. The responsibility, though, wore heavily on her. Bankers and chancellors of the Exchequer were by nature retentive; if she encouraged this man to be something different, then would he be an effective chancellor? What if he became liberal—profligate, even—with the nation's financial resources?

It was intriguing but nowhere near as interesting as the sessions she later had with one of the ministers in the Foreign Office. This man, although not yet Foreign Secretary, was clearly heading for that office, and was being tried in a junior, but nonetheless influential post. He was a vivid dreamer, and rather unusually had no difficulty recalling his dreams in fine detail.

"I was walking through a field," he said. "I was by myself, but I felt quite happy, perhaps even carefree. It was like that feeling you have at the end of term, when you're at school."

"Tell me about it."

"Well, it's a feeling of lightness, of possibility. You no longer have exams to worry about. Summer stretches before you in all its promise. It's a marvellous feeling—a feeling of complete freedom."

"I see. So you were in a field, and you felt like that. Free."

"Yes. And suddenly I looked up and saw house martins darting about the sky. They were not swallows—they were house martins. I remember saying to myself, 'Those birds are house martins.' You know how they fly? They swoop and dip, all so quickly, so very quickly. One moment they're above you and the next they're at the other edge of the sky."

She encouraged him to continue. "A field. House martins."

"That's right," he continued. "And then I saw that at the end of the field there was a line of trees. These followed the course of a river, a rather broad river, I think. And there was a group of people sitting on the bank having a picnic. I could tell even from the other side of the field that they were having a picnic. Rather like Monet's painting. You know the one? Where the women picnickers have no clothes on."

"Manet."

"No, Monet."

Berthea shook her head. "Monet's picnickers are all clad," she said. "Nobody has taken off their clothes in Monet's picnic. Or not at the stage when Monet painted it. Perhaps that came later; history does not record."

"Manet then."

Berthea nodded. Nudity was a common feature of dreams; there was no surprise in that. "So you saw a group of people on the bank of the river. Did you join them?"

He nodded. "I walked over and sat down with them. There were plates of sandwiches and glasses of wine. They welcomed me; I felt perfectly at home. Then one of them said, 'There is more than enough for all of us. Please join us. There is nothing to pay.'"

Berthea listened gravely. "And then?" It would not have surprised her had there been a sudden change in the tenor of the dream. Harmonious dreams were often abruptly spoiled by some dark development: a snake lurking in the garden.

"I joined them," said the minister. "But I remember asking, 'Are you sure there's enough for everybody?' They smiled, and reassured me that there was."

"I'm glad to hear it." She paused. "And who were they, these people? Did you know them?"

"They were Belgians," said the minister. "I knew this because one of them said, 'We are from Brussels.'"

Berthea said nothing, but she made a note in her records. *Dreams of the European Union*, she wrote. *Belgians enjoying a gourmet picnic, some unclothed.* She thought for a moment and then added: *Insecurity. Feelings of exclusion.* And then added: *Euro-envy?*

3. The Moment of Realisation

IN EVERY CHANGE that takes place—whether it be a change in human affairs or a change in the condition of the world—there is presumably some moment when a Rubicon is crossed. In the grand evolutionary scheme of things, there must have been a time—an actual day, no doubt—when, having emerged from the primeval slime, there were more of us who found dry land congenial than preferred the watery habitat we left behind. There must have been a moment, too, when more of us stood upright than on all fours; or when more of us could use jawbones as tools than could not. Or in language, the Great Vowel Shift that occurred in English over centuries must have known a point when more speakers used the new vowel sounds than the old.

Such significant changes may be almost geological in their pace, even if they do have their moment of no return. In human relations, time is considerably accelerated and feelings can change, if not exactly with the wind, at least quite quickly. And there, too, one might pinpoint the moment when we become aware that we no longer feel that which we felt only a few days, or perhaps even hours, before. So most of us have had the experience of coming to the realisation that we no longer like or love another whom we liked or loved before. *Eingang,* as John Betjeman observed in "In the Public Gardens," we were in love again, and *Ausgang* we were out.

Berthea could identify the moment when she admitted to herself her dislike of her son, Oedipus. It came at a curious moment, while she was talking on the telephone to Oedipus, who, having recently been adopted as a parliamentary candidate, was giving a party for constituency volunteers. These were the people who stuffed leaflets into envelopes and trudged around the streets putting these envelopes through the letterboxes of the voters. They were worthy people, Berthea thought; committed citizens who had ideas about the world and how it should be governed. They were not her type, of course; Berthea could not engage in the problems relating to drains and primary schools that fired the imaginations of these people, but she recognised the importance of such matters and could listen, though with a slightly glazed expression, while the faithful volunteers expostulated on them at some length. Most of what they said, of course, had an underlying theme, which was that society should, if at all possible, be given better drains and primary schools. This was unobjectionable enough—indeed it was positively laudable— but Berthea could not help but notice that such people devoted rather less energy to the issue of how we were to earn or make the things that we wanted to give to those who currently lacked them. If that issue was raised with the enthusiasts, as Berthea occasionally tried to do, then it was their turn to become glassy-eyed.

Initially, Berthea had had no idea why Oedipus had invited her to this particular party. It might have been pride, she thought; to give her the chance to see the adulation which he received from some of these volunteers.

"That nice Mr. Snark," she had overheard one of them say, "he's so *sensitive.*"

She had looked wide-eyed at the maker of this comment and felt a strong urge to correct her. "But he's far from nice," she wanted to say. "He really isn't."

She knew, though, that she could not say it, not even to herself . . . And yet, having *thought* the words, had she not uttered them to herself?

But she accepted the invitation to the party, which was held in the rooms in a run-down office building that the landlord, a Liberal Democrat, made available at a reduced rent. And then, once she had accepted, Oedipus disclosed his hand.

"Do you think you could possibly bring along a bottle or two?" Oedipus asked over the telephone.

Berthea was accommodating. "Certainly. It's a bring-your-own affair, is it? Would you like me to make cheese straws too?"

"Cheese straws? If you want to. I suppose some of them might like a cheese straw or two." He paused. "But wine would be more useful, I think. Could you manage a dozen bottles, do you think?"

She absorbed this request in silence.

"Mother?" asked Oedipus. "Still there?"

She tried to keep her voice even. "Yes. How many people are you expecting?"

"About thirty."

She made a mental calculation. The conventional wisdom was that one allowed one bottle of wine for every three guests. This meant that the majority who wanted, say, two glasses over the evening would get them, with a bit to spare. Now if Oedipus was inviting thirty people, and was expecting her to bring a dozen bottles, it meant that he himself would be providing no wine at all. This was tantamount, she realised, to his getting *her* to fund *his* party for *his* volunteers. The only reason he had invited her, she decided, was to get her to buy the wine. He had not asked her because he thought she might enjoy herself; he had not asked her because he was fond of her; he had asked her because he wanted something from her. And that was the way it had been not only with her but with everyone; all the way through. Oedipus was a user of people, including his mother.

And that was the moment when she realised that she disliked her son. At the end of the telephone conversation, having agreed to do as he asked, she went through to her bedroom and looked despairingly in the dressing-table mirror. It was a technique that she had often recommended to patients: Look at yourself, she would say. Look at yourself in the mirror and then tell yourself what you see.

She stared into the mirror. A middle-aged woman, quite handsome, with high cheekbones and eyes around which . . . well, wrinkles had begun to move outwards, little folds in the flesh, tiny fault lines; an intelligent face—she had to admit that—the face of one who had been trained for years to understand others . . . And now the time for self-understanding and honesty had come. "I do not like Oedipus," she said, whispering the words. "I do not like my son."

The effect of this admission was curious. Immediately she admitted it, she felt a weight lift from her. She was no longer in awe of him. She no longer felt guilty. She was free.

She went to the party, and was met by Oedipus at the door. He looked at her anxiously.

"Everyone's here," he said, sounding slightly peevish. He glanced behind her, as if expecting her to be accompanied by a retinue of some sort.

"Just me," she said. "Nobody else."

He frowned. "The wine?"

She shrugged. "Oh, that. Sorry, I was a little bit short of cash and decided not to get it. You'll have to make do with what you've brought along yourself. I'm sure that'll be fine."

"But I didn't bring any," he hissed. "The guests have nothing to drink."

Berthea smiled. "But there's a tap in there, isn't there? What about water? Surely Liberal Democrats are quite happy with water."

He raised his voice, attracting glances from a small knot of party volunteers standing near the door. "It's not funny!"

"Isn't it?" asked Berthea airily. "Actually I think it's really rather amusing. The same problem as the wedding at Cana of Galilee." She paused. "Perhaps there'll be a miracle and the water will turn—"

"What have weddings got to do with this?" snapped Oedipus. "You've really let me down, Mother. I trusted you, and this is how you repay me."

Berthea looked at him coldly. Was this how Liberal Democrats addressed their mothers? It was all very well occupying the moral high ground on electoral reform, but what really mattered, she thought, was how you treated your mother. Conservatives, she had observed, were very good to their mothers, and to their nannies as well. And Labourites were equally fond of their mothers, and sometimes made their mothers government ministers or put them in the House of Lords. So kind! Sometimes, though, they could be a little less than understanding when mothers made reactionary or *bigoted* remarks, as mothers sometimes do. But that was a small fault, as faults go.

4. In a Spirit of Failure

IF OEDIPUS SNARK was a flawed character, the same could certainly not be said of William French, Master of Wine (Failed). That particular failure—his regrettable performance in the MW examinations—was his own fault and nobody else's, and he certainly did not try to shift the blame. He had become intoxicated in the practical tests and completely confused the attribution of the sample wines. He recognised that it would have been a travesty had he passed, and he knew that he had a great deal of work ahead of him if he were eventually to obtain the treasured qualification.

Whereas Oedipus was unpopular with all those who got to know him at all well, the warmth of feeling that people had for William only grew as they spent time with him. It was difficult to put one's finger on the reason for this, but it was a quality of kindness, perhaps, that people most noticed: kindness, leavened with a large measure of charity in his attitude to others. One realised, of course, that William had a problem with finding direction in his life, but that counted for very little when one looked at the broader character of a person who had a strong sense of where he was going. The ranks of such persons were not entirely occupied by the ruthless, the selfish and the insensitive—but those characteristics were certainly well represented there.

His friend Marcia Light, who owned the outside-catering firm Marcia's Table, was well aware of William's lack of direction. For some years after William had been widowed, she had wanted him to marry her. She used every ploy known to woman to secure this end, but eventually admitted to failure.

"It's not going to happen," she had confided to a friend one day as they prepared a large selection of canapés for a reception at the Norwegian embassy. "The problem is chemistry. The chemistry's either there or it isn't. It's as simple as that."

"Are you sure?" her friend asked. She was an incurable romantic and believed, in the depths of her soul, that any man could be enticed as long as one knew what his appetites—in the culinary sense, of course—were. "There are ways, you know . . ."

Marcia knew what her friend was driving at. "It's not that simple," she said. "Yes, there are men who just want domestic comfort, who want somebody to cook for them. William's not like that."

"Pity," said the friend.

"Yes. But there we are. He's looking for something else."

William would not have disputed that assessment. He was aware of his problem of direction; he was aware of the fact that at the end of each day he made his way home to a flat in Corduroy Mansions that had developed a rather unlived-in feel; he was aware that if he were to attempt to sum up what he had achieved over the last six months, or even the last year, it would not be a long list of achievements. Indeed, he would be hard-pressed to find even a single thing to put on such a list.

Of course, there were very few occasions on which one was required to make a list of one's achievements. Some people went for years without listing their triumphs; others did it more regularly, often under the pretext of sending out a Christmas letter to their friends and acquaintances. William received a growing number of such letters each year, and he often blushed to the roots of his hair as he read the shameless blowing of trumpets that these entailed.

The previous year he had received a five-page letter in which an entire page was devoted to each member of the family. "It's been a rather successful year, as it happens," wrote his friend. "You may have read of my appointment in the newspapers, but in case you missed it I have scanned it in and attached it as appendix A! Well, that came as a surprise because I really shouldn't have got the job for another five or six years, and I'm afraid I did rather leapfrog—or I *was* leapfrogged—over at least ten people who were my seniors in the company. The chairman made a very generous remark about cream rising to the top . . . A bit of a joke, of course, but a sweet thing for him to say nonetheless. I do hope it sugared the pill for those who might have hoped to get the job but didn't (and I realise as I write this that a few people in that category will be reading this letter). Anyway, there was that, and then a few months later, in July, we had a simply wonderful piece of family news—the beatification of our late Great-Uncle Martin! It came as a complete surprise because, although we knew that there were quite a few people supporting his cause, not being Catholics ourselves we didn't know the ins and outs of it. The current Pope, however, is said to be very keen on the project, as was the last one, and so they have given the whole business a fair wind. Now being beatified is not the same as being canonised, but it's the first step and sometimes they fast-track these things. So I gather that there's a reasonable possibility that he might be made a saint if not in my lifetime then at least in the lifetime of the children, which would be rather nice as we currently don't have any saints (real ones, that is!) in the family. I gather that the ceremony in Rome is very moving and that they have special candles made for any members of the family who can get to the service.

"Of course, they need proof of a few miracles to get the thing nailed down, and I've told our Jane that the fact that she got *seven* A Level passes at A grade last year is *not* a miracle attributable to the Blessed Martin Blaise but more the result of hard work—and she *has* worked very hard over the last few years—and a certain amount of native intelligence. She was made a member of Mensa, as it happens, this year. For those of you who may not know about it, Mensa is the society for the super-intelligent. You have to do a very tough test to get in and, naturally, you need an IQ of the highest level. I served for some years as the secretary of our regional Mensa branch, and enjoyed it greatly. I could always be certain that the fellow members to whom I wrote about subscriptions and so on would understand my letter!

"On the subject of letters, I received an absolutely charming one from . . . well, modesty forbids my telling you exactly who it was from, but you might have seen his latest film—which I thought was really rather good. We were at the premiere, as it happens, where I bumped into . . ." And so it continued.

William realised he could never write a letter like that; he was far too modest and . . . Well, the other side of it was that he had nothing to write about. He would never get into Mensa, just as he feared he would never get his MW. William French, MW (Failed), Mensa (Failed): well, at least it was honest, and perhaps it would be no bad thing if more of us admitted to our shortcomings more readily—and in a spirit of genuine failure.

5. The Wali of Swat, Etc.

No, THOUGHT WILLIAM, what I need is *purpose*. It was all very well taking each day as it came, reacting to things that happened, but what sort of life did it amount to in the end? People who led lives like that suddenly discovered at the end of the day that they had nothing to show for their time on this earth except a pension— if they were lucky—a house—again if they were lucky—and children who might or might not have much time for them. That was it. And what would the obituary writers say of such a life?

William liked to read the obituary columns in the newspapers, not out of any morbid interest but because he appreciated potted biography. There were such extraordinary lives being led, he felt; it was a tribute to the inventiveness of humanity that people could devise such varied ways of passing the time. Unlike me, he thought, whose obituary might run to a few lines at the most and would make for very dull reading. William French, wine merchant, it would begin; and then what? There was no distinguished university record—no university record at all, in fact; there was no military service—unless one counted a short spell in the Wood-craft Folk as a teenager, and that organisation was decidedly un-militaristic in its outlook. His life had not even been touched by controversy; the obituaries of those touched by scandal often made very edifying reading, particularly if they recorded a come-back. The unfortunate Mr. Profumo, who suffered banishment because he did not tell the truth to the House of Commons, spent years thereafter doing good works and was justly rewarded in the end with a glowing obituary. Of course, he had the misfortune to mislead Parliament before it became standard practice for Parliament to be misled—on a daily basis—by half-truths and massaged figures.

William's favourite obituary was that of that great and good man, the Akond of Swat, also known as the Wali of Swat. His obituary in *The Times* following his death in 1987 was full of colourful detail. The Wali, who ruled over a territory that eventually ceased to exist, disliked lawyers and heard his subjects' legal cases personally, his door being open to all. He grew roses and wore elegant English suits. The obituary concluded: "In the eyes of his people, in an age of pygmies a giant has just passed away."

We could not all be a Wali of Swat; nor, thought William, could we be a Richard Branson, creating airlines here and there and fly-ing in immense balloons, or a Louis Mountbatten, running mili-tary campaigns in that titanic struggle against a *real* Axis, presiding over a crumbling Raj, dispensing advice to kings and presidents. By comparison with such lives, our days were inconsequential indeed, and yet even though our canvas was small, still we could paint a masterpiece—as long as we were content for it to be a miniature.

The real issue was that of acceptance. Most of us, thought William, are in the same boat as I am. Most of us have not done any-thing remarkable, nor are we likely to. Most of us are destined to lead life on a relatively modest scale. Yet that does not mean that we should resent the apparent smallness of our lives, which are as large, in their way, as the lives of those caught up in great events. A moral dilemma is equally absorbing whether the stakes are the destiny of nations or the happiness of one or two people—at the most. And the same was true of a love affair: romantic heroes may have their romantic heroines, and the resulting romances may take place against exotic backdrops, but the essential matter—the attraction of one to another, the search for completeness, the sad, insistent human longing—was the same wherever and however it occurred, had the same dignity, the same magnificence. The moping, lovesick teenager, blissfully unaware that his or her feelings were precisely those that his parents—and everybody else—had felt, might slip into solipsism, but surely must be forgiven because his teenage love affair, short-lived though it might be, was every bit as important, as magnificent, as that conducted by Romeo and Juliet or by Pyramus and Thisbe.

William glimpsed this insight. Doing what all of us should do from time to time, but which the demands of quotidian existence prevent us from doing—sitting down and taking stock of what his life was about and what it meant—he suddenly realised that if he felt that he had achieved nothing it was because he had failed to cherish what he had in fact done. He had filled his days doing ordinary, unexceptional things and thought nothing of them. But they were far from nothing: even the act of making his morning cup of tea as he looked, bleary-eyed, over the rooftops of Pimlico amounted to a small miracle: that there should, in this cold void of space, be a small blue planet on which he, a rather complex collection of cells, should be delighting in the dried black leaves of a plant that grew half a world away; that surely was astonishing and worthy of celebration and awe. And that was even before one started to address the mystery of consciousness—that this collection of cells, engaged in the making of tea, should trigger enough electrical activity to produce consciousness, of all things, even while being unable to explain exactly what consciousness was.

Yet what was the point of it? Unless one could subscribe to an explanation of the sort religion might offer, there appeared to be no point at all. We were born, we did what we found ourselves doing and then we died; a grim prospect, or certainly a dull one. And what was the point of having no point? So we should create a point, he thought; we should *impose* a sense of purpose. We could pick our cosmology and then put doubt aside. People had been doing so for a very long time, and half the world—at the least—wanted to carry on with this great act of self-administered and entirely understandable anaesthesia. They realised that belief of whatever sort—whether it was the faith in History and the State, as in the shattered halls of communism, or faith in a particular theology—at least made it possible to get through the day. And if one felt better in the belief that one's life made sense in these terms, then what was wrong with that? Was it weakness to allow oneself the pleasure of thinking that one *counted* in some way? And did this engagement not result, on balance, in greater human happiness? No, said the atheists, it did not. And yet where, William wondered, were the great works of those who believed in nothing at all? We *had* to believe, he thought, whether it was in some power beyond us, or in love, or art, or beauty. The need to believe was always there, and it would find expression, even if it attached itself to something paltry and shallow such as celebrity culture. And for many millions that was where their spiritual energy went—into a fascination with fashion and the lives of narcissistic entertainers. Viewed in this light, he considered, *Hello!* magazine was a religious tract, a work of theology.

William raised these questions with Marcia, who had called at his shop to place an order for a small reception she was in charge of that evening.

"Point?" she said. "Why think about it? Haven't we got enough on our minds as it is?"

"But . . ."

"And anyway, we know what we want in this life."

"Do you, Marcia? Do you know what you want?"

She looked at him. She could not tell him what she wanted in this life because try as she might to give him up—and she did give him up from time to time—he still came into it; indeed he occupied a very central place in that vision. But for many of us, she thought, it is difficult to tell those whom we love that we love them. We hope they notice, but we cannot spell it out. At least that was the situation if one was British: for others it was different, perhaps.

6. Eddie's Weltanschauung

WILLIAM'S SON, EDDIE, was quite different from his father. He was not troubled by doubts—not in the slightest—and would not have recognised the soul-searching that his father engaged in from time to time. "Barmy," he might say of such deliberations, "barmy" being the adjective that Eddie applied to anything unusual, creative or vaguely alternative. And if something went beyond barmy, it became, in Eddie's eyes, "bonkers." That which was barmy was at least understandable; that which was bonkers surpassed all understanding. Thus the United Nations was bonkers in Eddie's view, as was the European Union, the management of the football team from which he had recently withdrawn his support in disgust, various archbishops and the entire massed ranks of those self-appointed opinion-formers disparagingly referred to as "the chattering classes."

"You know how to ruin a perfectly decent country?" Eddie

would say. "You know how to ruin it? I'll tell you, mate. You put people who are bonkers in charge of it and then you stand back. That's how it's done."

William had long since ceased to reason with his son. He had tried, especially in what he believed were Eddie's formative years, to bring about a more sophisticated view of the world in his son's mind, but had given up. And that was when he realised that Eddie had already been formed by the time he reached those so-called formative years, and already it had been too late.

"I wish you'd think a bit more before you sound off about things," he once said to his son. "I'm not saying that you shouldn't express a view. I'm just saying that you might think a bit before you do so."

Eddie sniffed. "I know what's what, old man," he said. "Believe me."

William did not like being called "old man." "I'm not all that old," he said. "Late forties isn't old. Not these days."

"Maybe not," retorted Eddie. "But you aren't late forties, are you? More like fifty."

William could hardly deny his age—or at least he could not do so to his son, who knew his own father's date of birth—but he could resist his son's claim to knowledge of the world.

"I wonder if you know quite as much as you think you do," he muttered. "You haven't exactly done very much, have you?"

That, of course, was true, even if it was a somewhat uncomfortable fact. Eddie had never really settled to any job and had no qualifications of any sort. "What's the point?" he said. "What's the point in getting a piece of paper? All it says is that you knew something on the date they tested you. But things are changing, aren't they? You learn something today and the next moment it's out of date. So why bother to learn it in the first place? You'd have to be barmy."

"Or bonkers perhaps," sighed William.

"Yeah, that too."

Eddie had outstayed his welcome in his father's house, not moving out until he was well into his twenties. "You don't mind, do you?" he said. "Mum said I could stay, you know. She told me before she snuffed it. She said I should stay and look after you."

William gritted his teeth. He had largely recovered from the loss of his wife, but it did not help to hear his son referring to her death in this way.

"Your mother did *not* snuff it, as you so offensively put it."

"Oh yeah? So you're telling me she's alive?"

"And I'm not sure that she thought you should stay . . . quite so long."

Such suggestions that Eddie should move out proved fruitless, and even William's acquiring a dog, the Pimlico terrier known as Freddie de la Hay, failed to shift the known canine-aversive Eddie. At last, though, Eddie moved out to share a flat with a friend and William had his house to himself again.

He had his moments of guilt about his son, imagining him in a small and overpriced flat with malodorous drains and greasy, threadbare carpets. These feelings, however, turned out to be quite unnecessary, as Eddie then took up with a girlfriend, Merle, whose domestic circumstances were a very long distance from the world of malodorous drains and worn carpets. This girlfriend not only had a comfortable, airy flat in Primrose Hill, but also owned a house in the Windward Islands, for which she left the country each November to spend the next six months away from the trying and unpredictable British weather. Merle had inherited both of these properties from a well-placed but childless uncle, who had doted on her since her infancy; and with the legacy of the houses had come a large portfolio of shares and a substantial holding of Treasury bonds. "You know the government owes all this money," Eddie quipped to his friends in the pub. "Well, you know who they owe it to? I'll tell you. It's Merle. They owe the money to her."

As an heiress, even if one without some of the graces that are sometimes associated with heiresses, Merle could have been more cautious of the intentions of the men who took an interest. She was satisfied, though, that Eddie was interested in her and not in her money; Eddie was too direct, she felt, to conceal a motive. And there was something about him—a cockiness, perhaps—that attracted her in a magnetic, irresistible way. And they were happy together; Merle was quite content to keep them both with the ample proceeds of her portfolio, and Eddie was quite content to listen to Merle, who was a great talker, giving her opinion on a wide range of subjects. He never disagreed with her—not once—but said at regular intervals, "You're right, doll. You're right there."

Some women might have resented being called "doll," but Merle did not. The image this term of address conjured up was, in her eyes, an attractive one: a curvaceous woman with blonde hair and high-heeled shoes. That was a doll. And if that was how Eddie saw her, then that was flattering, and reassuring. Men did not run away from curvaceous blondes in high-heeled shoes; they ran *to* them. So, although she had often feared that her men would leave her, she now felt much more secure. Eddie was comfortable with her, and called her doll. She fed him well, cooking the greasy fry-ups that gave him particular pleasure, and provided him with all the support and consolation a man might wish for.

"You're marvellous, you know, Eddie," she purred.

"Thanks, doll," he said.

"You sure know how to keep a woman happy," she added. "Know what I mean?"

"Yes I do, doll," he said, winking broadly. "And thanks for the testimonial."

7. The Windward Islands

MERLE'S HOUSE IN the Windward Islands had been bought twenty years earlier by the childless uncle who had left it to her. The house, which overlooked a bay on the island of St. Lucia, had been more isolated in the past than it was now. Twenty years ago it would have been possible to walk in its garden by night and see no other lights puncturing the velvety darkness. Now the hillside behind the house had a road snaking up it, with houses off, and these at night made pinpoints of light.

The uncle adapted the house to his purposes, which were those of entertaining groups of friends who came out to stay with him, for weeks sometimes, occasionally for months. A swimming pool was created and an extension of bedrooms built to accommodate the guests at house parties. An additional shady veranda was added to the west side of the house to allow guests to enjoy sundowners while watching the sun sink into the sea. A gazebo, designed in no identifiable style by an eccentric architect whom the uncle had met in a bar, appeared in the corner of the grounds, surrounded by sea-grape trees, to be covered in an astonishingly short time by bougainvillea, and eventually to disappear, not to be missed because nobody had ever used it. With the house came a run-down marina and chandlery, which he put under the control of an enterprising local manager and which prospered greatly.

The uncle was a man of literary tastes, a voracious reader who expounded at length, to anybody who would listen, on the damp fate of books in the humid Caribbean climate. Merle was quite unlike him in this respect; she read virtually nothing other than the occasional beach novel, some breathless account of romantic yearnings or the racy couplings of hedonistic twenty-somethings. She wanted very little out of life except for one thing: a man. It did not particularly matter, she thought, what sort of man might be allocated to her by Fate; the only important thing was that he would be there, to be looked after and guarded from the depredations of other women who were not in the fortunate position of having a man. It was a curious, somewhat limited view of life, but not without a trace of dim nobility. Merle did not envy what others had; she bore few resentments; she did not wish to despoil the world in any way. All she wanted was a nest.

Eddie suited her perfectly. She regarded him as uncomplicated, and had indeed described him as such to her friends. "With Eddie," she said, "what you get is what it says on the tin."

"That's something," said her friend, before adding, enigmatically: "The trouble with my ex was that he didn't have a tin."

Merle was not sure what this meant but sympathised nonetheless. "Pity, that."

Eddie was content for Merle to look after him, and this quickly became her main concern. In this she manifested a selflessness which, had it been applied to a worthier project, would have seemed positively virtuous. The energy she poured into making sure that Eddie was well turned out, that his clothes were neatly folded and put away after he had tossed them down on the floor, was every bit as intense as that of the most devoted of nuns tending to the poor and sick. Her dedication was certainly as great even if its beneficiary was less meritorious. Not that Eddie himself regarded this as anything less than his due. He revelled in the attention shown him. It was, he thought, a stroke of the most extraordinary good fortune that he should find a woman like Merle, but it was nonetheless fortune that he had somehow always believed would come his way and he felt was, in some unexplained way, also his due.

Merle met Eddie shortly after he had moved out of Corduroy

Mansions. She was then living in London, in the Primrose Hill flat that belonged to her uncle, which he had offered to her when he began to spend most of his time on St. Lucia. Merle had a job helping a friend who ran a retro clothing shop on the Portobello Road. It was not well paid—in fact, the friend sometimes forgot to pay her at all—but it suited her very well as it enabled her to indulge her interest in clothing and at the same time to hone her quite exceptional skill at selling things.

This talent enabled her to persuade people that the clothing they were trying on was exactly the thing for which they had long been searching. Merle's power to do this was almost hypnotic.

"That is definitely you," she would say. "No, seriously, it looks just right. And you look fantastic in it—you really do. You owe it to yourself to buy it, you know."

Flattered in this way, and compelled by the suggestion that the purchase was somehow a tribute to themselves, the customers would do as Merle prompted and purchase the item. Of course there were consequences, mostly in the shape of disappointment on the part of the customers over the fact that they had bought such manifestly unsuitable garments, but these came later, in the cold light of home.

After the death of her uncle and the receipt of the news of the legacy he had left her, Merle continued to work in the retro clothing store, but as owner. Her friend, who had tired of the musty odour of the old clothes, of the old jackets and sad dresses, had readily accepted the offer that Merle was now able to make for the business, including the freehold of the shop itself.

Now that she was the owner, Merle decided to clear out the old clothing and rename the business Everything Olive. Where the racks once groaned under their weight of stoutly built old great-coats and morning suits, newly installed shelves now bore bottles of exotic and expensive cold-pressed olive oil, alongside jars of olives with every conceivable stuffing. Then there were bars of olive oil soap, bottles of olive oil moisturiser and tubes of olive oil hand cream. And all parts of the olive tree were used inventively, as captured whales were in the past, with displays of coasters, soprano recorders and desk sets made from olive wood.

Everything Olive proved to be a resounding success.

"I can't understand how retail places can fail," Merle remarked to Eddie one afternoon. "The business model is so easy. Buy something for one pound and sell it for two. Simple. You can't go wrong."

Eddie smiled. "Yeah, maybe. But sometimes people don't want to buy. That's the problem, I think."

"Then find out what they want to buy and sell them that," retorted Merle.

"Yeah, whatever," said Eddie.

He was not really interested in discussing retail theory with Merle. As far as he was concerned, such matters could be left entirely to her. She had a head for business, he had decided, which suited him very well. Money worries, and the indignities they brought, were not what Eddie had in mind for himself. He was looking forward to a life in which he did not have to bother about such concerns, and now, thanks to Merle, it looked as if just such a life was beginning.

"Marry me, doll?" he asked.

8. A Designer with an Eye

MERLE SAID NOTHING. It was not that she had failed to hear Eddie, who often mumbled, running his words together in the way of some speakers of Estuary English; she had heard his proposal perfectly well. Consequently this was not one of those embarrassing cases where the person to whom the question is popped has to say: "Sorry, I didn't quite get that. Are you asking me to *marry* you?" There have been many such cases, including some where the proposer, embarrassed by the incredulity to which his question has given rise, has replied: "No, of course not." And this has been followed by awkward silence, sometimes heralding the end of the relationship in question.

Eddie's question was followed by silence because Merle was thinking. She was pleased that Eddie had asked her to marry him, as she had entertained thoughts of marriage from the age of eighteen onwards and had been waiting for a man to propose. None had, or not until now, and it was inconceivable that she would turn down this offer. And yet there was something within her that prompted her to caution. It was not that she had her doubts about Eddie in particular—he was, as far as she was concerned, almost perfect—it was just that she had recently heard a disturbing statistic about the brevity of marriages entered into without a period of reflection beforehand.

So when at last she answered—about five minutes after Eddie's question had been posed—it was with a counter-proposal. "Let's get engaged," she said. "That gives us a bit of time."

"What for?" asked Eddie. "What do you need time for?"

"To think about things. To find out if we're compatible."

Eddie smiled. "We know that already. Know what I mean?"

"Oh I know, Eddie. You're really wonderful. It's just that it's best to wait a few months. Then we'll really know."

Eddie shrugged. "So we get engaged. OK, if that's what you want. We get engaged, and then we get married. Suits me."

Merle leaned forward and planted a kiss on his cheek. "What about the ring?"

Eddie nodded vaguely. "Yeah, a ring."

"Shall we go and choose one?"

Again, Eddie shrugged. "Whatever."

Merle had hoped for a more romantic response, but it was not to materialise, and they moved on to the next subject without further discussion of the ring. This conversation had taken place in the middle of a wider discussion of what to do about the house on St. Lucia. The marina and chandlery were doing well and needed no decisions taken; the house, though, required attention, or at least some view to be adopted as to its fate. Eddie had suggested turning it into a hotel, an idea Merle had originally greeted unenthusiastically but which she was now beginning to find more attractive.

"A hotel's the answer," said Eddie. "But we should keep a few rooms for ourselves—a flat at the back maybe, or in the grounds. Get somebody in to run it. A manager."

Merle liked the sound of a manager. "A manager," she said, savouring the reassuring qualities of the word. "Yes. Like the man who looks after the marina. A manager would be a good idea."

Eddie expanded upon this. "He can manage the place, you see."

Merle nodded. "That would be good."

"Hire the staff. Pay the bills. That sort of stuff."

"Important," said Merle.

"Yeah. And then we can check up that he's managing right."

"We'd have to do that," agreed Merle. "You want a good manager."

"We'd get the best," said Eddie.

The management structure having been decided, they passed on to the issue of decor and ambience.

"It should be classy," said Eddie.

"Of course."

"If it's classy," Eddie went on, "then you get the right sort of people staying there. No rubbish."

Merle thought he was right. "We don't want rubbish," she said. "They can stay elsewhere."

"Yeah. Not at our place. They can stay down the road."

"So, what . . . feel are we looking for, Ed?"

Already Eddie had an idea. "We need an angle," he said. "We need to get somebody to tell us what people are looking for, know what I mean? If we know what people are looking for, then . . ."

"Then we can give it to them," supplied Merle.

"Yeah. So we need to get a—"

Merle was thinking ahead. "A designer. I read an article in one of the mags about this guy who designs restaurants and hotels. It said he was the best there is. And he's here in London, I think. We could ask him. I've still got the mag."

She fetched the magazine—a bulky, glossily printed publication with advertisements for perfumes and fashion—and paged through it.

"Do you like this?" she said, holding up a picture of a large diamond ring. "Only joking!"

"One thing at a time," muttered Eddie. "This designer guy . . ."

The article was located. It was an interview with a man called Cosmo Bartonette, described at the head of the page as *London's sharpest design eye*. "I call myself a *design eye* rather than a *designer*," said Cosmo. "It sounds the same when you say it but the difference stresses the true nature of my calling. You have to have an eye for design."

Merle read this out to Eddie. "You see?"

"Yeah," said Eddie. "Carry on."

"'I start from the basic premise that there is nothing there. I look at a space and then I *subtract*. I call this the cleansing process—rather like eating a *trou normand* before the meal begins, rather than halfway through. I cleanse my palate, so to speak. I exclude the items that the client already has—because they clutter the room. Then I allow an alternative to emerge—organically.

"'People have said to me that the hallmark of my approach is to allow the space itself to do the work. And I think that's a good way of putting it. It's as if I interrogate the space and get *it* to tell *me* what *it* wants to have within it. Spaces are not inert. They breathe. They have their dreams. They have a destiny which their proportions, the materials they are made of, their positioning, all point towards. I simply unlock it for them. I open a door that would otherwise be closed by the preconceptions of the owner, or the designer for that matter. And it's extraordinary how many spaces give a shout of joy when this happens. *Look!* they exclaim. *Look! This is what I want to be! This is me! C'est moi!*'"

9. Cosmo Speaks

MERLE ARRANGED AN appointment with Cosmo Bartonette. It was not easy; Cosmo was not the sort of person one could phone directly—and his personal assistant proved elusive. Eventually she returned Merle's call and said that she would enter an appointment in Cosmo's diary for the following week. "You're lucky," she said. "There's been a cancellation—otherwise you would have had to wait for yonks and yonks. You can see Cosmo on Tuesday at nine, for an hour."

"Who does he think he is?" Merle said to Eddie. "Tuesday at nine. Yonks."

"Probably barmy," said Eddie.

"I suppose he *is* famous," she conceded.

Eddie appeared to have changed his mind. "You get what you pay for," he said. "I've always said that. This guy is something special. You don't get into mags like that without being something special."

They both went to the appointment, which took place in Cosmo Bartonette's studio off Old Church Street. The designer was in his late thirties, dressed relatively casually but with a studied elegance that seemed entirely right for his profession: neatly pressed chinos, a woven leather belt, a pink check shirt, small gold-rimmed glasses.

"Welcome to my studio," he said as he led them into a sitting area at one end of a large, airy room decorated with several large Hockney prints. Noticing Eddie's eyes go to these prints, he asked, "You like Hockney?"

The question seemed to be about something more than Eddie's taste in art, but Eddie did not pick up on this.

"Yeah. A bit. Yeah. Maybe."

"The lines he uses are so *clean,*" said Cosmo Bartonette. "And there are no more than are absolutely necessary. Yet he captures mood so well, don't you think? A few lines—zip, zip—and he's got a whole mood."

"Those boys look like they're good friends," said Merle, peering at one of the prints. "Nice."

Cosmo Bartonette smiled. "It's so hard to capture human closeness. Yet Hockney does it. Again, with just a few lines."

They sat down around a low glass table. Cosmo Bartonette folded his hands on his lap. "I hear from my assistant that you have a hotel."

"A house at the moment," said Merle. "It was left to me by my uncle. He had this house on St. Lucia and we—that's Eddie and I—thought we might turn it into a hotel. But we don't want just any old hotel—"

"We want something really special," interjected Eddie. "A really classy place. No rubbish."

"No, no rubbish," agreed Merle.

Cosmo Bartonette was watching them closely, his gaze moving from Merle to Eddie, and back to Merle.

"Well, we don't do rubbish," he said, a smile hovering on his lips.

"That's good," said Eddie.

"But I need to know a bit about what you have in mind. The setting. You've got some photographs to show me?"

Merle reached into her bag and took out a folder of photographic prints. "These aren't all that good, but they give a general idea of what it's like."

Cosmo Bartonette took the photographs and began to look through them. "Nice," he said. "Really nice. Not entirely unlike Mustique. I did a bit of work there for . . ."

He did not finish the sentence but returned to his scrutiny of the pictures. When he had finished going through them he passed them back to Merle. "You could make something really special out of that place," he said. "You're very lucky to have it."

Merle exchanged a look of satisfaction with Eddie. "You'll do it?" she asked.

"Natch," said Cosmo. "I'm already getting some *idées*. I think we need a theme."

"Like the Caribbean?" asked Eddie. "Pirates maybe?"

Cosmo looked at him and smiled. "Not quite. Nice idea, of course, but that's a bit on the *demotic* side, wouldn't you say? I'm thinking of something much more refined."

"That's what we want," said Merle. "Refinement. Remember what we agreed, Eddie? No rubbish."

"Something literary," suggested Cosmo Bartonette. "Something literary, but Caribbean. Have you been to Raffles in Singapore?"

Merle and Eddie both shook their head.

"Raffles plays on the connection with Somerset Maugham," said Cosmo. "Reasonably enough, because he did float around that part of the world. You should read him if you haven't already. God, he can write! And you can just *feel* the wickerwork chairs and *taste* the gin slings. Anyway, Raffles has got a Writers' Bar. People love it. How about something like that for your place?"

"Sounds good," said Eddie. "Maybe Wilbur Smith. Did you read the one he wrote about the Egyptian princess and this guy who was an elephant hunter in East Africa? You read that?"

Cosmo Bartonette flicked a strand of hair from his brow. "Not exactly. I must try him. Such bright covers—clearly a lot of action within."

"Yeah. Great stories. And that other guy who writes those books about codes and—"

"Not exactly what I had in mind," said Cosmo. "Thrilling books, no doubt, but not quite what I was thinking of for your place. I was thinking more of Hemingway. He used to go deep-sea fishing in the Caribbean, didn't he? Bull-fighting in Spain and fishing in the Caribbean. We could have a Hemingway Bar perhaps . . . serving twenty types of rum. Can't you see it? A slow-moving fan above the bar . . ."

"Could work," said Eddie.

"Of course it'll work!" Cosmo enthused. "And there'll be a Hemingway Suite, where he stayed for a few months while writing *The Old Man and the Sea* or maybe it was *Islands in the Stream*. Doesn't matter—one of them will do."

"But it belonged to my uncle," said Merle. "He bought it from a man called Edwards . . . Hemingway didn't go there, I think."

Cosmo Bartonette made a dismissive gesture. "My dear! *Quels* scruples! One doesn't have to be too *literal* about these things. I thought we might also have a Graham Greene Suite—the rooms he occupied while he was writing *The Comedians*, you know, the one set in Haiti—at that hotel, as chance would have it. And Papa Doc and those *frightful* Tontons Macoutes. Remember them? Those thugs that Duvalier used to frighten everybody out of their skins. *Très* voodoo! Perhaps we could dress the waiters up as Tontons, with dark glasses, just to give the guests a *frisson*. What do you think?"

"I really like what you're coming up with," said Eddie. "What do you think, doll?"

"Pretty good," said Merle. "I think we should leave it up to you, Cosmo."

Cosmo smiled broadly. "I shall give it further thought and come up with some sketches," he said. "I've got a really good feeling about this one, you know." He paused. "The Graham Greene Suite will have to be a little seedy, you know. Run down. Slightly lumpy bed and a tatty mosquito net, of course. But we can manage that, can't we? We can *distress* things, although perhaps when it comes to Graham Greene we should think about *depressing* them. And putting a bit of *guilt* into the decoration. The walls could be painted *guilty white*. You know what, my dears? I believe I've just invented a colour."

10. More About Boys

CAROLINE JARVIS LIVED immediately below William in Corduroy Mansions, in a flat shared with a number of other young women—"the downstairs girls" as William called them. Caroline had completed her master's degree in fine art at the Sotheby's Institute and was now working as an assistant to Tim Something, the photographer. It was not an ideal job from her point of view, but then, as her mother pointed out, "What job is ideal? Name one."

Caroline's mother, Frances, was not slow to give her daughter advice and had recently spoken to her about men, a subject on which many women feel they have something to say to their daughters; while many daughters feel that this is exactly the subject on which their mothers' views are likely to be unhelpful and outdated. Men had changed dramatically—anybody could tell that—and women too, with the result that the insights a mother might be expected to have acquired over the years were now of dubious value and relevance; or so Caroline had thought as she listened to her mother issuing a series of warnings in the parental kitchen in Cheltenham.

"That young man, James," Frances said. "The one you brought down here for the weekend. He's a case in point."

"Mummy, James and I are not—"

"Oh, I know that," said her mother. "And one couldn't have expected any other outcome, dear, could one?"

Caroline looked out of the window. Her parents' house was on the edge of the town and the kitchen looked directly onto a field in which horses were grazing. "I don't know what you mean," she said quietly.

Frances looked at her pityingly. "Oh come on, dear. No need to beat about the bush. James was a charming young man . . ."

"Yes. And he and I were really good friends."

"Which is exactly my point. Men like that—artistic men—are not good husband material. They're just not interested, you see. I know it's a pity because they can be quite charming. James played the piano beautifully, didn't he? But they are not the type to be interested in marriage, if you see what I mean. And sometimes it takes a woman a long time to admit that to herself."

Caroline said nothing.

"I knew a man like that," Frances continued. "He was a cousin of Betty Pargeter's. Remember Betty? Anyway, she had this cousin called Harold, if I remember correctly. And we all thought that he was just perfect. He was terribly handsome, even for those days."

Caroline frowned. "Even for those days? Did men look different in your day?"

"They can pay more attention to their grooming today," said her mother. "When I was your age, men were much less—how should I put it?—individual. And they all wore such dull clothing. Yes, men look rather different now, I can tell you."

"I don't see what this has got to do with James," said Caroline.

"It's just an observation, dear. If you don't want me to make any observations, then I'm quite happy to sit here in silence."

Caroline relented. "No, sorry, I didn't mean that."

"Thank you. Well, as I was saying, you have to remind yourself that those men are a waste of time—from the woman's point of view. What you have to do is find a man who *needs* you. No, don't smile. I don't mean it in any crude sense. I mean needs you in a practical sense. He has to need you to look after him, to make him comfortable, to give him a home."

Caroline shrugged. "I know all that. I really do."

Frances looked at her sharply. "Do you? I wonder."

"What do you mean by that?"

"I mean that your generation of young women have lost the place when it comes to men. You've befriended men. You treat men in the same way as you treat your girlfriends. And what happens then? Men are quite happy to think of themselves as one of your friends, and not as anything else. The result? Men don't see the point of settling down with one particular woman because they have all these women friends. They've stopped treating women as some-thing special—they're just the same as their other friends. Nothing special."

Caroline stared at her mother. Did she really think that? She sighed.

"It's no good sighing," said her mother. "Sighing doesn't change the truth."

Caroline tried to explain. "I really don't see it," she said. "I'm not sure if I understand what you're driving at."

"Well, let me explain," said Frances. "You know Peggy Warden. Do you remember her son, Ronald? He's more or less exactly your age. Well, Peggy told me that Ronald brought home this very nice girl whom he'd met at university in Exeter. Peggy said that she really was charming, and of course her hopes, as Ronald's mother, were raised. But she said nothing, and off they went. Then Ronald brought her home again a few weeks later and Peggy had the chance to speak to him privately. She said that she asked him about this girl and he said that they were just good friends. So she said that this could change and she told him how much she liked her. But apparently he just shook his head and said that he couldn't possibly make a romance out of it precisely because they were friends. Peggy said to me that he then said, 'You don't sleep with your friends.' Those were his exact words. So you see what I mean?"

Again, Caroline shrugged. "Just because Ronald says—"

Her mother interrupted her. "The point is, Caroline, that men and women can't be friends. We have to keep up these . . . these psychological barriers between us because if we don't then we're never going to get men to agree to marriage—or even partnership, if you will. That's why there are so many people living on their own. That's why so many women find it difficult to get a man these days."

Caroline looked out of the window again. "Is it very difficult? Are there all that many women looking for men they're not going to be able to find?"

"Yes, there are. Thousands in this country alone. Millions. And it's their own fault, much of the time. They've let men get what they want without giving anything in return. Men—our friends? We think they are but let me tell you, dear, they most definitely aren't!"

Caroline closed her eyes briefly; she found that it helped to close her eyes when talking to her mother, or indeed when participating in any argument. The closing of the eyes somehow equalised things. And while her eyes were closed, she thought: Of course men and women can be friends—it was ridiculous to assert otherwise. Of course they could. There were so many examples of such friendships, and she told her mother so, forcefully, and with a conviction that perhaps matched that shown by her mother.

But Frances was not convinced. "Give me an instance," she said provocatively. "If you're so sure about that—give me an instance."

11. He's My Friend

FRANCES HAD CHANGED the focus of the conversation, as she often did. She had started talking about the difficulty of moving from a relationship of friendship to something more. Now the topic seemed to have broadened to that of friendship between the sexes— and its apparent impossibility. Caroline was sure that her mother was wrong about both: she saw no reason why a friend should not become a lover, just as she saw no reason why a man and a woman should not have a firm and uncomplicated friendship.

It was tempting simply to agree with her mother. Parents can be so wrong, Caroline thought—about virtually everything—and it was therefore best just to steer clear of matters of disagreement and concentrate instead on keeping relations uncontroversial and consequently affable.

She gave in to the temptation. "No, you're right," she said quietly. "I don't suppose that . . ."

She did not finish. "You're being evasive, Caroline," said Frances. "Don't think I can't tell."

Caroline sighed. "I'm not. All I'm saying is . . . Well, what I mean is, why argue?"

Frances laughed. This discussion was taking place in the kitchen, where the two of them were seated at the kitchen table, shelling peas.

"Why argue?" Her mother's voice rose perceptibly. "I was not aware that we were arguing. I was under the impression that we were having a perfectly reasonable discussion. But if you think that you can't *discuss* anything with me, then . . ."

Caroline put down the pod she had been stripping. She turned away.

"Caroline?"

She said nothing. Her mother, pushing aside the bowl of shelled peas, reached out across the table for her daughter's hand. "Darling. Darling."

Caroline looked up. "I'm sorry." She wiped away a tear. "I'm just . . ."

"Oh, darling. Of course you are. We all get upset from time to time. The world . . ." She shrugged. "The world can be so hard, so difficult, can't it? And things are never quite right, are they? Is it . . . is it a boy? Is that the trouble?"

Caroline nodded. "Yes."

Frances fished a tissue out of her pocket and passed it to her daughter. "Well, darling, you can talk to me, you know. It's obviously not going well but these things can change, can't they? Tell me about him. Who is he?"

Caroline blew her nose. "My nose runs when I cry," she said. "Stupid nose."

"Everybody's does. But tell me about him, darling. Who is he?" There was an edge to Frances's question; the sympathetic mother could be the inquisitive mother too—the same mother who had talked about boys being suitable and who had, ever since her daughter had started taking an interest in boys, sought to bring her into contact with the right sort of boy, a *nice* boy.

"You know him already."

This answer piqued her mother's curiosity. "Oh I do, do I? So he's local . . ."

Caroline shook her head. "London."

Frances frowned. "So . . ."

"It's James, Mummy. James!"

"Oh, darling!" Frances shook her head. "No, darling, no! We've been through that. Surely you see—do I have to spell it out to you? And you said, anyway, that there was nothing between you and him—you said it just a few moments ago."

"There's nothing between us at the moment," said Caroline stubbornly. "But that doesn't stop me wanting him, does it?" That was precisely the problem; she still yearned for James. She had recently met another boy—one who seemed completely suitable—but it had not worked out. Her feelings had been hurt, and she had thought: James would never have done this to me.

Her mother sighed. "There are bags of people, bags of them, who go through life wanting what they can't have. And what does it bring them? Nothing. It's a complete waste of time."

"That implies that there can never be anything between James and me."

"Well, that's the case, isn't it?"

Caroline looked up. "Why? Why do you say that?"

"Because I don't think he's interested. Don't you see that?"

Caroline shook her head. "No, I don't. James is just not sure at the moment. He . . . he may be a little bit that way, but not everybody is one hundred per cent one way or the other. You can be a bit of both. Look at . . ." She searched for an example. "Shakespeare. Yes, look at Shakespeare."

Frances picked a handful of pods out of the colander and began to shell them aggressively. "Shakespeare was happily married," she said.

Caroline remembered the sonnets, which she had studied in one of her university courses. "The twentieth sonnet?" she challenged.

Her mother was unimpressed. "I don't care what he wrote," she said. "It's what he did that counts. And he got married."

Caroline reached for some peas. "The point is, Mummy, that I think that James and I are perfect for one another. I used to think it wouldn't work, but I've changed my mind. I'm never happier than when I'm in his company. When I'm not with him, I wonder what he's doing. And when we do meet up, we get on so well. We talk about everything. He bares his soul to me. He's my friend, Mummy, my best, best friend."

"Then keep him as a friend, if you must. Not that I think men and women can be real friends, as I've just said . . ."

"No."

Frances stared at her daughter. "Are you setting out—deliberately—to make yourself unhappy? Do you want to be one of those women who spend their lives hankering after some man they can't have because he's gone off with somebody else or never looked at them in the first place? Is that what you want?"

"No. I don't want that. I want James."

Frances sighed. "Are you going to see him?"

"Yes. We're going to meet up next week. We're going to have dinner."

"And the approach came from him?"

Caroline hesitated. Her mother was watching her. "Not exactly . . ."

Her mother smiled. "I thought not."

Caroline ignored the provocation. "I phoned him. I said that we hadn't seen one another for a while and did he want to have dinner."

"And?"

"And he said he'd like that very much. He's coming to Corduroy Mansions next week. He's going to cook."

"What's he going to cook?"

"Risotto. He makes lovely risotto."

Frances rolled her eyes. "Oh, darling, can't you see? A man who goes round cooking risotto . . . It's just not going to work."

12. The Mothers Take Action

"I DESPAIR," FRANCES said to her husband later that evening. "She sat there, shelling peas, talking about that young man she brought here—remember him?—and completely refusing to accept that she's barking up the wrong tree. Why do young people do it? Why can't they see that some boys are possible and others don't even get close to the starting line?"

Frances was alone with her husband in their drawing room, Caroline having gone out for the evening with a couple of school friends who remained in Cheltenham. Rufus Jarvis was only half listening, being absorbed in watching a game of golf on the television. A player had just sliced a ball into the rough, giving rise to a groan from the Greek chorus of spectators.

"You tell me," he mumbled.

"Tell you what? Why young women can't see things that are staring them in the face?"

"Yes. You're always telling me that men and women are equally competent. Now you're telling me that women have a problem in sorting out the sheep from the goats, so to speak."

Frances gave her husband a disparaging look. "In emotional matters it's different."

Rufus fiddled with the remote control. "She needs to meet a decent boy," he said. "Isn't there anybody?"

"You know what it's like," said Frances. "There are so many completely unsuitable young men . . ." She paused. Her conversation with Caroline had moved on from James to more mundane issues, and Caroline had told her that she was looking for new flatmates to replace two of the girls. That peculiar vitamin girl, Dee, had moved on now that she had sold her business, and the Australian girl had gone too, at least for a few months. So that meant two rooms needed to be filled.

Now it came back to her: Peggy Warden had said that her son Ronald was going off to London to take up a new job in a firm of architects and was looking for somewhere to live. He had made some sort of arrangement with a friend who owned a flat, but the friend had fallen behind with his mortgage payments and was having to sell up. "He's rather worried," Peggy had said. "He thinks he may have to commute for a few weeks before he finds anywhere. It's not easy, you know."

Frances had been unable to give any advice. Caroline had been lucky in finding her room in the Corduroy Mansions flat, but presumably not everybody had such luck. Now, as she remembered the conversation, an idea came to her.

She looked at her husband. "If only she were to get to know some suitable boys a bit better," she said. "Ronald, for example; Peggy and Tufty's boy. What do you think of him?"

Rufus was non-committal. "All right. A bit conscious of being bright, I suppose."

Frances knew what he meant. Ronald was intelligent and probably knew it. And if he made a bit much of it, it might be a reaction to being the son of such dim parents. Peggy, bless her, was not exactly an intellectual; she had once said something which revealed that she thought Stravinsky was a *place* in Russia. "I've never

46

been to Stravinsky," she said. "But I do hope to go there one day. St. Petersburg too." Frances had wondered to herself, Should I tell her that Stravinsky's a *writer*? but had said nothing; one does not like to embarrass others by revealing their ignorance. Poor Peggy!

"Ronald's rather nice, I think," she said. "I wonder whether he might not take an interest in Caroline . . ."

"Don't!" whispered Rufus. "Just don't!"

"Why not? If she's not going to do anything herself about meeting the right sort of boy, then I don't see what's wrong in giving her a bit of a push."

"She won't listen to you," said Rufus.

I won't ask her to listen to me, thought Frances. I shall do this myself.

She left the room and went up to their bedroom, where there was a phone beside the bed. She paged through her address book and identified the Warden number.

Peggy listened with interest to her proposal.

"It's a complete coincidence," Frances began. "Caroline has a room—maybe even two—coming up in her flat in Pimlico. You said that Ronald—"

"Oh, that would be marvellous," said Peggy. "If Ronald could—"

Frances interrupted her. "I haven't spoken to Caroline herself. You know how touchy they can be about this sort of thing."

"Don't I know it. They're worried that we're trying to lead their lives for them."

"And all we're doing is trying to provide a bit of help."

"Exactly."

"You tell him you've heard that Caroline's looking for a flat-mate. Don't tell him I told you. Make something up. Then get him to phone her—they do know one another vaguely, after all. They were at that dance a couple of years ago in the same party, weren't they?"

"They were. That was when the Ellis girl got pregnant, wasn't it?"

"So they say. Anyway, Caroline could hardly refuse to let him at least look at the place."

Peggy raised the possibility that she might be looking for a female flatmate. "I could understand it if she were . . ."

"Not at all," said Frances. "These days they all live together, as friends."

There was a pause. Both women were thinking the same thing but neither could admit it to the other. And Frances, in addition, was wondering whose lawn would be more suitable for the marquee: theirs or the Wardens'? Theirs was on a bit of a slope, and although the marquee-hire people claimed that they could erect their tents on sloping ground and compensate for it in the setting up of the floor, she was not convinced that this always worked. She had been at a wedding once where the marquee had been so placed and there had been several collisions on the dance floor as dancers, unaware of the subtle slope in the floor, failed to adjust their steps. Bumping into people on the dance floor—metaphorically—was one thing; bumping into them in the physical sense was quite another.

The two mothers finished their conversation and rang off, Frances uttering these parting words to her friend: "Tell him I just happened to mention that Caroline's flat has a vacant room. Happened to mention. I would prefer for Caroline not to think that I was interfering."

"Perish the thought," Peggy said.

Which was reassuring, thought Frances. Peggy might not be unduly bright, but she was not dim; if that was possible. Not bright but not dim—somewhere in between, like one of those lights controlled by a rheostat.

13. A Literary Agent

BARBARA RAGG BEGAN her day, as most people do, with a routine. Hers was to change into her jogging outfit—black Lycra leggings and loose-fitting sports sweater—and run the five blocks that separated her flat in Notting Hill from the corner newsagency where she purchased her morning paper and a pint of semi-skimmed milk. These would be placed in an environmentally sound hemp shopping bag and she would run home, or rather run three blocks and walk the final two. The point at which she changed from running to walking was always the same, and although she realised that it was a superstition—of much the same order as the superstition that keeps children from stepping on the pavement cracks lest they be eaten by bears—she nonetheless observed it scrupulously. She knew it was irrational, but she believed that were she to run for a block more or a block less, then she would be seized by some vaguely imagined impending doom. Such beliefs, she had been told, spring from our inherent understanding that our lives hang by a thread. Things may be going well and we may be successfully negotiating the perilous shoals that beset any human life, but we are acutely aware that at any time, quite without warning, our run of luck can stop. And did stop for many people, suddenly and without warning, as the perusal of any daily newspaper would reveal. That which separates us from the unfortunates who perish in accidents is only the merest of chances. One may cross a busy road without incident; the next person may coincide with a carelessly driven car, or a car driven by someone who at the crucial moment closes his eyes in a sneeze and brings to an end, in that second, a whole cherished life. Or a swimmer enjoying the surf on an Australian beach may emerge from the tumble of waves exhilarated and refreshed, while another, only a short distance down the beach, may find that he shares his wave with a great white shark that just happened to be cruising past that particular place at that particular time. Neither deserves his fate; sharks and other agents of Nemesis pay no attention to the claims of moral desert. A selfless campaigner for social justice tastes much the same to a shark as a ruthless exploiter of others; not especially delicious—in shark terms, we are told—but good enough to eat in the absence of a seal or sea lion pup.

That morning, the feeling that the hand of fate should not in any way be tempted was strong and nothing would have persuaded Barbara to run even half a block more than habit and superstition dictated. This was because she was happy—blissfully so—and did not wish in any way to imperil her happiness. The happiness came from the fact that she would that evening be seeing her fiancé, Hugh, who was travelling down from Scotland to spend several days with her in London. This, then, was double good fortune: to be engaged and to be facing the prospect of dinner with the man who had asked her to marry him. Me! she thought. Me! It was a simple thought, but one that the blessed must often think: that this should happen to me, of all people.

When they had first become engaged, they had planned to live together immediately in a cottage on the farm. In the clear light of day this had seemed to be a rather impetuous decision, and they had opted to take their time. Barbara would return to London and, rather than packing up there and then, would wait a year or so. She knew, of course, that this would cause problems as she had already told her business partner Rupert that she would sell her flat to him more or less straight away. Telling him of the change of plan was going to be awkward.

Hugh had stayed behind in Ardnamurchan. There were two decrepit cottages on the farm that they were doing up, and much of the work was being done by Hugh, who was in the process mastering skills ranging from pointing and plastering to replacing broken Ballachulish slate on the roofs. There was no alternative, he explained: contractors in that part of Scotland were few and far between, and anyway, the budget did not run to their exorbitant charges. So Hugh, who as a farmer's son had always been good with his hands, was obliged to become even better.

He sent her photographs of his handiwork, and she emailed back for more. She looked at these photographs with wonder, not because the building work was in itself especially interesting but because it was *his* work. The slates were grey and uninteresting but had been put there by *him*. The plaster looked as any plaster looks but was special to her because it was Hugh—her Hugh—who had smoothed it into position. And then, very occasionally, there was a photograph in which, at the edge, she saw his hand, or perhaps the toe-cap of his work-boot. She would look at this with a still deeper sense of wonderment, savouring the thought that this was him, and he was hers. And these photographs in her eyes became almost sacramental in their significance.

Tonight they would eat in. Hugh enjoyed going out for meals, but preferred to have dinner with her in the flat. She was touched by his appreciation of her culinary skills, which had never been exceptional but which she now set out to improve for his sake. She had purchased several volumes of Delia and studied them conscientiously. "If there is one person who will help you keep your man, it's Delia." That had been said by a friend of hers, and Barbara had initially thought it was a joke. But then she had reflected on it and realised that it expressed a folksy but nonetheless profound truth.

She reached her flat and went to run her bath. As she did so, she glanced at the front page of the newspaper and saw an item that made her stop in her tracks. *Snark Accepts Ministerial Post*, the copy line read.

She read the news report, which was fairly lengthy, impervious to the fact that the water was approaching the top of the bath. Oedipus Snark had been Barbara Ragg's lover. He had not cared for her, and she had eventually freed herself of him. And now here he was, a government minister.

She closed her eyes. The bath continued to run.

14. Justice and Her Colleague, Nemesis

THE NEWSPAPER ITEM on Oedipus Snark put Barbara in a thoroughly bad mood. It was not the tone that had this effect; the newspaper did not welcome the appointment, it simply reported it. She was galled because she knew what Oedipus was like: she knew the contempt he had for the electorate; she knew that it was personal gain rather than public service that motivated him. If she had no difficulty is seeing this clearly, why did others who had dealings with him miss it? Were they completely ignorant of his character? Was the Prime Minister, who presumably had made the appointment, such a poor judge of men that he should think Snark worthy of ministerial office?

But it was not only these questions that caused Barbara to despair; what made her truly despondent was the fact that unworthy people could succeed—and often, as in this case, did so spectacularly. Like most of us, she believed in the existence of Justice. She believed that, by and large, the wicked and unworthy could not prevail for long and that Justice, although overburdened with an impossible case-load, would eventually get round to invoking Nemesis. Barbara really believed it, and could, if pressed, call to mind numerous cases where precisely this had happened. Sometimes these were major instances—as when a florid dictator was overthrown or put on trial; sometimes they were more modest—as when an outsider won against impossible odds, the victory of a little man against a bully and so on. And yet, if Justice were to accomplish her goals, she needed support, and specifically she needed somebody to whisper into her ear what she needed to know.

As she stepped into the bath that morning, it occurred to Barbara that it was she who should be the invoker of Nemesis. She had been making a deliberate effort to put the issue out of her mind, but she had knowledge of something that could end Oedipus Snark's political career within days. It had never really occurred to her to use this information but now she thought the time had come. She would have to use what she knew; it was her duty to do so.

A few lines of Yeats came to her, something about the best lacking all conviction and the worst being filled with passionate intensity; she would not be so immodest as to list herself among the best, but those lines, she thought, had some bearing on the situation. Oedipus got away with it because nobody *did* anything. And that was always how evil triumphed; it counted on the inaction of those who, although they might have no taste for it and its works, did nothing to thwart it.

She lay down in the bath and closed her eyes. She had added a few drops of Penhaligon's Lily of the Valley to the water and now she luxuriated in the rich embrace of the bath oil. The warmth of the water and the delicious scent calmed her, and her mind began to drift back to a weekend three years earlier when Oedipus Snark had come to stay. He often did that then, arriving at her flat in time for a late dinner on Friday and staying until Sunday afternoon.

She was pleased by the company. On Saturday mornings they did some shopping, sometimes traipsing across town to a food market before returning to laze about the flat for the afternoon. Oedipus liked crosswords and would spend several hours with one of the more difficult newspaper puzzles, all the while congratulating himself on defeating a compiler's wiles.

"Infantile," he would say, tossing aside a completed crossword. "Predictable. Tedious. Infantile. Composed for ten-year-olds." It did not occur to him that this might be a tactless remark to make in the full hearing of Barbara, who, although not unintelligent, found it difficult to get more than a few clues.

"They don't want to make them too hard," she said. "We can't all be . . ."

"Geniuses?" said Oedipus scornfully. "Clearly not. You don't need to tell me that, Barbara. I have constituents!"

She wanted to retort: *Who voted for you; who pay your salary.* But she did not.

Barbara would read, or spend time in the kitchen preparing the evening meal. Or she would sometimes wash the car, carrying hot water out in her old red bucket with the uncomfortable handle . . . It was bliss, even if she felt that this shared domestic existence could never last. She did not trust Oedipus even then, but tried as hard as she could to put this distrust out of her mind. Oedipus was an attentive lover; he could be amusing—in a waspish sort of way; he made her feel less alone. In short, Oedipus fascinated her, just as a cobra might fascinate its prey.

Then, one Sunday after Oedipus had said goodbye and returned to his flat, she found that his briefcase, which he had placed under a coffee table in the living room, had disgorged a small pile of documents. When he came to leave, he had picked up the briefcase without noticing the spillage, and these were the papers that Barbara now discovered.

She had not intended to read them, but her eye was caught by the name at the top of one of the papers—a very well-known name; a public figure, although not a politician.

She could not help herself. Picking up the letter, she began to read. "Dear Mr. Snark," the letter began, "I am writing to thank you for all that you have done to assist the passage of my company's planning application. We have now been informed that we have been given approval, even if there were one or two members of the council who made shocking allegations in the course of the debate. The usual stuff—the revenge of failure, I call it. Socialists to a man, of course.

"I would like to mark my appreciation of your assistance by increasing the unofficial retainer, bearing in mind we last reviewed this over two years ago. Assuming that the approval is indeed going to reach us this weekend, I would suggest that next weekend you and I meet to finalise things."

Barbara took the letter to her computer and scanned it into the memory. She did not ask herself why—she had no clear plan, but somewhere, in the depths of her mind, a small voice of self-interest, of self-preservation perhaps, bade her act. At that point she was still in love with Oedipus, and had no desire to compromise him. A retainer? Well, lots of politicians were paid retainers of one sort or another, which they openly declared . . .

Barbara happened to know a young woman who worked as a House of Commons researcher. This woman undertook freelance editing to enhance her income and was occasionally given a manuscript by one of the Ragg Porter clients. When Barbara saw her next, she asked her to find out whether Oedipus had declared any payments in the Register of Members' Interests. It was not a difficult request, and the reply came quickly: Oedipus had declared no payments of any nature. "He's clean," said the researcher.

Barbara smiled. Clean, as in dirty, she thought.

15. A Suppressed Memory

OEDIPUS SNARK HAD not been the only difficult man in Barbara Ragg's life. The other was Rupert Porter, her co-director of the Ragg Porter Literary Agency. Rupert was the son of Fatty Porter, who had founded the agency with Barbara's father, Gregory Ragg. The business association between Fatty and Gregory had been a successful one, even if Gregory had always harboured a slight distrust of Fatty and had warned Barbara to be on her guard.

"Remember one thing," he had said. "Like father, like son."

She had pressed him to explain.

"Just remember in your dealings with Rupert: like father, like son. These old adages have an uncanny habit of proving to be true."

She had smiled. "Like: 'All cats are grey in the dark'?"

"Yes, and don't be so superior. The cats are metaphorical; the saying is telling you that you can't be too sure about something when you can't see it properly. Good advice, if you ask me."

She apologised. "I wasn't laughing at you. Sorry."

"No offence taken. Say no more. Least said, soonest mended."

They both laughed at that.

"But going back to Fatty and the firm: you think I should be careful of Rupert?"

He hesitated, but eventually nodded. "Fatty was the sort of man to bear a grudge. He found it hard to forgive."

"An example?"

"Plenty, but here's one. Fatty represented a client, a rather well-known author who died and left a fairly substantial literary estate. The main beneficiary was a young man, the client's nephew. This nephew held a wake for his uncle and didn't invite Fatty. It wasn't an oversight—it was an intentional slight. He had never liked

Fatty and had referred to him as Billy Bunter, the Fat Owl of the Remove, and so on. This got back to Fatty and so the detestation came to be fully reciprocated. The non-invitation to the wake was the final straw.

"Anyway, Fatty nursed that particular grudge, and a few months later he had the opportunity to wreak his revenge. He had received an offer for the film options on some of the late client's books. Remember that as literary executor Fatty had unfettered powers to do what he saw fit, and so he accepted this offer although it was derisory. The films were eventually made and took millions. The estate got virtually nothing.

"Of course, the nephew was furious. He wanted to sue Fatty for breach of fiduciary duty, but the lawyers told him that it would be difficult as there had been no other offers for the rights and Fatty would argue that a bird in the hand et cetera.

"I asked Fatty why he had done it and he looked about him melodramatically to see that nobody was listening. Then he gave me his reply. One word: 'Punishment,' he said."

Barbara thought about this. She would not act like that—no reputable agent would: the nephew was quite within his rights, in her view.

"I'm not suggesting that Rupert will necessarily do anything like that," Gregory said. "But just be aware. Watch him. I have a feeling, for instance, that he resents my passing on the flat to you. Bear that in mind."

Gregory proved right, although he was not to live to see his prediction come true. Rupert bitterly resented the fact that his father had sold Gregory the flat currently owned by Barbara. "Pop would never have sold it," he complained, "if he had known that Gregory was going to pass it on to her. He wanted to help Gregory out, not his daughter. Morally, that flat's mine."

Barbara ignored the snide remarks that Rupert regularly made about her ownership of her flat. She paid no attention when Rupert let drop the fact that he and his wife had expected to have a little bit more living room, and would have had it, had things worked out "as we expected."

Then came the engagement to Hugh, and her offer to sell the flat to Rupert. The plan had been perfectly sensible: she could just as easily work at a distance if she had access to a broadband connection, and all she would need in London was a *pied-à-terre* to use when she came down for meetings.

Rupert had been overwhelmed by the offer and appeared to put all resentment behind him.

"That is astonishingly good of you," he said. "I know that in the past I might have brought up certain issues, but . . ."

"Water under the bridge," she said. "Don't let's even think about all that."

"It's really kind of you," he said. "When shall we . . . ?"

"Would you mind giving me a bit of time? I need to sort everything out."

He had readily agreed. "Take as long as you like. This is a major life-change. You need to sort everything out, especially if you're going to be working away from the office. We need to get the modalities of that all worked out."

Rupert liked the word "modalities" and made frequent use of it. Barbara imagined that even his shopping list contained modalities. *Soap powder. Milk. Bread. Kitchen modalities . . .*

"You don't see any difficulty with my working up there? These days, with broadband conferencing and pdfs and so on, one doesn't really have to be in the office."

"No problem," said Rupert. "None at all. You get the authors to submit in electronic format. Press the print button. Have a glance at the dreary, introspective rubbish. Send the rejection letter back that day by email."

"Very funny!"

"But on the nose. Have you noticed how many unpublishable memoirs of awful experiences we're getting these days? Three a day. Four sometimes."

Barbara thought he was being unsympathetic. Rupert was a man, and men, in her experience, did not like to read about the misfortunes of others. Women, by contrast, loved to do just that, drawing on the vast wells of feeling built up over the generations. "But lots of people have dreadful things happen to them," she objected. "In their childhood, for instance. All sorts of cruelty and insecurity."

"True. But lots don't. How about some memoirs from them for a change?"

She wondered whether Rupert had ever suffered. He was so self-assured, so apparently pleased to be Rupert Porter . . .

"Nothing nasty ever happen to you, Rupert?" she asked. "When you were a boy?"

Rupert shook his head. "Not really."

"Never bullied?"

"Not that I remember. The odd fight in the playground, of course, but who didn't have that sort of thing? Part of growing up."

He paused, and for a moment she thought that he was going to say more. He did not, but he was remembering something now: how his father, Fatty, had once punished him for some transgression. His father had sat on him, forcing the wind out of him under that great, crushing weight. "Do it one more time," Fatty had warned, "and I'll sit on you again!"

The moment passed, and the suppressed memory of darkness and a struggle for breath faded.

16. Her Own Decision

BARBARA HAD NOT told Hugh immediately that the buyer she had in mind for her flat was Rupert. When she did eventually reveal this to him, though, he frowned and looked doubtful.

"Why him?" he asked.

"Because he's wanted it for years," she explained. "He has this bizarre notion that it's his by right because his father sold it to my father. He thinks about it all the time and can't resist any opportunity to bring it up. Snide remarks. References to his flat being too small, and so on. It's really tedious stuff, and so I thought that I might as well put a stop to it by giving him what he wants."

Hugh's frown deepened. "Is there any merit in his claim?"

"None at all. It's ridiculous. Just because your father owned something doesn't mean that it should be yours. It's nonsense . . ."

"Then don't do it," said Hugh. "You haven't signed anything yet, have you?"

She had not.

"Then you're in the clear," Hugh went on. "Remember that when it comes to houses you can say what you like right up until the moment at which contracts are actually exchanged. It all means nothing before that. People agree to sell flats all the time and then change their mind when a better offer comes along, or when they decide they don't want to move after all."

"But I told him," said Barbara.

"Tell him that you've changed your mind."

"But I haven't."

"Then you should."

"Why?"

Hugh's concern registered in his expression. "It would be a very bad mistake, I think, to sell your flat right now. The market is tricky. If you hold on to it, then you would probably get a much better price a couple of years from now. Everybody's saying that. Read the papers. They're all making the same predictions: a recovery in prices won't happen for quite a few years."

She was silent. She was not one to change her mind arbitrarily and she certainly was not one to go back on her promises. She told Hugh so, and he listened gravely.

"I know that," he said. "And I admire you for it. I wouldn't want to marry somebody who changed her mind about important things, somebody fickle or untrustworthy. No. But this is different."

"Why?"

He reached out and took her hand. She marvelled at his touch; she still did. "Listen," he said. "There are promises and promises. Some things we say bind us; others don't. A solemn promise is binding, but an offer to do something that we don't really have to do is . . . Well, there's a certain amount of discretion there. We can change our minds because it's understood that there's flexibility. There's no moral obligation to do favours to others."

"Moral obligation?" she said. "Isn't there a moral obligation not to disappoint others when we've said we'll do something for them?"

"It depends," said Hugh. "If it's implicit that we may change our minds because of the nature of the promise, then we can. As I've said, a promise to sell a house is always like that. The other person *knows* you're entitled to change your mind. That makes a big difference."

He saw that she was not convinced and tried another tack. "He brought pressure to bear on you, you said? Over the years."

She nodded. "I suppose you could say that."

Hugh spoke triumphantly. "Then your position is even stronger!

You have absolutely no moral obligation to see this through. It's a promise extracted under duress. He's ground you down—taken advantage of you; pushed you into making the offer."

"Do you really think so?"

He did.

"I don't know, Hugh. It's going to be very awkward."

"Darling, would you like me to do it for you—would you like me to tell him?"

She considered this offer for a moment before rejecting it. "I don't think so. This strikes me as being dirty work that one should do oneself."

"Except it's not dirty," he objected.

"Really?"

"You're being taken advantage of by a man who has tried to wear you down over the years. He has behaved badly and frankly he doesn't deserve what you offered him. Now, on more sober reflection, you're deciding to withdraw your offer. That's all."

She had eventually been persuaded. Hugh, she felt, was right, and she should not have been so impetuous in her original offer. She would tell Rupert, who would be angry, of course, but he had been angry about things before and she had weathered the storm. I do not need to be frightened of him, she said to herself. Rupert is a bully. I shall stand up to him.

Thinking this was strangely liberating. She realised that she had been bullied by men twice in her life—by Oedipus and by Rupert. Now, with Hugh—a good and kind man—at her side she felt so much stronger, so much more capable of dealing with male pressure.

The conversation with Hugh had taken place in Ardnamurchan when Barbara had gone up for a weekend. She decided that she would tell Rupert of her change of mind when she returned to London. But then, on the train down from Fort William, the thought occurred to her: If she withdrew her offer to Rupert, was she not simply repeating the old pattern—*doing the bidding of a man*? Hugh was her fiancé and she loved and trusted him, and yet here she was, doing what he told her to do. Was this not yet another case of female inauthenticity? And if she did as Hugh told her now, would the rest of her life—her life with him—be characterised by the same behaviour? At their wedding, might she not just as well use those now-abandoned words from the marriage service and promise to love, honour and *obey*?

The thought was disturbing, and presented her with a real dilemma. If she rejected Hugh's advice she would implicitly be saying that she wanted to do as *she* chose. But in so doing, she would end up acting as another man—Rupert—wanted, and that would mean that she had complied with a man's wishes in any case.

Barbara had plenty of feminist friends—or friends who claimed feminist credentials; perhaps she should ask one of them. The friend would give advice, no doubt, but then if Barbara took it, would that not be a case of her doing the bidding of a *woman*? And if you were a woman was there any difference—any real difference—between doing what a woman tells you to do and doing what a man tells you to do? There was a distinction, she thought, but she was not quite sure she could put her finger on it. Was it the case that there was a presumption that a man would advise you with an eye to his own interests, whereas a woman would be more likely to take your interests into account? Yes, she thought. But then she wondered: Why should we think that men are inevitably self-interested? Could men not believe in the right of women to autonomous decisions? Of course they could.

She made up her mind: I shall tell Rupert it's off—and I don't care what he does. My decision. Made by me. Authentic. Autonomous. And within her a small voice added: *Disastrous*.

17. The Friendship of Dogs

WILLIAM RARELY USED his car, which he kept in a distant lockup bought before the prices of such places had become unaffordable. He knew that the rational thing would be to sell the garage for the absurdly inflated price it would doubtless command, but for the moment inertia reigned, along with a certain attachment to the contented Saab that the lockup contained.

The main reason for the infrequent use of the car was the fact that he very rarely had anywhere to go. Apart from work, to which he travelled by tube, and wine tastings, to which he took a taxi, William went virtually nowhere—evidence, he thought, of the profound rut into which he had fallen. London, it appeared to him, was full of people rushing around on journeys that merely underlined the point that they were not only doing far more than he was but also having more fun in the process.

But late that Friday afternoon he, too, was about to go somewhere. With his weekend bag packed in the back of the Saab, he settled Freddie de la Hay into the front passenger seat. Freddie was thoroughly in favour of outings of any description, and the prospect of a spin in the car was particularly appealing. His mouth open in the enthusiastic grin that marks out a dog anticipating a treat, Freddie stared steadily ahead through the windscreen, focusing on the stained rear wall of the garage as if it were a vista of the utmost promise for dogs and humans alike.

"Right," said William, as he closed the door and strapped himself into his seatbelt. "Here we go for a weekend in the country. Suffolk to be precise. You know Suffolk, Freddie?"

Freddie gave a small growl of encouragement that William interpreted as a yes.

"Aldeburgh, Freddie," William continued. "Or close by. Know that part?"

Again, Freddie gave a receptive response.

"And I'm pleased to say that Geoffrey and Maggie have invited you too," William continued as he turned the key in the ignition. It was always an anxious moment when the underused battery decided whether or not it had the willpower to bring the engine to life. This time it had, and William heaved a sigh of relief.

They drove out through the sprawling outskirts of London, a landscape that at the same time expressed and refuted the premise of its creation: a dream of *rus in urbe* realised in a bit of half-choked greenery, a tiny patch of ground, low walls and fences around box-like houses. William found himself depressed by these surround-ings and felt grateful that, for all the crowding and expense of town, he was not part of this suburban world. And yet he knew that most residents of these suburbs would never wish to exchange their life for his; would hate to give up their gardens, their tiny driveways and their patch of sky for a life in a flat with shared staircases and neighbours on either side, below and above, hearing one's breath-ing, taking a bath, boiling a kettle, living.

"À *chacun son goût*, don't you think?" he remarked to Freddie.

Freddie looked at his master and gave a weak canine grin. He was one for whom suburbia would be infinitely preferable to a city existence. One's own territory, no matter how small; an en suite lamppost virtually at the front gate; a doorstep on which one might sit in the sun; a postman who provocatively came up to one's very door, whose ankles cried out to be nipped if only one had the chance; these were the things that counted for a dog.

William looked fondly at Freddie de la Hay. He had not had the dog for more than a couple of years, but he had become so ac-customed to his company that it was difficult to remember how life had been before Freddie. He had mentioned this to Marcia—whose feelings for Freddie were not without ambiguity, she believing that the dog prevented William's feeling *really* lonely. That, in Marcia's view, was both good and bad: good because Freddie de la Hay made William happy, and bad because the lonelier William was, the more he would relish her company. She was a realist, of course, and knew that at present there was little chance of their friendship becoming anything more that just that, a friendship, but if William were to become desperate with loneliness . . . And it *could* work, she felt, it really could . . .

William found that the bond between him and Freddie de la Hay raised a wider question of the relationship between man and dog. Freddie had never been asked whether he wanted to devote himself to William; he just did so. That was what made canine friendship so remarkable: a dog gave its friendship—and its devotion—without any thought as to whether the person to whom these were given deserved them. In that respect the dog acted without calculation as to what it might receive in return. How different, then, from human friendship, which in many cases is dished out sparingly and only with a great deal of forethought as to what might be got from it. That was why the beautiful and the rich had so many friends, and so easily acquired, whereas the less blessed in looks and the poor had to work much harder to win the friendship of others.

Dogs did not care what their owners looked like. The most un-prepossessing of people might have the most elegant of dogs look-ing up at them as if they possessed the beauty of Greek gods. The most wretched, the most materially deprived, might have a dog—admittedly a thin dog—that remained loyal in the face of pinching poverty. How dogs showed us up, thought William; they took what fate allocated to them and made the most of it.

"So, Freddie," said William. "I'm the straw you've drawn in that lottery. Thanks for being so good about it."

Freddie de la Hay was aware that William had addressed a remark to him but in his ears it was just a noise, even if a noise in which one recognisable element—his name—had occurred. People, Freddie had observed, made these noises constantly. They were like fridges that gurgled and hummed away during the day, a background noise that dogs found reassuring. Only when these noises stopped and there was silence did a dog have to look out. That was ominous—when the gurgling stopped and disapproval set in. But that was not happening now, thank heavens, and he could turn his attentions to the smells that were wafting in from the outside. The car was now on the very outskirts of London and the countryside was making its olfactory presence felt. Freddie de la Hay shivered in anticipation as he sniffed at the rush of air from his inadequately closed window; old cars like William's were good for dogs, as they let the outside in. And this outside air was a form of aerial palimpsest for Freddie, with layer upon layer of intriguing smells, and traces of smells: rabbit, cut grass, pheasant, rabbit, horse manure, blackberry, green wellington boots, rabbit . . .

18. Old Friends

THE HOUSE TO which William and Freddie de la Hay had been invited belonged to William's old friend Geoffrey Chiswick and his wife, Maggie. Geoffrey and William had known one another since boyhood, when they had been together in an alternative to the scouts, the Woodcraft Folk. William had been encouraged to join the movement by his father, who had belonged when he had been evacuated during the Blitz; his father had sought to impart to his son his own enthusiasm for camping but William had never taken to it. He had, in fact, met Geoffrey on a Woodcraft camp in Sussex, both aged ten, and both homesick and afraid of being attacked by the cattle occupying the neighbouring field.

"Is it best to play dead if you're attacked by a bull?" William had asked.

They were in their shared tent at night, grimly aware of the scant protection that the thin canvas offered them from anything, including stampeding cattle.

"No," said Geoffrey. "That's bears. If a bear comes at you then you have to lie down and play dead, you jolly well have to, even if the bear begins to bite you. They go away if you play dead."

"Bears . . . ," said William.

"But there aren't any," said Geoffrey, trying to sound convinced. "Bears are extinct."

Geoffrey had been slightly more confident than William, promising to protect him from the hidden dangers of camping in a large English field with forty other children, and this had been the tenor of their relationship ever since: it was implicit that Geoffrey would *look out* for William. Their friendship had survived—as they had—the camping expedition, and at the age of seventeen they had gone together to a pop music festival in the Netherlands, where Geoffrey had been arrested for no apparent reason and William robbed of his wallet and passport. The help they gave each other on that occasion had further cemented the relationship, and in due course Geoffrey had acted as best man at William's wedding, with William returning the compliment four months later. When, after twenty years of marriage, William lost his wife, it was Geoffrey and Maggie who insisted on spending the first raw days of widowerhood with him, taking him up to their house in Suffolk after the funeral, walking with him on the stony beach and putting their arms about him when he cried, which he did, voluminously and despairingly.

Their careers could hardly have been more different. While William did the one thing—wine—Geoffrey rarely spent more than three or four years in a job. He had trained as an actuary, but could not bear office life in the City of London. He had become an insurance broker in Cambridgeshire, and after that had bought, with the aid of a large loan, a garden centre in Suffolk. That had prospered, and he had sold it on and bought a country hotel. The hotel had failed, and he and Maggie had been reduced to near-penury, to be rescued by a friend who took him into partnership in a building-supply firm near Newmarket. This coincided with a rash of development in East Anglia that allowed an extraordinary expansion of the business and, in a very few years, a takeover bid by a larger firm. The proceeds of the sale of Geoffrey's share were such that no further business activities would be required on his part unless he really wanted to do something, and he and Maggie had bought an old farmhouse in the country. Geoffrey, however, did not fancy a life of idleness, and so he acquired a pig farm about five miles from their farmhouse. He installed a manager, a young man from the village whose obsession—and sole topic of conversation—was the raising of rare-breed pigs. This venture, like many ventures run by passionate enthusiasts, proved highly successful, and also gave great pleasure to Maggie, who approved of British Saddleback pigs and enjoyed smoking hams in the old barn behind their house.

"No more change for us," said Geoffrey. "It's pigs and more pigs from now on."

The farmhouse was of uncertain age, the safest conclusion, in Geoffrey's view at least, being that it had "been there for ever." And, unlike many modern buildings, which seem to have been imposed upon the land in an act of conquest, this house appeared to grow out of the land, as naturally as does a plant, or a hedgerow, or a tree. It was the materials used for its construction that gave this impression, of course: wattle and daub for the second of its two storeys, the daub being clay and sand from the land about, while the pinkness of the wash applied to it was obtained, at least in the beginning, by the mixing of the blood of oxen and the juice of sloes. The first storey was made of brick—tiny bricks, red as the land itself, uneven in their dimensions, fitting neatly into the hands of the men who laid them.

The house was concealed from the road by trees that had been planted higgledy-piggledy, or had seeded themselves and been allowed to persist. A pond, overgrown at the edges by reeds, lay a few hundred yards away, and beyond that was a meadow, another meadow, and then a somnolent village with church and pub. It was, thought William as he drove down the farm road that evening, a perfect distillation of rural England; it could be nowhere else. And the beauty of it, the quiet, the utterly unassuming serenity of the place, made him catch his breath and swallow. It did that to him every time he visited, which he did two times a year, once in summer and once in winter.

He drew up on the small gravel circle at the front of the house. Geoffrey's car, an ancient and shabby Renault, was parked under a tree to the side of the house. Even this French car seemed reassuringly English in this setting: well used, understated, unthreatening in its functionality, going nowhere but not the slightest bit worried about that.

19. Moral Meaning and Iris Murdoch

THE DOOR TO the farmhouse was open, as it always seemed to be whenever William visited.

"Don't you lock?" he had once asked Geoffrey.

"No. Not since we came here. We locked the door in Newmarket. Not here."

William, for whom the act of locking was second nature, shook his head in wonderment. "I have two locks," he said. "And I know people with three."

Geoffrey looked regretful. "It seems such a pity to lock, doesn't it? It makes you feel as if you're living in a fortress."

"Which we are, I suppose." And it would get worse, he thought; much worse.

Geoffrey agreed. "Yes. And what about these panic rooms that people have in their houses now? Talk about fortresses . . ."

"I don't know anybody who has a panic room," said William. "Or not just yet . . ."

Geoffrey, who had read about them in the newspaper, launched into an explanation. "You have a sort of walk-in safe in the middle of the house. When the intruders come, you gather the family together and climb into this safe and lock the door behind you. That means that the burglars can't get at you."

"And you phone the police?"

"Yes. That's how it works."

William thought about this. "Perhaps one might have a panic room to use when you have unwanted guests—people whom you can't stand. If they come to visit you, you could retreat into your panic room and close the door behind you until they go away."

"Those exist," said Geoffrey. "They're called studies."

They both laughed. "You would let me know, wouldn't you, if my visits were ever unwelcome?" asked William. How often, he thought, do we question whether our old friends still *like* us.

"Your visits are never unwelcome," replied Geoffrey. And William believed him.

And now here was William opening the door of the car and

letting Freddie de la Hay out after the long journey from London. The dog shot off into the undergrowth bordering the small lawn to the side of the house, giving a bark of delight as he did so. William unloaded his bag from the back seat of the car and walked towards the front door. Underfoot, the gravel made that crunching sound that always delighted him, and reminded him, indeed, when he heard it elsewhere, of here.

Maggie came to greet him, embracing him in the hall, keeping her hands off his jacket, though, as they were covered in flour.

"Pastry," she explained. "For a pie. For you to take back to London on Sunday."

"Darling cook," said William, planting a kiss on her cheek.

"You need feeding up," said Maggie.

"Do I?"

"Probably not. But I'm making you a Melton Mowbray pie, or an imitation of one now that we can't call our humble pies by that name any more. Or so Brussels says."

"It's the people of Melton Mowbray who say it," said William. "Not Brussels."

"I suppose so. They don't have much else, do they, poor dears? Just their pies."

He followed her through to the kitchen, leaving his bag on a chair in the hall. Freddie de la Hay was still outside, but clearly remembered the house and would find his own way in once he had finished his preliminary investigations in the bushes.

Maggie dusted her hands on her apron. She was a tall woman, still auburn-haired at forty-six; attractive, thought William, but in the habit of wearing rather old-fashioned steel-rimmed glasses that gave her a vaguely scholarly air, like that of a displaced librarian. And she was indeed scholarly, he reminded himself: when Geoffrey had married Maggie she had been a postgraduate student at the University of East Anglia, writing a doctoral thesis on moral imagery in the novels of Iris Murdoch. This thesis was never completed, marriage—and life in general—being responsible for many an uncompleted doctorate, but it still lay, a pile of neatly stacked typescript, on a desk in Maggie's room upstairs. And then, to add to the thesis-inhibiting effect of marriage, there came the distraction of two children, a boy and a girl, both now away from home studying subjects that William could never remember: something to do with product-engineering in one case and psychology in the other.

"Your thesis?" William once asked her.

She rolled her eyes. "Maybe one day." She paused, looking at him through the steel-rimmed glasses. "I still want to finish it, you know. Oh, I won't get a degree from it—it's too late for that. But I do want to complete it."

"Like my Master of Wine qualification," said William. "The one I failed. At least you didn't fail your Ph.D. You just . . . moved on."

"You were drunk, weren't you?"

William shrugged. "That's the trouble with doing a practical wine exam. You have to taste samples."

Maggie was sympathetic. "I can understand why you'd like to do it again. Unfinished business—most of us have something we haven't finished, even if it's something small, like completing the decoration of a room, or sorting out a cupboard. Small things— small *unfinished* things."

"How much more Murdoch is there?"

Maggie opened her hands in a gesture of helplessness. "The more I read her," she said, "the more I discover. Her books are like quarries—you can dig away for as long as you like and keep finding new material, new dimensions to her work. She believed in good, you know. How strange it seems today that anybody should believe in good!"

William had read some of the novels, but not for a long time. He remembered swimming scenes, for some reason. There was a lot of water, he thought.

"I sometimes wonder," Maggie went on, "how she would regard me, if she met me now. Would she think that I was a bit of a failure, having spent all that time thinking about her work and then ending up here, raising pigs, making pies in the kitchen . . . ?"

"I don't think she would," said William. "I saw a documentary about her once. I remember that, even if I don't remember the novels very well. She was sitting there, with rather short hair, and her eyes were moving as she spoke, darting about in a tremendously intelligent way. But I thought she seemed very down to earth, very matter of fact. She wouldn't disapprove of people who gave up philosophy or literary theory to do ordinary things."

"Maybe not," mused Maggie. "If we eat pies, then we should never, not for one moment, look down on the making of them."

"I don't," said William. "I never have."

20. Rupert's Disclosure

BARBARA RAGG SAT at her desk and looked at the open double page of her diary before her. It was not a busy day, the morning's only noted commitment being a brief meeting with a publisher at ten-thirty, over a cappuccino in one of the coffee bars which that part of Soho still allowed to flourish among the dubious bars and overpriced restaurants. Barbara was a member of the Ivy Club, some fifteen minutes away in West Street, and the publisher, who was notoriously mean, had angled for an invitation to lunch there, knowing that with a club lunch the member always pays.

"It would be nice to meet for lunch," he had said. "I'd take you to my club, but it's closed for renovations. Any suggestions?"

She had smiled. The publisher's club must have been renovated several times in the course of her dealings with him; perhaps it was like the Forth Bridge, which, until the invention of miracle paints, had needed to be tackled all over again by the time the painting crews reached the far side.

"Your poor club," she said. "Wasn't it being renovated earlier this year?"

There had been a pause while the question was assessed. "That was the basement. A new . . ."

She waited. "Yes?"

"Set of bedrooms."

She frowned. "That's strange. It can't be much fun staying in the basement. Not much natural light, I would have thought. So what are they working on now?"

"Oh, heaven knows. But we can't go there, I'm afraid."

She rolled her eyes. "Then let's have coffee. Ten-thirty?"

So there was that, and then at two o'clock she was expecting a visit from one of her authors who had telephoned to say that he had had an idea. This was all that was in the diary, and neither of these appointments would be remotely stressful. But unrecorded was a further and infinitely more worrying duty: a session with Rupert. It could be put off, but she realised that it would then only prey on her mind. So she closed her eyes, mentally counted to ten, then twenty, then thirty; prevarication enough, she thought, and rose to her feet.

Rupert's office was down the corridor. While Barbara kept her door open so that any member of the agency's staff might drop in with a query or for a chat, Rupert's door policy was distinctly less encouraging. Not only was his door always closed, but there were occasions when, although everybody knew that he was within, he resolutely refused to answer a knock. "If people want to speak to me," he once observed, "then they can speak to me about speaking to me. This casual, everybody's welcome approach is an utter waste of time. Believe me." This comment was accompanied by a look in Barbara's direction—a look that she intercepted and met with a challenging stare.

"Saying 'believe me' all the time is a sign of insecurity," Barbara had observed to one of her colleagues. "You say it because you doubt that anybody's going to believe you. And why should nobody believe you?"

"Because you tell so many lies," said the colleague.

"I didn't say that," said Barbara, and laughed, adding: "Believe me."

Now, standing in front of Rupert's door, she drew a deep breath and knocked firmly. There was no reply, and so she knocked once more. Again there was no answer.

She took another deep breath and tested the handle. The door was not locked. She pushed it open.

Rupert was sitting back in his chair, his feet on his desk. He was reading a manuscript, which he barely lowered as Barbara came in.

"I wish you'd knock, Barbara," he said from behind the manuscript. "It doesn't take much effort, you know."

"I did," she said. "Twice."

"Oh, sorry," he said. "I didn't hear you. I could have been on the phone, you know. It might not have been convenient."

"Well, you weren't," she said briskly. "Which was most fortunate, as I need to have a word with you, Rupert."

Rupert lowered the manuscript and took his feet off the desk. "Fine," he drawled. "My door is always open. Metaphorically, of course. What can I do for you, dear R— Barbara?"

Barbara knew that he referred to her as Ragg, or la Ragg, but it rarely slipped out in her presence. She drew up the chair beside his desk and sat down.

"It's about the flat."

His manner changed immediately: he was now all solicitude. "Of course. Have you decided on a date? You know that we'll be happy to do anything to help you. I'm even prepared to shift furniture, you know—an alternative to going to the gym. Really. Yes, I really am."

She shook her head. "No. There's not going to be a date, Rupert. I've decided to keep the flat after all. I'm so sorry to have raised your hopes, but I know that you'll understand."

For a moment Rupert said nothing. She watched his face, though, and saw the colour rise. Rupert had always been like a piece of litmus paper, she thought, his complexion revealing his emotional state with immediate and striking clarity.

"So," he said at last. "You're going to break your promise to me. Just like that. Pouf! Promise gone."

"It wasn't exactly a promise, Rupert," said Barbara mildly. "As I recall, all I said was that I had decided to sell the flat and you could buy it. Your ability to buy it was dependent on my initial decision to sell, and relied on that. When my decision changed, your interest fell away."

Rupert's eyes opened wide. "Don't you come the hair-splitting scholastic theologian with me, Ragg," he shouted. "You promised, and you're now going to break your promise. Fine. That shows me what sort of partner I've got. My father was right. He warned me that no Ragg could be trusted. That's what he said, you know. He said you were as unreliable as gypsies."

"That's a shocking thing to say, Rupert. Are you saying that gypsies are unreliable? Is that what you're suggesting?"

"I didn't say they were unreliable, I said that *you* Raggs were unreliable."

"You didn't. I heard you, Rupert. You said that gypsies were unreliable. You can't say things like that these days, you know. It's insulting."

He stared at her venomously. "What do you know about gypsies, Barbara? Nothing, that's what!"

"So you're the big expert on gypsies, Rupert? Like so many other things."

He looked away. "I'm going to get even with you, Barbara, I promise you. And just you remember: I, unlike some I could name, keep my promises." He paused. "There's something you should perhaps know, Barbara. You interested? Well, since you started this, I might tell you. My father knew more about your father than you do. Yes, it's true. And you know what? He told me that your grandfather was a gypsy. He never told *you* that, did he? Well, he told Pop, and Pop told me. So you should go away and think about that little bit of information, Barbara!"

21. On Who We Really Are

BARBARA RAGG MANAGED to meet the publisher for coffee at ten-thirty as planned, but only just. She had thought all along that her conversation with Rupert would not be easy, but she had not imagined that it would be quite as uncomfortable as this, and she had certainly not anticipated that Rupert would make a disclosure as to the identity of her grandfather. She left his office reeling. Outside in the corridor, she turned first one way, then the other. She looked up. There was the office accountant, staring at her anxiously.

The accountant, a thin woman with a permanently worried expression, reached out to touch Barbara's arm. "Is everything all right, Barbara? You look a bit upset."

"I'm fine. It's just that I've exchanged a few words with Rupert, and . . ."

"Oh, I know what it's like talking to him. Impossible." Her hand shot to her mouth. "Sorry. Didn't mean that."

Barbara reassured her, but her manner was distracted. "No, don't apologise. Rupert is . . . Well, we all have our ways."

The accountant gave a weak smile. "We need to gang together," she whispered. "We women need to stand up to him. It's the only way with bullies."

Barbara nodded. "Do you think it felt like this during the Battle of Britain?"

"Of course it did," said the accountant. "It must have been like this every minute of the day. And they stood up to the bullies, didn't they? Those young men—half of them barely out of short trousers; they stood up against the bullies."

The accountant patted Barbara's arm and went on her way. Barbara, still dazed, returned to her room and sat down heavily in her chair. I have gypsy blood, she thought. Rom. Traveller. Whatever it's called these days—that's me. *That's me.*

There was no doubt in her mind that what Rupert had said was correct. Her grandfather on her father's side had died some years before her birth, as had his wife, her grandmother. It was not until she was about eight that she had started to ask her father about his parents—questions brought on by the conversation of coevals at school who saw their grandparents regularly.

"What happened to your parents?" she asked directly. "They're my grandparents, aren't they?"

Gregory Ragg had looked away. "They died, darling. Terribly sad, but there we are. Went to heaven."

He did not seem to wish to continue the conversation, but she persisted. "Where did they live?"

He had sounded a bit vague. "Here and there. They moved about a bit."

Now, remembering this exchange all these years later, her father's words came back to her. *They moved about a bit.* Of course they did: that's what travellers did—they travelled.

"So what did Granddad do for a living? Was he a literary agent, like you?"

"Not quite, darling. My dad was keener on the outdoor life. He liked fresh air."

"So what did he do? Was he a farmer?"

"Not really. He had business dealings with farmers, though. He loved horses, your granddad. He was a very good judge of horse-flesh. He took a lot of them . . ." And there he had faltered.

Took a lot of horses. What did *that* mean? The meaning was quite clear now, of course, and she felt foolish that she had not understood then. Nor had she understood the significance of her father's remarks on his education. "I had terrifically good luck with my education," he explained to her. "There was a bit of a mix-up, you see, and I was left by mistake under a hedge when I was three. And this terrifically kind man whose hedge it was found me and took me in. He sent me to a little school nearby and then on to an expensive boarding place. It was a really good education and I made the most of it. My parents would never have been able to afford it."

"Did you see your parents again? Your real parents, that is."

"Yes. The man who took me in had a good idea who they were, and he made a point of keeping in touch with them. So my father came to see me every so often, right up to the time he died."

It seemed strange to her that a father might leave a son in a hedge and still be interested in him. "But he left you in a hedge," she said.

"I like to think that he knew what he was doing," said Gregory. "I like to think that he was very well aware that my stepfather would find me and look after me. I think of it as an act of generosity on his part. He wanted the best for me, and he knew that the way to secure it was to abandon me. It was an act of self-sacrifice. A noble act."

Barbara had lost interest and the matter was not pursued. Nor did her father make subsequent reference to his parents, and she picked up on the prickly feeling of discouragement that surrounded the subject. But it all made sense, all fitted so neatly into place, now that she knew.

Her first reaction, of course, was shock. But, sitting in her office, she reflected on the meaning of what had been revealed to her. There was nothing wrong in being a gypsy, anything more than there was anything wrong in living a settled life in a house made of bricks and mortar. We were all the same, were we not, when we came into this world: we were all equal in our vulnerability and our malleability. And we did not *ask* for the bed in which we were born: that was one of the things over which we had no control at all, just as we had no say as to whether we would be redheads, or tall or short or somewhere in between; or whether we were born Polish or Zambian, Catholic or Muslim or Jewish. We had no choice in all this. And it was this, precisely this, that made it so wrong to think the less of another for what he or she *was*. There was no moral obligation to *like* others, nor necessarily to enthuse over them, but we did have to recognise their equal worth.

Barbara stood up. On the wall beside her bookcase there was a mirror that she used to tidy up before a meeting. Now she saw herself reflected in it, and she leaned forward to peer more closely at her face. "*Gypsy*," she muttered under her breath. And what looked back was the face of her ancestors: long-dead judges of horseflesh, occupants of colourful wooden caravans, the victims of all sorts of abuse and bad treatment. She reached out and touched the reflection. "Hello," she whispered, as one who, for the first time, acknowledges some aspect of self long denied or unknown. *Hello.*

22. Coffee with George

WHAT DIFFERENCE, BARBARA considered as she made her way to the coffee bar, what earthly difference does it make who my grandfather was? Or my grandmother, for that matter. Rupert had not mentioned her, and neither had Gregory, now that she thought of it: her father had only spoken of his own father, and it had never occurred to her to ask him about his mother. Perhaps that was just another example of the fate of women in those days—to be eclipsed by men. Was her grandmother also a gypsy—or traveller? Should she be using the word "gypsy"—was it an act of discourtesy towards her own people? She rather liked the word, which she had never seen as offensive, but then that was before the . . . the revelation; for that is how she thought of it—a profound and over-whelming revelation. *I am now something special,* she thought. *I am Rom . . . I come from somewhere else, from outside all this.* This answered the question as to what difference the revelation repre-sented: in a curious way it freed her.

The publisher whom she was due to meet was already in the cof-fee bar when she arrived, seated at one of the small tables near the window. As she entered, he looked pointedly at his watch.

"I was about to give up on you," he said.

Barbara glanced at the clock on the wall behind the counter. "Sorry, George. It's only ten minutes. I had a meeting."

George looked at his watch again. "I have to be away in twenty minutes, I'm afraid."

She ordered coffee for both of them and returned to the table.

"You're Australian, aren't you, George?"

He looked at her with surprise. "Of course I am. You know that. We did the Melbourne book with that author of yours. Remember—

we took him out to lunch, and we discovered that he and I had been at the same school."

She remembered. She had paid the bill on that occasion too, and now she felt like saying: *I* took him out to lunch actually.

"You always knew you were Australian, of course."

He looked at her sideways. "Always knew I was Australian? Of course I did. How could I think otherwise . . . ?" He paused, and frowned. "Oh, I see what you're driving at. Cultural identity—that sort of thing. Yes, well, I suppose in my case I grew up just after Whitlam and Australia was beginning to ask itself that sort of question. But I never thought of myself as British, as my parents did. They were both born there and yet they thought of themselves as British, at least for the first part of their lives. Then suddenly all that stopped and we thought of ourselves as Australian and nothing else. We grew up. End of the cultural cringe and all that. Finito."

She listened. "And now?"

He smiled at her. "What is this? The cricket-support test? Whom do I cheer when I watch England versus Australia?"

"No, not that. It's just . . . well, I've had a bit of a shock this morning. I've discovered something about myself."

The proprietor brought their coffee to the table. George lifted his spoon and dipped it into the top layer of foamed milk. "You don't have to tell me," he said. "We publishers have a don't ask, don't tell policy." He grinned.

"Nothing to do with that."

He lifted his cup to his lips. "So you've discovered you're Australian? Is that it?"

She hesitated. It was the first time she was mentioning her new knowledge to anybody, and she might have chosen somebody other than George—Hugh, ideally—but George was in this place at this time and she had to speak about it.

"What do you think about gypsies?" she asked.

He lowered his cup. "Have you been drinking, Barbara?"

"What?"

"It's just that you've made very little sense since you came in here. Asking me whether I always knew I was Australian. Then you mention a personal discovery of some sort. Then suddenly you ask me my view of gypsies, of all people."

Barbara had to admit that it sounded strange. But it all made sense, she explained, because . . . "Well, you see, I've just discovered that I'm at least one quarter gypsy. Just this morning. An hour or so ago."

George shrugged. "So are lots of people, I imagine."

"But it's important . . ."

He shrugged again. "Not really. Gypsies look pretty much like anybody else to me. Two arms, two legs, a nose." He paused, look-ing at her in a way which made it seem as if he were assessing her. "Of course, people are pretty hung up on these things in this coun-try, aren't they? In Australia it makes not the slightest bit of differ-ence. Half the population can trace their roots back to some poor cattle thief, and so we don't put much store by such things. And what's wrong with being a gypsy, anyway? Rather colourful life, I would have thought. Free as air. No taxes. They don't pay income tax, do they?"

Barbara said that she was not sure whether they paid taxes. "I wasn't saying there's anything wrong. It's just that it makes me *feel* different, somehow. It gives me a sense of being, well, a bit of an outsider."

George laughed. "Imagination. You're no different from what you were when you got up this morning. Don't fantasise about gyp-sies or circuses or whatever. If you want that sort of stuff, go and read Enid Blyton." He looked at her severely. "And now we have to get down to business, Barbara, as we can't sit here indefinitely talk-ing about you. That manuscript you sent me, the Errol Greatorex one. We want him to finish it as soon as possible, and we're going to do something big with it. But first we need to know: Is it fiction or non-fiction? By which I mean, is there really a yeti and did he really dictate his memoirs to this Greatorex character?"

Barbara took a sip of her coffee. "George, I'll be absolutely straight with you. It's non-fiction. And yes, the yeti exists." She put down her cup, and added, "He really does. Would you like to meet him?"

"Of course." He looked at her and smiled. "You know something, Barbara? I really don't believe I'm having this conversation. How strange is that?"

"Very," she said.

"And I've got a feeling you're going to offer to tell my fortune. Or sell me a bunch of lucky heather."

Barbara wagged a finger at him. "Don't think in stereotypes," she said. "But I may ask you for the price of a cup of coffee."

23. A Walk in the Country

THE EVENING SUN was warm on the pink-washed walls of the Suffolk farmhouse in which William stood chatting with Maggie, his hostess and the wife of his childhood friend, Geoffrey.

"Where's Geoff?" he asked as Maggie washed her hands in the large Belfast sink.

"Looking at the pigs, I think," she said. "He usually checks up on them at this time of the evening. Our pig-keeper, Wally, goes off for his tea round about now, so Geoff takes the opportunity to spend a bit of quality time with the pigs." She reached for a towel and dried her hands energetically. "Geoff's trying some Gloucester

Old Spot and Tamworth crosses at the moment. Nice-looking pigs. He'll be back soon."

"Geoff's a happy man, isn't he? He's got his pigs, this place, his stamp collection . . ."

Maggie, who had removed her glasses in the final stage of preparing her pie, now replaced them. "Yes, I think he's happy. Although sometimes he wonders whether he isn't getting in a rut with the farming thing and shouldn't do something different with his life while he's still got the energy for new projects."

"The worst question to ask oneself," said William. "Therein lies regret after regret."

Maggie nodded. "Yes. The only point in asking that question is to sharpen up how one approaches the rest of one's time. Having the odd regret might warn us against wasting our chances." She paused, moving across the kitchen to gaze out of the window. The sun was on her face now, creating a halo effect through her slightly disordered hair. "I've often thought that the worst regret must be to think that one's spent one's life with the wrong person. It must be terrible, truly terrible."

William agreed. "And yet many people must feel that, mustn't they?"

"Yes. They must. Though these days, most of them can get out of their relationship—and do."

William thought about this. He had friends who acknowledged that they were staying together for the sake of their children. He thought it noble. Maggie, though, seemed uncertain. "Noble? I suppose that any form of sacrifice has a certain nobility to it. And yet foolish may be an equally good way of describing it. Throwing away twenty years of your life, or however long, could be viewed as downright silly rather than noble."

"Except it's not throwing away twenty years—it's setting them aside for a higher cause."

No, she was even more unsure about that. "What did Horace say? *Dulce et decorum est pro patria mori.* It's sweet and fitting to die for one's country. Is it really? Or is it just bad luck?"

"I'm uncomfortable about that, Maggie. Really uncomfortable. Giving your life for something can be a magnificent thing to do, heroic . . ."

She was silent for a moment. "Yes, you're right," she conceded. "That was going too far. It depends on the cause, though. What if your country's fighting an unjust war, or even a useless one? What then?"

"It may still be the right thing to do."

This brought a sideways look from Maggie. "Maybe . . . But look, shall we go for a walk? By the time we come back Geoff will have returned from the pigs, and the two of you can have a whisky together before our guests arrive. We've invited a few people over for supper. Freddie de la Hay would like a walk, wouldn't he? Where is he by the way?"

He had not seen Freddie since he came into the house. The dog had gone off to sniff about the garden, and William knew that he was unlikely to go far: Freddie de la Hay was no wanderer. "If he wants to come, he'll turn up," he said. "Otherwise he'll be perfectly happy investigating your garden. You don't mind, do you?"

Maggie did not. She fetched an old Barbour jacket—"Such a cliché," she said, "but so comfortable and practical. Please don't judge."

"I have one myself," said William. "And green wellingtons too."

"Good. Then we'll both sink into our stereotypes."

They went outside. The summer solstice was six weeks in the past, as the slant of the evening sun revealed, but the air was still warm and heavy. Maggie had planted lavender in profusion and its scent was all about them, mingling with that of recently cut grass. William sniffed at it as he would at a good Médoc, savouring the fragrance. The olfactory treat made him think of Freddie, and he called the dog several times.

"Nowhere to be seen?" asked Maggie.

"He'll turn up," said William. "He always does."

They set off down a path that led past the barn and into one of the fields. As they walked, Maggie returned to the subject of her thesis.

"You know what I feel when I sit down to write about Iris Murdoch? You know what goes through my mind?"

William shrugged. "The ideas?" he suggested. "All those ideas you talked about?"

"No," said Maggie. "I feel sad. I think sad thoughts."

"Why?"

"Because she's no longer with us. Because such a wonderful intelligence is silent. But mostly because the intellectual elite that used to be at the centre of our national life here is changing and there's no room for such figures. What we have instead are sound-bite merchants."

William was puzzled. "But there are plenty of people with opinions."

"Are there?" asked Maggie. "Or are those who come out with something slightly different shouted down? Don't you think there's a certain hegemony of opinion these days? An approved way of thinking? Don't you think that it's considered almost indecent now to voice an opinion that deviates from the consensus?"

"Perhaps. Perhaps it's a bit like that."

Maggie said nothing for a moment. "Perhaps. But . . ." She hesitated, as if weighing whether or not to continue. "You know what you said back there about unhappiness. You talked about Geoff's happiness. But you didn't ask about me, did you?"

He was slightly taken aback. "Didn't I? Well, that's very rude of me. I suppose it's because I've always assumed that you're perfectly happy. You have your . . ." What did Maggie have—her thesis on Iris Murdoch? Her Melton Mowbray pies? Her family?

"My kitchen? Is that what you were going to say?"

"No. Certainly not. You've got your thesis. But it's not just a question of what you have—it's a matter of attitude. And I think that your attitude, your disposition, is fundamentally happy."

Her voice was quiet. "Well, it's not. I'm not happy, William. I'm not happy."

He stopped. The stick he was carrying, a bit of oak branch, fell to the ground. He did not bend to pick it up. "Why?" he asked. "Why do you say you're unhappy?"

She was looking at him directly, staring into his eyes. "Because of you," she said softly. "Because I'm in love with you, William. I've loved you for years—for years—and I've never had the courage to confess it to anybody. Well, now I'm telling you."

24. Things That Didn't Happen

FOR WILLIAM, MAGGIE'S declaration was the cause of a mélange of feelings: in the space of a few seconds astonishment vied with embarrassment, which was quickly tempered by sentiments of pleasure, sympathy and affection. There were no words to describe this succession of reactions—no words other than "Oh" and something that sounded like "Ah" but could have been a simple exhalation of breath.

"So there you have it," said Maggie. Her tone was matter of fact—the tone of one who has simply pointed out some mundane and totally unremarkable fact, such as "It's about to rain" or "It's Tuesday today."

William cleared his throat. "I see," he said. "Well, thank you for telling me."

It was a trite thing to say, and he felt immediately ashamed that he was not able to rise to a more momentous acknowledgement of her declaration. She was, after all, talking of years of denial, years of frustration, and all he could do was to thank her for telling him. Well, he thought, at least that's better than saying, "Thank you for sharing that with me." That expression was the ultimate anodyne.

Maggie indicated that they should continue with their walk. "It's only a bit further," she said. "We come to a pond where we've tried to keep ducks for the last few years, but the fox outwits us, I'm afraid."

They walked on. "Maggie . . . ," William began, but she reached out and touched him lightly on the forearm.

"No," she said. "Don't say anything. The subject has been aired, and now it's closed. Permanently. No need to say a thing."

He protested. "But I think that we—"

"No," she said, more firmly. "I suggest that we treat my words as never having been uttered. What happened back there simply never occurred. All right?"

He did not respond. It was something he himself had done on more than one occasion—said to himself that he would pretend that something he found uncomfortable just had not happened. Willed amnesia, he believed it was called, and it could be invoked at an intimate level—as when we stop ourselves thinking of some situation of acute social embarrassment, or obliterate some act of unkindness or gross selfishness from our personal record; or it could be resorted to on a grander scale altogether—as when an entire nation denies some dire period in its history. It worked—human memory was tactful, and could be persuaded to be more sympathetic yet. And even if it was a dangerous recourse, as historians are quick to point out, there could be situations in which it was the best and most productive thing to do; getting through life could be difficult enough even without a burden of guilt and self-loathing to drag us down further than we already were.

For the rest of the walk, conversation was sporadic, and shallow. Maggie pointed out a tree that found favour with wood pigeons; William observed that the hedgerows seemed in good health; Maggie said that she had read *The Cloudspotter's Guide* and now knew what to look for in a cumulus build-up; and so on. In between these undemanding exchanges, William reflected on her revelation. He had had no idea of her feelings—not the slightest inkling. They were friends—close friends, indeed—and he enjoyed the relaxed intimacy of their relationship. They could talk about anything, more or less, and their conversation had always had the amiability and ease that marked out the conversation of old friends—people who had known one another for years, for so long they could not even remember how they met, and knew the preferences and prejudices of the other as well as or even better than they knew their own. An old friend, William thought, could *vote* in the place of his friend; could choose his breakfast; could write an entirely credible letter in his voice . . . could—and here the appalling, unwelcome thought intruded—could take his place in a marriage. No! No! It was not going to be like that.

Geoffrey was William's friend; Maggie was the wife of his friend, and he could never entertain any thought of having an affair with her. How could he? How could he sit in the same room as Geoffrey, talking to him as he had always talked to him, harbouring all the while that secret knowledge? It was impossible. He could not do it.

And yet, he reflected, people did precisely that. People did it with astonishing regularity—they had affairs, which they concealed from others; they lied, not just occasionally, but for days, months, years on end. They maintained the façade, he supposed, by some sort of interior bifurcation, which meant that they could be one person one moment, and another the next. And they did not think of the disloyalty involved, the dirtying deception, or, if they did, they put it from their mind. More denial.

He was not naïve. He did not believe that he could do this personally, but he knew that the sheer power of love could quite easily drive one to such extremes. There was an adage that he had once seen inscribed on the label of a wine bottle: *Amor brevis furor est.* Love is a brief madness. It was true; it was. But even in the grip of madness, one could retain some sense of what was right and what was wrong; of who was one's friend, whose trust one would never betray. One could retain that through all the tempests of love, couldn't one? Couldn't one?

They reached the house. "Geoffrey's back," said Maggie. "You go and see him while I check on things in the kitchen."

He noticed how she spoke as if nothing had happened—*I'll check on things in the kitchen*—when she had only a few minutes ago revealed that the whole structure of her life was undermined by a reckless, hopeless passion. Now, it was as if the revelation had never been made; as if those feelings were simply not there. Things were exactly as they seemed. She was happily married to an engaging and personable man. She had two children who loved both parents. They had an old friend, William, whom they both liked and who was almost a member of the family. Everything was as it had always been and as it should be.

But it was not.

25. Where Is Freddie de la Hay?

MAGGIE LEFT WILLIAM in the hall. He stood still for a moment, like a man at an unfamiliar crossroads, uncertain as to whether or not he should follow her into the kitchen and insist on clearing the air. It was all very well for her to announce that the subject was closed, but she had broached it in the first place and therefore could not simply walk away from it. He felt a degree of irritation, wondering what could have possessed her to blurt out her confession if she intended to become silent only a few minutes later. Or—and this was a disturbing thought—had she imagined her words would have met with a rather different response from that which they had actually elicited? If William had responded more warmly, then perhaps she would have been prepared to discuss the matter; but he had not concealed his shock, and this reaction might have been what silenced her. And if that were true, then his insensitivity had made things much worse for Maggie; rather than helping her, he had returned her burden to her not lightened, as burdens should be, but only made all the heavier.

He was still standing in the hall, seemingly paralysed by these questions, when his host appeared.

Geoffrey broke into a smile. "William! Old friend . . ."

Involuntarily, William winced. *Old friend.*

Geoffrey looked concerned. "Are you all right?"

"Of course. Of course."

"It's just that you looked as if . . . well, you looked as if you were in pain."

He was in pain, he realised, his pain being the entirely familiar discomfort felt by the guilty. It was difficult to see why this should be; he had been completely ignorant of Maggie's feelings for him

93

and had done nothing to encourage them. There was no reason, then, for him to feel guilty—and yet he did.

For a moment he questioned whether to tell Geoffrey about what had happened. If he did not, he would be concealing something from him, and one did not hide things from old friends. But if he were to reveal Maggie's secret, it would be an appalling breach of confidence—an implied one, of course, but a confidence nonetheless. No, this was a miserable situation, whichever way one looked at it.

"In pain?" said William, trying to smile. "No, not really. I was just standing and thinking."

"Thinking about what?" asked Geoffrey.

About your wife, William said to himself. *About your wife—who has just revealed that she's been in love with me for years.*

"Nothing important." And then he said to himself: *Nothing important, other than your marriage and your wife's happiness.*

Geoffrey smiled. "Ready for a Scotch?"

They went together into the low-ceilinged drawing room. On a table behind a sofa was a small array of bottles and decanters from which Geoffrey took a bottle of whisky. He poured two drams, adding a small quantity of water to each. "I don't have to ask you about the water," he said. "I know what you like."

William raised his glass to his friend. "Your health."

"And yours."

Geoffrey looked at him. "You know, I was reflecting the other day on how long we've known one another. It's getting to the stage where one doesn't want to count the years."

His friend's words rang in his ears like the terms of a formal indictment. "Yes, it's been a long time," agreed William. He inhaled the aroma of the whisky before taking a sip. The thought of his friendship with Geoffrey weighed heavily on him because it was now dawning on him how difficult it might be to carry on. Geoffrey

94

and Maggie came as a package, so to speak—he could not conduct the friendship solely with one and not with the other; and while he had no desire to fall out with Maggie, at the same time he felt that it would probably be just too awkward to continue to see her with this unresolved issue hanging over them, an elephant in the room of their friendship.

Geoffrey was talking about his plan to plant truffles. "A long shot," he said, "but I've got a bit of woodland that apparently could support them. Tricky things, though. Temperamental. Maggie can't stand them." He smiled. "Her tastes have always been a bit unsophisticated."

William felt himself blushing. Was that why she had fallen for him? He finished his whisky hurriedly and looked at his watch. "I need to go and change," he said.

"Me too," said Geoffrey. "Where's Freddie de la Hay, by the way?"

William had had other things on his mind, and now he realised that the dog had been outside for rather a long time. "I'll go and call him," he said. "He's probably persecuting rabbits."

"He's welcome to do that," said Geoffrey. "They're a perfect pest at the moment. But I hope he's careful. My neighbour lost a dog a few weeks ago. It went down a hole and never came back up. Everybody was very upset. They tried to dig him out, but you know what it's like down there—a bit of a rabbit warren, as perhaps one might expect."

"Freddie is very careful about these things," said William.

"I hope so," said Geoffrey.

William put down his glass and went outside. The sun had moved further down the sky, and although it was still light, the farmhouse was no longer bathed in gold. He looked up—the evening sky was quite empty, and was now that attenuated blue which occurs just before dusk sets in. One can so easily forget about the sky in London, he thought.

He called Freddie's name, using all four words. This was how he normally summoned him, as he believed that the operative word that Freddie recognised was "Hay." Dogs, he had read somewhere, pick up short words rather than long ones. He might, therefore, with equal effect simply shout "Hay," but he felt it would sound ridiculous. One could not go about shouting "Hay"; one could not.

When there was still no response after he had called out six or seven times, William made his way onto the expanse of grass beyond the shrubbery. He called out again, half expecting, half hoping to hear an answering bark, but there was silence. A solitary gull, blown in from the sea, rose from a field somewhere and mewed over something that was not quite right.

William walked further away from the house. He found himself in a patch of stinging nettles, and he negotiated his way through it with great care. He remembered that on one of his previous visits Maggie had complained that Geoffrey was not assiduous enough in his spraying and that there was a limit to the amount of nettle soup she could make. It was strange what one's memory brought back.

If Freddie had gone this way then he would have left some trace in the undergrowth. But there was nothing; no sign of flattened grass to reveal that an animal had passed through. William began to feel concerned. There were plenty of rabbit holes: he could see them all about him now, and one seemed to have freshly disturbed earth at its mouth, as if an inhabitant of the warren—or even a passing dog—had energetically and messily strived to enlarge the entrance.

How many of us dig our own graves, thought William. We dig them with vigour and determination, unaware of the implications, but with all the conviction of those who do not really know what they are doing, who are impervious to the dangers that others can see so clearly.

26. Ronald Telephones

IT WAS NOT that Caroline did not know Ronald at all; it was just that their acquaintanceship was slight, and certainly not intimate enough for him to have the number of her mobile phone. A mobile telephone number is not one to be bandied about: if one has the mobile phone number of another, one has his ear, or at least his pocket, or bedside table, or wherever the telephone itself happens to be.

So she was surprised when Ronald phoned her as she was walking past the flower shop round the corner, and it took her a moment or two to work out which Ronald it was. There was Ronald Evans, who had been on her course and was an obsessive jogger: she occasionally saw him running on the pavements, dodging pedestrians, glistening with sweat. He would have no time to telephone people, she thought, or might do so perhaps while on one of his runs, speaking—or gasping—into one of those headsets that enable taxi drivers to conduct what appear to be long soliloquies while negotiating the traffic.

"Are you sure you're not running away from something?" she had once asked him.

"Ha ha, Caroline," he had retorted. "Very funny. But since you ask, yes."

She had been taken aback, and had not wanted to ask him what that something was; nor had he offered any explanation, and the matter had been left where it was.

But this was not Ronald Evans.

"Ronald Warden."

"Of course. Well, hello . . ." When had she last seen him? Last year, at a party in the house of an old schoolfriend in Cheltenham, Emmy, and he had been with that Irish girl, the one with the teeth . . .

"I got your number from my ma. She was talking to your mother . . ."

Caroline stiffened. A mental picture had come to her of the two women gossiping on a copious chintzy sofa with a large flower arrangement in the background.

"Yes." Her voice was guarded.

"You know what they're like," continued Ronald. "Old bats. Sorry—my poor ma is, not yours . . ."

Caroline relaxed. "Sure."

"And my ma told yours that I was looking for a place to stay in London. She said that you might have a room in your flat. You don't by any chance . . . ?" He trailed off.

Caroline hesitated. Dee had generously paid two months' rent when she left, "to give you time to find somebody nice," and they were therefore in no hurry. Dee could afford it, of course, since she had sold the rights in that ridiculous Sudoku Remedy of hers for an astronomic amount, but still it was good of her as their agreement specified that only a month's notice was required. Jo, her remaining flatmate, seemed happy enough to leave it up to Caroline to find a replacement, which was just as well: Jo had very peculiar taste when it came to friends and almost certainly would have come up with somebody difficult to live with.

And the one thing one did not want, Caroline thought, was a flatmate who was *odd*. A friend of hers had taken the first person who answered her advertisement and then discovered that he was electronically tagged following an unspecified offence and could leave the flat for only twenty minutes a day. She had found him poring over the layout of a building and become convinced that he was plotting some further crime. "I'm really interested in design," he said hurriedly as he put the plans away. "Of banks?" Caroline's friend had asked. Thereafter the arrangement had become distinctly tense, and the friend had herself moved out.

And another friend had taken a flatmate on the recommendation of a cousin and discovered that the new flatmate was an enthusiast for a contrived international language called Interlingua. That was unexceptionable enough, but it had become a bit trying when this new resident insisted on using nothing but Interlingua to address his flatmates, and labelled everything in the house with a small sticky label on which he printed the Interlingua word for that object.

"I wish you'd speak English to us," said Caroline's friend. "After all, this is England."

"*Anglaterra*," he corrected. "*Un bon numero de parolas in Interlingua es similar a parolas anglese.*"

RONALD, OF COURSE, was neither a criminal nor an Interlingua enthusiast, and so her hesitation did not last. If he became wearing, after all, she could always complain to his mother, who was given, she remembered, to organising her son's life.

"Yes, we do have a room coming up. In fact, it's already come up—would you like to take a look at it?"

Ronald accepted, and Caroline noted the relief in his voice. "Is it hard to find somewhere at the moment?" she asked.

"Immensely," said Ronald. "Or anywhere semi-decent, or semi-central. I've just looked at a place in Tooting. Tiny. And over an hour from where I'm working."

"I've always liked the sound of Tooting," said Caroline. "But not to live there."

Ronald laughed. "I don't care what a place is called," he said. "I'm sure Tooting's fine—but maybe not for the whole weekend."

Caroline laughed too. "You know this place we live in, Corduroy

Mansions, isn't at all posh. You do know that, don't you? Pimlico's a bit of a mixture, and we're not one of the grand bits. But it's got character and there are nice shops nearby, and you can just about get to work on foot if your office is fairly central."

"Sounds great," said Ronald. "Can I see it?"

They made an arrangement for him to come that evening, an hour before James was due to arrive to cook risotto. Caroline explained that she had a friend coming round but it would be all right if Ronald did not mind restricting his visit to half an hour or so. He had no objection, he said. He was going to see a film at the South Bank and it suited him not to stay too long.

"It's a film about Le Corbusier," he said. "You know him? The French architect."

Caroline knew him—vaguely. "I've seen photographs of his work in art history books," she said. "Long buildings that look as if they've been squeezed out of a tube of toothpaste."

"That's him," said Ronald. "My God, I hate him, I really do. I hate him."

"Then why go and see a film about him?" she asked.

"Because I enjoy horror movies," said Ronald.

He laughed again, and so did Caroline. There was something about Ronald that rather appealed to her. Perhaps it was the same thing that she saw and appreciated in James, and this made her wonder: Was she destined to admire men whose wit and entertainment value set them apart from that other, more ubiquitous class of dull and uninspiring men, the sort of whom her mother approved, the sort who were unambiguously—and depressingly—available? Yes, she decided, she probably was.

27. Ronald's Interview

SHE BARELY RECOGNISED Ronald.

"Your hair . . . ," she began. And then, "You . . ."

His hand went up involuntarily to the side of his head. "Oh, this."

Last time she had seen him he had been unkempt, with long, rather straggly blond hair tied up at the back in a ponytail; now his hair had been barbered just short of a crew cut. It was, she thought, a great improvement—a transformation from the awkward territory of late teenagerdom to the firmer ground of early adulthood. Ronald was her contemporary—or close enough—but always seemed younger, as if he had just stepped off a skateboard. There was no metaphorical skateboard now.

"You've had a haircut," she said. "It really suits you."

He smiled at the compliment; the smile was still boyish. "Thanks. I had to become respectable, you see, when I started work. Corporate image and all that."

She invited him in. "I thought architects could dress casually," she said as they made their way through to the kitchen.

"It depends. Most wear a sort of uniform, of course. Slightly preppy, for want of a better word. You know the style? But with a bit more colour maybe. Linen jackets are pretty important."

"Linen crumples," said Caroline.

Ronald nodded. "Big problem for architects."

She gestured to a chair. "Coffee?"

He accepted. "I used those big tins of Colombian coffee too when I was at uni. Have you been to South America?"

She had not.

"Nor me. I can't wait to go to Colombia. The firm I'm working for has a contract to design a museum in Cartagena. I asked if I could be put on that project, and they just laughed. They said I had to do at least five council buildings in Hackney before I could get onto an overseas project. Or Tooting."

"Tooting," she said. "We seem to talk about Tooting a lot."

"Yes. We must stop."

She switched on the kettle, and as she did so she cast a glance at Ronald. He was taller than she remembered him—perhaps he was still growing. Did boys carry on growing longer than girls? She noticed his high cheekbones for the first time. Did cheekbones change, or was it the effect of the haircut? He was very . . . She looked away guiltily. The word came unwanted to her mind: gorgeous. Oh no, she thought. Don't think he's gorgeous: just don't. This is a *flatmate*, and flatmates should not be gorgeous.

"What's your work like?" she asked.

He sat back in his chair. "I enjoy it," he said. "Even the buildings in Hackney, which I'm not actually working on. I'm doing a bit of an office block in Maidstone, down in Kent. It's pretty routine stuff, of course, but I don't mind. Specifying windows and insulation and so on. There are lots of green considerations these days and I like that. But I don't want to do it for the rest of my life."

"Windows and insulation?"

"I want to do domestic stuff. Houses. Flats. Living space. That's what interests me." He paused. "I don't suppose you've ever heard of somebody called Christopher Alexander? No? I just wondered—you did art history, didn't you?"

She nodded. She had to remind herself sometimes that she used to consider herself an art historian; and now she was just a photographer's assistant—the girl who carried the lighting stand.

"I thought you might have come across him," Ronald went on. "He wrote a terrific book called *A Pattern Language*. I've got two copies of it, in case I lose one. I love it that much."

She felt the side of the kettle with the back of her hand; it was getting warm. "Should I have read it? There's a massive list of books I should have read."

"No, there's no reason why you should even have come across it. It's about building, and about how we can make our houses more habitable, more humane." Ronald looked about him. "This kitchen, for instance."

"It's a bit of a mess," said Caroline. "Jo cooked last night and she never washes up." She bit her tongue. She should not have said that; she wanted Ronald to move in, after only these few minutes she wanted it desperately, and she should not give him the impression that one of his future flatmates was messy.

She need not have worried. "I lived with somebody like that in Exeter," Ronald said. "He lived out of a tin. All his food was canned, and he left the empty cans lying around. It was disgusting, especially the ones that had contained pilchards. He loved pilchards."

"Nobody eats pilchards here," said Caroline.

"I'm pleased to hear it," said Ronald, smiling. "But I wasn't talking about tidiness. I was talking about light."

Caroline looked up at the light fitting. She had meant to clean it weeks ago.

"Not electric light," said Ronald. "The free stuff. The light that comes from outside."

Caroline looked at the window. She had meant to clean that too.

"Light should come from two sources," said Ronald. "Go into a room where there is only a single window and you'll see how lifeless the light is. It's static. Whereas if you go into a room like this kitchen, where you've got a window there and that window on the side, it's different, isn't it? Chris Alexander points that out, together with hundreds of other rules. He calls them principles, actually."

The kettle boiled, and Caroline busied herself with pouring the water into the cafetière. Waiting a few moments for the grounds to settle, she pushed gently down on the strainer. "We can take our coffee with us as I show you round. Dee's room is at the back. It's nice and quiet."

"I get the feeling already that I'm going to like it," said Ronald. "In fact, I want to live here!"

Caroline felt a surge of pleasure. "All right. Live here."

They both laughed. He sipped at his coffee. She noticed his mouth, and his lips. She looked away again. This was *unplanned*, she thought.

Ronald glanced at his watch. "I'm going to have to skip that film about Le Corbusier," he said. "It's starting half an hour earlier than I originally thought."

"Oh well, it would just make you cross, wouldn't it? There's no point in going to see something that would just make you cross."

"No, you're right." He was looking up at the ceiling now. "You were tied up with something, weren't you? Are you still, or could I . . ."

She waited for his words. Already she had decided on her answer.

". . . could I take you for dinner somewhere? I got paid today."

She looked into her coffee mug. "As it happens, yes. Thanks. I was going to be doing something, but not any more."

"That's great. Well, could you show me the room? Not that I'm going to turn it down but I suppose I should take a look."

She turned and led him to Dee's old room. She felt light-headed. She would phone James and . . . and put him off. She could tell him . . . something, and he wouldn't mind—or not all that much.

28. Honesty Is Sometimes the Best Policy

THE LIE WAS very easy, as so many lies are. Of course, Caroline did not tell James that she was going out, simply explaining that she did not feel "one hundred per cent" and would prefer him to cook for her "some other time." The words "one hundred per cent" were carefully chosen: none of us, she told herself, ever feels one hundred per cent—a state of health beyond the dreams of even the most cheerfully fit. Ninety-five per cent, perhaps—that was feasible, and would be a state of well-being spoiled only by the occasional physical twinge from the provinces of our body; but one hundred per cent, no, that was a state of bodily nirvana which none of us could claim. So she was not telling a lie, she reasoned, even if it *felt* like one.

There was concern in James's voice. "You haven't got this bug that's going round?" he asked. "A friend of mine had it and he said he felt really awful. He brought up this green stuff, you know, and he hadn't eaten anything green for ages. So where did it come from? Do you think it was bile? Bile's green, isn't it? Like envy."

"No, I haven't brought up any green stuff. It's not like that."

James was relieved. "Good, because that bug lasts for ten days. And you feel really washed out afterwards. Like a rag." He paused. "You don't think it would cheer you up to be cooked for? I don't like to think of you sitting alone in your garret feeding yourself warmed-up gruel. Let me come and do the Florence Nightingale thing."

"No!" She spoke rather quickly, and it sounded rude. "I mean, no thanks. I'll be fine—I really will."

"Well, I'll think of you. I'll keep the Arborio rice I bought, and the bottle of wine. But I don't think the mushrooms will keep.

They're rather old, I'm afraid—not that it's easy to tell with mushrooms, as you know. Sometimes they get so *traumatised* by being taken out of the forest that they look quite *discouraged.*"

"It must be a shock for them. Poor mushrooms."

There was a silence. "You're sure you're going to be all right? Quite sure?"

She closed her eyes; James was not making it any easier for her. "Quite sure."

"Shall I phone you a little later?" James asked solicitously. "Just to check you haven't taken a turn for the worse."

"No, don't phone." Her reply was once again too quick, and she immediately backtracked. "I might phone you. But let's leave it . . ."

"In case you're sleeping," supplied James. "Of course."

They rang off, and Caroline sank her head in her hands. She had left Ronald in the kitchen while she made the telephone call, having told him that she needed to go to her bedroom to change. Another lie, even if one of no consequence and not rationalised, as had been her excuse to James, as some sort of half-truth. Lying could become second nature, she thought, as it was with some people—with spin doctors, perhaps, those manipulators of truth who must become accustomed to twisting everything; like a bowler who cannot bowl straight, or a pastry chef expert in the making of plaited bread rolls.

She stood up, combed her hair and looked in the mirror. She decided to change her top, and to add a necklace—the one with the single pearl and the gold heart. She picked a top with straps from her wardrobe and then slipped the necklace round her neck. She glanced in the mirror again, and froze. The gold heart caught the light and winked back at her. James had given her the necklace two birthdays ago; she had forgotten, but now it came back to her. He had denied himself lunch for three weeks in order to buy it, and now . . . She felt herself blush—a hot feeling of shame—and then unfastened the necklace and put it back in the small leather-covered jewel box her grandmother had given her. Her grandmother would never have behaved like this with one of the young men she had coyly described as her *beaux*. She would never have cancelled an evening because something more exciting had turned up.

But it was different now. Today it was every girl for herself, and if that meant the occasional *ruse*, then it was within the rules, such as they were. If James had been a girlfriend there would have been no difficulty: she would have telephoned and explained the situation, and the girlfriend would have understood. The prospect of dinner with a man always trumped prior commitments to one's own sex; everybody knew that.

But James was a man, and the rules about cancelling one man for another were very different. In fact, they forbade it, unless of course one was getting rid of the cancelled man. If a relationship had come to an end, then the outstanding commitments it entailed could be brought to an end too. If one had, for example, agreed to go on holiday with a boyfriend and then split up before the holiday took place, one certainly did not have to go; it was obvious. And yet, Caroline was not getting rid of James—she wanted to keep him— and therefore the analogy did not apply. It was all very complicated.

She was looking for another necklace when she heard a knock on the door.

"Caroline?"

"Yes."

The door opened slightly. "Do you mind?"

Ronald stood in the doorway. She was not sure whether she minded or not.

"You didn't show me your room," he continued, advancing hesitantly. "Gosh, it's really nice. Feminine but not . . . well, not too girly. What a view."

She smiled. "Yes, it is nice, isn't it? You'll approve of the light, I suppose."

"I'll be perfectly happy with the room I'm getting," said Ronald. "But of course it would be nice to be in here."

For a sudden, heady moment she imagined keeping a boy in her room—a boy such as Ronald—like some handsome, exotic pet.

"We should go," she said. "I'm actually quite hungry."

29. Ronald Talks with His Eyes in the Underground

RONALD HAD A Greek restaurant in mind—a place in Islington that he had found a few weeks previously, when he came to London for his placement interview. It was cheap, he told Caroline, but the food was "absolutely genuine" and served in generous quantities. "None of your *nouvelle cuisine*," he said, "so we won't go hungry."

They made the journey by tube. Ronald said very little on the way, but Caroline did not find the absence of conversation uncomfortable. James would have talked non-stop, and been more or less oblivious of his surroundings; Ronald, though, *watched*. And he was not uncommunicative; Ronald, she discovered, talked with his eyes, exchanging glances with her that conveyed a great deal. When a man with an eye-patch and a Salvador Dalí moustache entered the carriage, the look that Ronald exchanged with her was more eloquent than words, and when the Dalí-esque passenger got off and a nun carrying a guitar boarded the train, there was another meaningful look that said everything that needed to be said.

In the restaurant, Ronald ordered a bottle of wine that they broached while perusing the menu. Raising his glass, he smiled at Caroline. "To living together," he said, and quickly added, "Well, sort of—you know what I mean."

"To sharing," she said.

"Yes," he said. "That's it. To sharing."

They placed their orders and while they were waiting for their first course, Ronald asked Caroline about the others in the flat. Why had Dee left? Where was Jo? Did people share the cooking?

Caroline told him about Dee and her enthusiasm for vitamins. "You'll still find little plastic bottles of vitamins all over the flat," she said. "And colonic irrigation bits and pieces. That was another of her enthusiasms—colonic irrigation."

Ronald blushed. "Oh. Well, I suppose we all need a hobby."

"We don't need that one," said Caroline. "And then there's Jenny. She sort of lives in the flat at the moment, but is away a lot with a new job she's got. It's half in Brussels, and so she's over there most of the time. She's some sort of *fonctionnaire*, and she says she has nothing, but nothing, to do all day. She's very well paid, though. So until Jo gets back from Western Australia, it'll just be me and you."

Ronald sipped at his wine. "That'll be nice."

She caught her breath. There was only one way of interpreting that remark: he wanted to be alone with her. She found the thought oddly exciting, and while she knew that she should be cautious, she had no hesitation in enjoying the thrill it gave her.

Ronald looked about him. "Not very busy," he said. "I suppose it's Tuesday and people don't go out on a Tuesday. Except people like us. Sad, Tuesday people." He laughed. A small basket of bread had been brought to the table, and he selected a piece to dip in olive oil.

"Have you ever been to Greece, Caroline?"

She told him that she had been once—during a university vacation she and a friend had travelled to Rhodes.

"I used to go a lot," he said. "Greece and Sweden. That's where I liked to go. Still do. I remember my first trip to Greece. I had just discovered *The Magus*. You know it? John Fowles. I remember reading it with complete fascination, although in retrospect I'm not sure what the story meant. But for those few weeks I was under its spell."

"And Sweden?"

"I first went to Sweden when I was fourteen. My father's sister—my aunt—married a Swede and so I've got Swedish cousins. They used to invite me to stay with them in the summer. They had a cottage on one of those islands in the Stockholm archipelago. Do you know they have about twenty-five thousand islands there? Imagine that. Twenty-five thousand islands.

"On the Swedish side of the family," Ronald went on, "there was a great-uncle who was very friendly with the sculptor Carl Milles. The great-uncle bought quite a number of Milles's works and I remember seeing them just sitting out in the garden—these gorgeous floating figures. I took it all for granted.

"We used to swim from a jetty in front of the house. You simply dived into the water and swam. It was very clear and really quite warm. All of us—all the cousins—used to swim together. I remember thinking: I wish I were Swedish. It's marvellous being Swedish, you know. It's such a rational country and everything is so beautiful."

Caroline listened intently. There was something seductive about Ronald's conversation and, listening to these observations, it seemed to her she was being shown a richer, more engaged way of relating to the world.

"But you can never really become Swedish," Ronald went on. "You can become American; you can become British. But you can't be a Swede just by living there or speaking the language. It goes deeper than that."

The waiter lowered plates onto the table in front of them and flourished an impossibly large pepper mill over the food.

"I don't know why they have those ridiculous pepper mills," said Ronald when the waiter had gone. "Such clunky design."

"To stop people stealing them," said Caroline. "We have become so dishonest in this country that even the pepper mills aren't safe any more."

"Are we more dishonest than anybody else?" asked Ronald.

"Yes," said Caroline. "I think we are. We didn't use to be. But we are now. I read about it in the papers. It's official."

And at this point, as Caroline was pronouncing on dishonesty, forgetting her glaring lie of a couple of hours earlier, the door of the restaurant was pushed open and James walked in, accompanied by another young man wearing large-framed glasses.

James and Caroline saw one another at the same moment. James stood quite still. He looked at Caroline, who could not bring herself to meet his gaze. She looked away, and then, when she snatched a quick glance a moment or two later, James was still staring straight at her. She thought: The odds against this are ridiculously high; this restaurant, tonight, this exact time. *This shouldn't have happened.*

"Do you know them?" asked Ronald, looking over his shoulder.

"Yes," muttered Caroline. "Or one of them."

James was conferring discreetly with his companion. The other young man listened, and then nodded. They turned round and left the restaurant.

"Are you all right?" asked Ronald.

It took her a little while to answer. "Yes, I suppose I am. Don't worry. I'll be fine."

Ronald reached for his glass again. "I wouldn't mind working in Sweden," he said. And then, changing the subject rather quickly, he asked Caroline if he could stay in the flat that night. "I've been staying with a friend in Hounslow," he said. "But it's such a long way out, and it would be easier to stay in Pimlico. I've got spare things in a bag at the office, and I can shower there. We have these showers, you see, for the workaholics. That is, if you don't mind?"

She thought for a moment. She felt raw from being found out

by James and did not relish the prospect of returning to the flat by herself.

"Of course you can stay," she said. "You can have Jo's room if you like, because the bed's made up."

There was a momentary flash of disappointment in his expression, but it passed so quickly that Caroline thought perhaps she had misinterpreted it. He thanked her, and raised his glass again. "To Corduroy Mansions," he said.

She returned the toast, but even as she did so she was thinking of the look James had given her before he left the restaurant: it was predominantly one of reproach, but there was sadness and regret too. She had lost the friendship, she realised, of her closest friend in London; and replaced it with what? The interest of a young man about whom she knew very little, and whose feelings for her—if any—were uncertain and untested. It was hardly a good exchange. *You stupid, stupid girl*, she said to herself; but not in her own voice, oddly enough—her mother's.

30. Terence Moongrove Issues

ON THE DAY when Caroline lied to James and consequently lost his friendship, Berthea Snark travelled across the country by train to Cheltenham, where she planned to spend a few days in the company of her brother, Terence Moongrove. She did this about once a month now, having come to the conclusion that Terence, who was a mystic engaged in a long and fruitless journey of self-discovery, might take it upon himself to do something even more foolish than that which he had done so far. And that was a fair number of things, she reflected, as the train made its way across Oxfordshire. There had been the dreadful incident when Terence had attempted to recharge the battery of his Morris Traveller car— directly from the mains. That had resulted in a near-death experience, and several nasty burns and bruises. Then there had been the worrying episode of those two fraudsters who had almost got away with persuading Terence to make over his valuable Queen Anne house to a bogus meditation centre that they had cooked up. That had required quick footwork on her part, and the assistance, of course, of Lennie Marchbanks, Terence's mechanic, who had been a firm and reliable ally to Berthea in her task of protecting Terence from himself.

Terence required watching, and Berthea had decided that a monthly visit of at least a few days' duration was now necessary to ensure that nothing too drastic happened. She had to be discreet, though: Terence did not respond well to direct intervention; he was sensitive to direction on her part, and readily accused her of being bossy. It was understandable enough, of course—not because she was bossy, but because childhood roles are rarely abandoned when siblings reach maturity, and indeed a great deal of Berthea's professional time as a psychotherapist was spent in dealing with the consequences of imbalances and pathology in those vital early relationships. Earlier that same week she had taken on a new patient who had consulted her because she felt unable to make any decision without telephoning her sister in Newcastle to ask for advice.

"I know I should be able to stand on my own two feet," this patient had said. "But the problem is, if I try to take the decision myself I spend hours, yes, hours, thinking about it, and I tend to avoid deciding one way or the other."

Berthea had asked what sort of decisions required to be made by this committee of two.

"Oh, just about everything. When I go to the shops, I need to consult Lizzie about what to buy. Even if I see that there are no eggs in the fridge, I have to ask her whether she thinks it's a good idea to get eggs today or tomorrow."

"Even when you know that you're going to need them today?"

"Even then."

Berthea made a note. "When you were children, was she the one who told you what to do?"

"Of course." There was a pause. "Well, at least I think so. Perhaps I should ask her. Do you mind if I ask her about that and tell you next time?"

That answer required a rather longer note.

It was different with her and Terence. She had certainly been the one in charge of their games as children; she had invariably been the leader and Terence had followed. But that did not mean that he still accepted these arrangements: the underlying dynamics might be the same, but the problem itself was different. Terence now felt inclined to do the opposite of what Berthea suggested because, unlike her patient, he resented Berthea's leadership. This, however, did not compromise any theory of the persistence of childhood relationships: if anything, it underlined the phenomenon. So Berthea, conscious of what was going on in Terence's mind, knew that in order to secure his compliance, she merely had to suggest the opposite of what she wanted. Or so it had seemed until recently, when Terence appeared to develop some insight into her strategy and started to do exactly what she suggested, knowing that this was what she did *not* want. So if she advised him to do B rather than A, he would follow her suggestion to do B because he twigged that A was what she actually wanted him to do. He subsequently made the calculation that Berthea might realise that he had tumbled to her device, and therefore when she proposed that he do

B rather than A . . . Here he had faltered, uncertain what to do if she knew that he knew. Should he go back to doing the opposite? Would that work?

There were currently two Terence-related issues preying on Berthea's mind. The first of these was his car—the Porsche that Lennie Marchbanks had reluctantly obtained for him from Monty Bismarck; it was a constant worry, even if Terence tended to drive it at not much more than twenty-five miles per hour. There was still the potential to go much faster should he ever decide to put his foot down hard on the accelerator; and Terence was so uncoordinated, in spite of all that sacred dance, that his foot could conceivably go down without his intending it.

That was one worry. The other was India, and the references that Terence had recently made to the possibility of visiting an ashram he had read about in one of his New Age magazines. Berthea had gently pointed out the complexity of visiting India, the need to have inoculations and to avoid the monsoon season.

"And you have to get a visa," she said. "And that's terribly complicated. You should see the forms, Terence—very complicated. Hardly worth bothering, I would have thought."

"I won't need a visa," he said.

"Yes, you will. Everybody needs a visa. The Indians are very strict about that."

Terence shook his head. "No. I think they let you in as long as your karma's good. They'll assess that at the airport."

Berthea had stared at her brother. Where did one begin with somebody like Terence? And, more importantly, where did one end?

31. Lennie Marchbanks
Utters a Warning

THE LOW-SLUNG PORSCHE was waiting for Berthea as she emerged from Cheltenham station. She waved: dear Terence, what a great effort it cost him to be punctual—with all his metaphysical concerns—but he had managed it, bless him! And now that he had this car, the eventful journeys in the Morris Traveller, during which they had more than once run out of petrol between the station and the house, were a thing of the past.

As she approached the Porsche, the driver's door opened and a figure stepped out to greet her. It was not Terence Moongrove, but his *garagiste*, Lennie Marchbanks, who smiled warmly at Berthea, his ill-fitting false teeth projecting slightly as he did so. She remembered those teeth—how could she forget them?—as she had briefly kept them in her coat pocket when Lennie had gamely played the part of the Green Man in her elaborate plan to save Terence from the New Age fraudsters. The knowledge that one has had the false teeth of another in one's pocket lends a strange intimacy to a relationship, Berthea mused.

Lennie stepped forward to help with her bag.

"Not much luggage," he said as he took the well-packed grip Berthea was carrying. "You should see Mrs. Marchbanks when she goes off for a day or two to her mother in Bristol. You need a camel to carry everything."

"People have different requirements, Mr. Marchbanks," said Berthea. She had only met Lennie's wife once, but felt that she must defend the travelling habits of her sex in the face of this rather old-fashioned comment. "I'm sure that your wife packs only what she needs."

"I'm not," said Lennie cheerfully. "She takes half her wardrobe, so she does. I see her packing. She just empties whole drawers into the suitcase."

They got into the car. It was very badly designed for getting in and out of, thought Berthea, at least for people like her. But then she realised that Porsches were not for people like her in the first place but for rather younger, lither people—the sort of people who wore sunglasses when it was not strictly necessary. The unnecessary wearing of sunglasses, of course, was a sure sign of neurosis, as her training analyst had told her years ago. This belief had been confirmed by her own experience.

"I must ask you to remove your sunglasses during analysis," she had said to one patient. He had done so, and she had seen the anxiety in his eyes as his protection against the world was laid aside. She had felt momentarily guilty, and assured him that it was for his own benefit. "We cannot shelter during this process," she explained. "The whole point of analysis is to see behind that which stands between us and the social world."

The patient had looked at her reproachfully. "I need them," he said. "Like as the hart desireth the waterbrooks."

Lennie turned the key in the ignition. "Lovely sound, this motor," he said. "You hear that, Dr. Snark? Gorgeous sound." He looked at her and smiled. "I've come to collect you because I had the car in the garage for its service. Your brother phoned and said I might as well pick you up since I was going to be bringing the car back to his place. So here I am."

"You're very kind, Mr. Marchbanks," said Berthea. "My brother, as you know, is not quite as other men. I'd be very worried about him if I didn't know that you were keeping an eye on him."

"You're quite welcome, Dr. Snark," said Lennie. "I do my best, and I'm fond of Terence, you know. He's got some unusual ideas in that head of his, but nowt so queer as folk, as they used to say. Wouldn't you agree?"

"People are very strange," agreed Berthea. "But it's certainly true, I think, that some are stranger than others. My dear brother possibly belongs in this latter category."

"Could be," said Lennie, as he changed gear. "Listen to that gearbox. Smooth as a baby's bottom. You have to hand it to the Germans: they make a very fine gearbox."

"I don't doubt it," said Berthea. "And I'm perfectly happy to give them the credit for it."

There was silence for a few moments. Then Lennie said, "Actually, Dr. Snark, there's something that's giving me cause for concern. Your brother's got a little scheme brewing."

Berthea's heart sank. "Tell me," she sighed. "It's best that I should know."

"It's that Monty Bismarck," Lennie went on, frowning as he spoke. "He's got no business getting Mr. Moongrove all excited. I had a word with his dad, you know, Alfie Bismarck, but he said that Monty was a grown-up and he couldn't really tell him what to do any more. He said that he'd tried but it hadn't worked."

Berthea remained tight-lipped as the mechanic continued.

"It's to do with a car," said Lennie.

Berthea was relieved. At least that was manageable, and could presumably be dealt with by Lennie Marchbanks. Was Terence planning to get a newer Porsche, perhaps? Well, that was not exactly the end of the world: he had survived this one, and would probably drive the next one in much the same way.

"That doesn't sound too ominous," she said. "You can manage a new car, can't you, Mr. Marchbanks?"

Lennie shook his head. "He's keeping this. He's not getting rid of it."

"Well?"

"He's getting another one, Dr. Snark. That's the problem. Monty has managed to persuade your brother to invest in a syndicate to buy a vintage racing car."

"With a view to selling it on? Does he know what he's doing?"

Lennie's false teeth made a strange clicking sound. "Oh, Monty Bismarck knows what he's doing all right. The syndicate consists of himself and Mr. Moongrove—that's all. Monty's putting in two hundred quid, and Mr. Moongrove's putting in one hundred thousand."

Berthea looked out of the window. Terence had been left well provided for by their father and there was no shortage of money, but one hundred thousand pounds . . . For a car—and a second-hand one at that!

"It's a Frazer Nash," Lennie continued. "Lovely machine, actually, and I'd buy it like a shot myself if I had the cash. The 1932 model, and those aren't two a penny, I can assure you. But it is a racing car, you know, and . . . Well, Monty intends to race it."

Berthea shrugged. "Well, I suppose those old cars don't go too fast. And it will be on a racetrack, I take it."

"They can get going," said Lennie. "It's not Formula One stuff, but they go fast enough with the wind behind them."

"Well, I suppose there are more dangerous sports."

"Yes, there are," conceded Lennie. "But the point is this: Monty's agreed to have Mr. Moongrove as his co-driver. There are lots of these old car races that are for two-driver cars. So your brother's actually taking up motor racing, Dr. Snark. That's the problem."

32. Oily Deposits

TERENCE MOONGROVE CARRIED his sister's bag upstairs. "You'll be pleased to hear I've put you in your usual room, Berthy," he said. "I had a friend staying last week. He loved the view from that window, you know, the one that Uncle Edgar painted when he unearthed that old watercolour set in the attic."

"Oh yes," said Berthea. "I remember the painting. What a pity he had absolutely no talent. Quite devoid of it, in fact. Poor Uncle Edgar."

Terence admonished her. "Naughty!" he said, nonetheless allowing himself a smile. "Be careful what you say about Uncle Edgar, Berthy. I believe his spirit is still here somewhere. He's very close to us. Even now, as we speak."

Berthea crossed the room to open the window, in case Uncle Edgar might wish to get out. There was a curious, rather sweet smell in the room; the smell, she thought, of an exotic, over-scented pot pourri. Was Uncle Edgar *wearing something*? Or *smoking* it perhaps?

"You've seen him?" she asked her brother. "Do you have any evidence?"

Terence put the bag down on the end of the bed. "Oh, you may mock, Berthy," he said. "You and your reductionist, materialist outlook: the reason you never see anything is that your eyes are closed to things that clearly exist on another dimension. You are one-dimensional, Berthy, that's what you are."

Berthea sighed; with her generous figure, she would have loved to be more one-dimensional. "Where exactly is Uncle Edgar?" she asked. "And when precisely did you see him?"

"I've seen him twice over the last six months," said Terence, using a matter-of-fact tone, of the sort one might use to describe the spotting of a friend on the street. "I saw him outside the kitchen window one evening, looking in at me from the garden. I waved to him and he—or his spirit—waved back. Then he dematerialised and I didn't see him again until I caught a glimpse of him cleaning his teeth in the downstairs bathroom. I spoke to him on that occasion but he did not reply. Spirits rarely do."

Berthea raised an eyebrow. "Strange that one would have to clean one's teeth in the spirit world: I would have thought that one of the perks of being disembodied would be not to have to clean one's teeth, not to use deodorant, perhaps. But still . . . What did you say to him, Terence?"

"I asked him whether he was happy in the other dimension."

"And did he reply?" asked Berthea. "Did he complain about a shortage of whisky on the other side? Remember how he loved his favourite whisky—any whisky, indeed."

Her levity clearly annoyed Terence. "It's all very well for you to laugh, Berthy, but this is not an amusing subject at all. Just you wait until you cross over yourself. Would you want people making fun of you, just because you were a spirit?"

Berthea tried to look contrite. "I'm sorry. What did he say, Terence?"

"He was unable to comment on the precise arrangements on the other side," said Terence, "because he dematerialised again—rather quickly. One moment he was there, and the next he was gone."

"How unfortunate," said Berthea. "And in general, don't you agree it's somewhat unfortunate that we have so little *quality time* with spirits. You'd imagine they might occasionally make themselves available for interview, perhaps, on the more hospitable television programmes. They need not agree to be interviewed by anybody aggressive, but it would be so helpful . . ."

Terence gave her a sideways look. "They're very busy," he said.

"You can't expect them to spend their time with those of us on this side when they have all those things to do on the other side. It's kind enough of them to give us the occasional glimpse, and we should be grateful for it."

Berthea did not pursue the matter. "Oh well. Tell me, Terence, who was the friend who stayed here last week?"

"My friend Jasper," said Terence. "I haven't known him long, but we get on very well together."

Berthea's eyes narrowed. "And how did you meet him?"

Terence smiled. "In the car. I was driving over to Glastonbury to do some healing, and Jasper was standing by the side of the road, indicating that he wanted help in getting somewhere. So I stopped and asked him where he was going. And he said, 'That depends on where you're going, my friend—our journeys are converging, I think.' Those were his exact words, Berthy, and I thought them very beautiful words indeed. So I opened the door for him, and he hopped in."

"And?" said Berthea, through pursed lips.

"And I drove Jasper all the way to Glastonbury. We talked a lot on the way there, and he told me that he had been a coracle-maker in Wales—or apprenticed to one—when the call came."

"What call?"

"It was a call to stop making coracles and to take up another project altogether."

"Which was?"

"To map the ley lines of the west of England. Do you know, Berthy, there isn't a full map of ley lines and other energy fields in England? People know about them, of course. I pointed one out to Monty Bismarck the other day; it ran straight through his father's living room—not that Alfie Bismarck is at all sensitive to these things. Nor Monty, for that matter: all Monty asked was whether it would interfere with the television reception. Honestly, Berthy, some people . . ."

Berthea was keen to find out more about Jasper. "So this new friend of yours, this Jasper, is working on a map?"

"Yes," said Terence proudly. "And he's asked me for advice on relevant features of the countryside round here. He wants to put in not only ley lines but sacred wells too."

Berthea suddenly felt very tired. She had experienced this sensation before when talking to her brother, and so it was familiar enough. It sprang from despair; despair at not knowing how to penetrate the fog of magical thinking that seemed to envelop Terence Moongrove. It was how the parent of an estranged teenager might feel, struggling to find some way of penetrating a consciousness that would admit of no rational exchange.

"The bed," said Terence suddenly. "I haven't changed the sheets since Jasper was here. It's a new policy I have to help protect the environment. And Jasper is perfectly clean, so there's no reason why we should change them just yet."

Berthea's jaw dropped. "You mean, I'm to sleep between some . . . some *man's* sheets?"

Terence nodded. "Why not? He only used them for three days."

"But . . . but people like clean sheets," protested Berthea. "There'll be . . ." She struggled to find the right word. "There'll be bits of skin on the sheets. We all shed bits of skin, you know. And oily deposits too."

Terence looked puzzled. "Oily deposits? You know, Berthy, you do sound rather *fussy*."

Berthea's voice was now raised. "Fussy! That's rich, Terence."

He stood his ground. "Yes, fussy. How do you know that Jasper has oily deposits? Yes, go on, how do you know? You tell me!"

33. You're My Brother, and I'm Proud of You

DINNER WAS A trying occasion for Berthea. Terence was in a talkative mood and insisted on giving her long and detailed accounts of issues dividing his sacred dance group.

"Most of the members are easy enough to get on with," he said. "Very easy. They're not interested in political intrigue. They just . . ."

"Just want to get on with the dancing," prompted Berthea.

"Exactly," said Terence. "But there are *always* some people who see committees as a way of advancing themselves. You know the type, Berthy? They plot and scheme. They use all sorts of devices to get themselves into positions of power. I've no time for people like that, Berthy—no time at all."

Berthea suppressed a yawn. She wondered what issues could arise in a sacred dance group: personality clashes, perhaps? The issue of unconventional steps? It was possible that there were even theological divisions between those who stuck to that Bulgarian mystic—what was his name?—and those who were open to other influences. People had an insatiable appetite for disagreement, she felt; whenever two or more were gathered together it seemed inevitable that they would find something to differ about. And there was always politics—even, it seemed, in the sphere of sacred dance.

Berthea toyed with her soup. Terence had put far too much salt in it, making it virtually undrinkable. She took a sip, and spat it back into the spoon. "What are these issues, Terence?" she asked.

Terence appeared to be having no difficulty with the salty broth. "Good question, Berthy. There are quite a few, as it happens, but the thing that has really set the cat among the pigeons is morris dancing. That's made things jolly difficult for everyone, Berthy, I'm telling you."

Berthea stared morosely at her soup. The salt made it impossible to divine exactly what sort it was, but she was beginning to suspect it was based on tripe. Tripe soup was unheard of, surely, but then anything was possible with her brother.

"Yes," Terence continued. "There are some on the committee— that horrid Jones woman being the ringleader—who want us to accept an invitation to dance with a group of morris dancers who perform outside the Lamb and Flag every other weekend. That Jones woman had a letter of invitation from the leader of the morris men and she's frightfully keen that we accept."

Berthea shrugged. "Well, it would be nice, wouldn't it? You're all interested in roughly the same thing—and you all wear similar white outfits, don't you?"

Terence put down his spoon. "Berthy!" he exclaimed. "You couldn't be more wrong if you tried! Morris men are *pagan*—their dances are all about fertility and things like that. We're above all that. Far above it."

Berthea inched her untouched plate of soup away from her. "Nobody is above reproduction, Terence," she said quietly. "Even you and me. We are the result of reproductive passions. We need to remind ourselves of that."

Terence would have none of it. "Beings of Light do not come about in the same way as ordinary people," he pronounced. "Our dances are pure. There is no trace of the bodily side. That is the whole point of sacred dance, Berthy, and I thought somebody like you would understand that."

The conversation drifted on along these lines, and then Terence suddenly said, "You should eat your soup, Berthy. It's jolly rude not to eat it when your host has spent hours making it for you. Jolly rude indeed."

"One can't drink soup that has far too much salt in it, Terence. I'm sorry, but it's just not possible."

Terence glowered at her. "You don't drink soup, Berthy, you *eat* it. Remember how we were told that when we were really small? Aunty Bee, who knew all about manners. Remember? It's the same as not saying serviette for table napkin."

"Nonsense," said Berthea. "Liquids are drunk, not eaten. You don't say 'Eat your coffee,' do you? You say, 'Drink your coffee.'"

Terence responded hotly, "Oh you think you know better, do you, Berthy? You think you know better than everybody, don't you? Better than Mummy knew, better than Daddy or Aunty Bee; better even than the Queen, I shouldn't be surprised."

"Oh Terence," sighed Berthea, "I do wish you'd grow up."

There was silence. Then Terence muttered, "You're jolly rude, you know. It's all very well for you. You live in London and have hundreds of friends. I'm stuck here and I haven't really anything much. You'd think that . . ."

The words trailed away, and in a sudden awful moment Berthea realised that she had reduced her brother to tears.

"Oh Terence," she said, rising to put an arm about her brother. "I didn't mean to upset you. Come, come."

The volume of the sobs rose. "I know I haven't done much with my life, Berthy. Other chaps have done much more. But I'm doing my best, Berthy, I promise you I am."

"Of course you are," said Berthea. "Of course you are. And I'm really proud of you—I hope you know that. We may have our little disagreements, but I'm so proud of you, Terence."

He looked up at her, wiping at his eyes with a large blue handkerchief, threadbare and unironed, which he had removed from the pocket of his jacket, where it had been tucked in an attempt at raffishness. "Are you proud of me, Berthy? Are you really?"

"Of course I am," she said. "You're my brother, and I'm proud of you."

He produced a second handkerchief from another pocket and blew his nose. "Well, I'll make you even prouder, Berthy. Once I start my racing, I'll make you really proud. Our Frazer Nash is going to be jolly fast."

"I wonder whether that's such a good idea, Terence," said Berthea, her tone at once tentative and tactful.

"It's too late," said Terence.

"Oh?"

"We've already bought the Frazer Nash. I gave Monty the cheque this afternoon, and he's going over to see Richard Latcham tomorrow."

"Who is this Richard Latcham?"

"He's the man we've bought it from," said Terence. "He's restored it very well, and he's promised me that nothing will go wrong with this car."

He looked at Berthea, his eyes now bright again. "And I'm going to make you proud, Berthy, by winning my first race. You just watch. You just watch."

34. The Leporine Challenge

WHEN FREDDIE DE LA HAY first picked up the scent of rabbit, he stood motionless, his nose into the wind, his whole body quivering in anticipation. He remembered, of course, that he was not meant to wander; that he must stay within the general curtilage of the house to which William had brought him. He knew that if he interpreted too broadly the permission that William had implicitly given him to investigate the lawn and shrubs around the house, then there would be recriminations. There would be raised voices and other signs of displeasure, and for a dog like Freddie, in whom a conscience, even a merely Pavlovian one, had been instilled, the displeasure of the humans he loved was like a great cloud of thunder: dark, forbidding and centred directly above one's head.

But this was not an ordinary situation—there were rabbits here; not merely lingering traces of ancient rabbits, but real living and breathing rabbits. Only the best-trained dogs, those disciplined to stay at their owners' sides whatever the circumstances—experienced gun-dogs, for example—can resist the temptation of readily available prey. Freddie de la Hay was not untrained, but his education, such as it was, had encouraged him to go after significant smells. As a sniffer dog at Heathrow, he had been rewarded for running after a tempting suitcase as it was carried along a conveyor belt; that was the whole point of his being there. So now that he smelled the rabbits, although he knew that he should not go too far, there was also a strong and ultimately irresistible urge to ferret out these annoying creatures and deal with them in the way he felt they deserved.

It did not take long, then, for his indecision to be overcome. Uttering a yelp of excitement, Freddie ran straight towards the first of the rabbit holes. This was not very large, and he managed to get his snout into the entrance, but there was not much more he could do. Besides, once he had sniffed the earth at the entrance to the hole, he found that the scent he had picked up so strongly was fainter here. Rabbits had passed this way—there was no doubt about it—but they had done so some time ago.

He sniffed at the breeze, picking up the stronger scent that wafted over from a further point of the field. Giving another yelp, he rushed off in that direction, and soon found exactly what he was hoping for: a commodious, inviting entrance into the main rabbit warren. This hole clearly served a whole colony of rabbits and was easily large enough for even a medium-sized dog such as Freddie de la Hay to penetrate.

In the darkness of the hole, Freddie sniffed at the dank air: there was so much to take in—the smell of earth, of roots, the whiff of other creatures—moles—whose tunnels intersected the rabbit highway. He pushed himself forwards, scrabbling his way past a curtain of hanging roots. These bore the evidence of recent rabbit passage, and the scent served only to urge Freddie on to more frantic burrowing. Had he paused to consider the consequences of his actions—something beyond the intellectual competence of most dogs—he would have realised that the only way he could retreat from the tunnel, which was growing rapidly narrower, would be by going backwards; that is unless he found a chamber of some sort in which he could turn round. But he did not think of this, his mind being completely occupied with the task of getting closer to the source of this rabbit smell—the rabbits themselves, who had to be in there somewhere, taunting him with their proximity.

He moved forwards in the darkness, more slowly now as the tunnel roof grew lower at this point and pressed upon his shoulders and his back. After a few minutes during which he made very little progress, the urge to get back to the light and fresh air became stronger than the urge to find the rabbits. He stopped, and tried to turn round; of course, there was no room, not even enough to make the slightest turn. He tried again, but succeeded only in wedging himself still more tightly in the constricted space.

Next, Freddie de la Hay tried to move backwards. This proved every bit as impossible as turning. He paused, and the realisation dawned on him that something was seriously wrong. He closed his eyes and then reopened them, in the hope that he might simply find himself elsewhere. Such rapid and inexplicable transitions could occur; he had once been in a train and had closed his eyes, gone to sleep, and then when he awoke discovered himself in an entirely different place. If such a thing could happen once, then there was no reason why it should not happen again.

But it did not, and on opening his eyes he was in exactly the same place. Now he began to whimper, and these whimpers, soft at first, became louder and louder until they were a full-blown wail. Freddie was not only bemoaning his fate, he was calling for William. In his mind, William was all-powerful and perfectly capable of bringing his durance to an end. William would come, would come down from above, would come with shovels, would come to pluck him from this earthly tomb. William would brush the earth from his coat, take him in his arms and tell him that he was a good dog and that dinner would be ready shortly, would let him be with him, which was all that Freddie had ever wanted, and what he wanted now with all his heart.

But there was no William. There was only darkness and discomfort, and a sense that whatever was happening to him was something final and irreparable. This thing was the death that every creature so instinctively resists. Freddie de la Hay had no word for it, but knew its face, and knew that it was his companion in this subterranean prison. He whimpered, and instinctively licked at his paw, which was tucked up unnaturally under his chin, forced into that position by his attempts to turn round. He licked at his paw as if to comfort himself, but there was no comfort for him, none at all, just a growing terror.

35. Freddie Digs His Way Out of a Hole

IT WAS TERROR that eventually drove Freddie de la Hay to start digging again. He had no alternative but to go forwards, and he did so now with fervent energy, scratching with all his power at the yielding earth, ignoring the showers of debris that covered his head and neck. He closed his eyes; he struggled to breathe; he was as a creature possessed, acquiring from deep within him the strength and determination of ten dogs or more.

For the first few minutes, he made little progress. The ground seemed harder now, and his claws sent stabs of pain shooting up his legs; he ignored the pains, redoubling his efforts when he suddenly felt the ground become more yielding. And then the wall of the tunnel gave way and opened out into a chamber. Freddie de la Hay opened his eyes and saw, at the end of the chamber, a shaft leading upwards. And from this came the smell of fresh air, of grass, of creatures other than rabbits.

Freddie shot forwards, at first entangling and then disentangling himself from a hanging skein of roots. His paws were painful and there was grit in his nostrils, but he ignored these discomforts in the urgency of his efforts. There was light now—not bright light, but a filtered sort of gloaming, a vague glow. He scrabbled frantically, pushing with his hind legs, wiggling to give himself extra purchase on the soft floor of the chamber. He could still smell rabbits, but he ignored them, yearning only to break free and emerge from the nightmare into which he had so foolishly launched himself.

That is not to say, though, that Freddie de la Hay felt any inclination to reproach himself. The past for a dog is just that: the past. A dog sees no point in dwelling on things that have happened; the important thing is that they are not happening *now*. In that respect, they have something to teach us: we so often feel that then is now, and this leads us to prolong the suffering of yesterday into the suffering of today. Dogs do not do that.

With a final effort, Freddie pushed himself up through the gradually widening opening above his head. He was free, and the sudden evening light made him blink in confusion. Without thinking, he set off across the field in which he found himself as fast as he could manage, giving several exultant barks as he did so. He did not stop until he reached the far side, where a thick hedge blocked further progress. He sat down momentarily, looked up at the sky and then gave another bark before launching himself through a gap he had just spotted in the hedge.

Now he was on a road—one of those small, winding roads that seem to go nowhere in particular but in fact connect village to village, in their own time. Freddie had no idea where he was, nor did he know where he was going. He trotted along, from time to time sniffing at the verge; not unhappy, perhaps, but not happy either.

There was a noise that he registered as an approaching car. Freddie cocked an ear, listening to see whether he recognised the note of the engine. He did not, and he sat down to wait for the noise to become louder.

There was the squeal of brakes, followed by the sound of a car door opening.

"You silly dog!"

It was a woman.

"Yes, you! I'm not talking to any other dogs—I'm addressing you! You silly, silly dog, sitting there in the road like that. I had to brake, you know, and if I'd been going any faster I would have run over you."

Freddie looked at the woman who had stepped out of the car.

He realised that what she had to say concerned him, but he had no idea what it was. The word "dog," however, was familiar, and he knew that this, in some vague way, referred to him. It was not his name, of course, but it was close to it, and he wagged his tail in response.

The woman bent down to look more closely at Freddie. "You're wearing a collar, I see. Let me take a look."

Freddie allowed the stranger to turn the collar round his neck so that the nameplate, a small steel tag, could be read.

"Freddie de la Hay," she read aloud. "Now that is very interesting. Are you, I wonder, Freddie de la Hay—an unlikely name for a dog, I'd have thought—or do you belong to somebody called Freddie de la Hay?"

She straightened up, still gazing down on Freddie.

"Freddie!" she called out.

Freddie looked up sharply and gave a bark of recognition.

"That settles that," said the woman. "So you're Freddie de la Hay." She paused. "Well, Freddie de la Hay, you're clearly lost and so I suppose . . ." She looked about her, scanning the fields that bordered the road. Although the light was fading, it was clear that there was nobody to be seen. "I suppose I can't leave you here. So . . . come along, Freddie de la Hay. Hop in."

She clicked her fingers and began to make her way towards the open door of the car. Freddie immediately understood what was intended and obediently trotted past her, peered into the car and jumped inside. The woman settled herself in the driver's seat and slammed the door shut.

This was the signal for Freddie, seated in the passenger seat beside her, to do as he had been trained during his period of indoctrination as a "new dog." Half turning in his seat, he took the seatbelt in his mouth and drew it across his front. Then nuzzling the red clip at the side of the seat, he pressed the metal connector home.

The woman watched in astonishment.

"Did you just strap yourself in?" she stuttered. "Did I see what I think I saw?"

Freddie smiled at her, his pink tongue hanging out of the side of his mouth. A small stream of saliva dropped down onto the seat. He bent his head apologetically, licked up the spittle and then turned to face his new friend once more.

"Amazing . . . ," she muttered, slipping the car into gear. "Let's go, Freddie de la Hay!"

36. An Unrevealed Source

IF FREDDIE WAS about to venture into the unknown, then so too was Barbara Ragg. What she did next was nothing to do with her recent discovery of her gypsy roots, although that revelation had certainly left her feeling quite light-headed; this, rather, was the result of the decision she had already taken to bring Oedipus Snark's political career to an end. Or, if she could not end it entirely, then she could at least lead it down an alley from which it might never emerge. She had not discussed this plan with anybody—she did not want to talk to Hugh about a former boyfriend—and so she had received no advice about it. Had she sought such counsel, of course, it might well have urged caution: Oedipus Snark was a formidable opponent with a reputation for the ruthless pursuit of self-interest; not for nothing, people said, was he known as the only nasty Lib Dem MP in recent history. But now it was too late for such reservations, and even though the journalist to whom she had spoken warned her of the possible consequences, she felt that she had gone too far to back-track.

The journalist she had approached was a client of the Ragg Porter Agency. Tom Maxwell was the deputy editor of a popular daily, and a widely read political columnist. Some years earlier he had uncovered a circle of influential freemasons who had been using connections to secure contracts. He had published a book on the subject, which had led to parliamentary questions and an official inquiry. He had used the Ragg Porter Agency to negotiate publication, and it was in this context that he had come across Barbara. They got on well, and she had even wondered at one point if their friendship might become something more. But Tom was not interested; there was somebody, she found out—a woman in Amsterdam whom he had known for years and with whom he lived sporadically. Barbara's being aware of this woman at least made things easier for her; she could meet Tom and enjoy his friendship without the complication that romantic possibility inserts into any relationship.

They met early one morning in a coffee bar off Brook Street. Tom had an interview to conduct at the Dorchester—he was due to talk to a visiting German businessman who was circling an ailing drinks company and whose real intentions had yet to be uncovered.

"There's a possibility that he would just close it down," he said. "It would be one way of knocking out the competition."

"And throw how many people out of work?" asked Barbara.

Tom shrugged. "Three hundred, give or take a few."

"Awful," said Barbara.

Tom sighed. "Yes, but that's capitalism for you. Money doesn't sit in a hole, you know."

"And what does that mean?"

"It means that money has to work, or it's not doing its job. And being used to buy things—including companies—is part of that work."

Barbara did not approve. "And one just ignores the human consequences?"

Tom sighed again. "One does not ignore them. One can lament them, but ultimately money has its own logic. Ultimately, it finds the most fruitful place to be and it flows in that direction. It's the way of the world, Barbara."

Barbara stared into her coffee. "I thought that the whole point about civilised capitalism was that you brought money under control—you stopped it behaving ruthlessly. Can't we do that?"

Tom smiled. "People try. You may recall that unions which have attempted to resist the force of economics have a tendency to find themselves without an industry to control. Remember coal? And that was before full-scale globalisation. Now . . ." He made a gesture of helplessness. "If unions put up their costs too much, economic activity simply migrates. And there's always somebody to do things more cheaply than we can. China. You know what it's like."

She nodded. "Yes, but listen, I didn't plan to meet you to talk about economics. I wanted to give you something. Some information." She glanced about her, to check whether anybody might overhear.

"You look very sweet when you clutch your cloak and dagger," said Tom, smiling.

"Don't patronise me," she muttered.

"Sorry. So what is it? Remember that I'm really a columnist these days. I'm no Bob Woodward."

"Oedipus Snark," said Barbara simply.

Tom frowned, as if trying to remember something. "Snark? The junior minister for . . ."

Barbara named the ministry, and Tom nodded. "Ridiculous-sounding name. Not my favourite member of the House of Commons, if the truth be told."

"That's what I want," said Barbara. "I want the truth to be told."

Tom broke into a wry smile. "Don't we all?" He looked at her quizzically. "Do you know something about our friend Mr. Snark?

You know him?" He paused. "Hold on, weren't you . . . close friends for a while?"

"Yes."

He raised an eyebrow. "If this is some sort of exercise in revenge, Barbara . . . That's not what newspapers are for, you know."

"I thought that was exactly what they did," replied Barbara.

"Some of them, maybe. But not ours."

"Ah, I see! Too high-minded?"

"Something like that," said Tom.

For a few moments they looked at one another in silence. Then Barbara said, "I won't say that I bear Oedipus Snark no ill will. I do. I bear him a great deal of ill will."

"Hell hath no fury—" Tom began.

She cut him off. "I asked you not to patronise, Tom. You have no idea what transpired between Oedipus and me. You really haven't."

"All right. It wasn't good. So?"

"I want to stop him," she said. "Not because of what he did to me, but because of what he might do in power. I just can't bear the thought of Oedipus being anywhere *near* power."

Tom took out a small notebook. "You do realise what you're doing, Barbara?"

"Yes."

"I'm not so sure. People think that they're safe in this country, that nobody could ever have them . . . harmed. Well, I've seen that this is not true at all. There are plenty of people who come to a sticky end because they've taken on people in power—or people who have money. Same thing, really. Money and power occupy the same bed."

Barbara looked down at the floor. She asked herself what she felt about Oedipus. Did she hate him? The word "hate" could be used lightly—as in "I hate vanilla ice cream"—but it had a very different feel when used in its strong sense. Should we not feel ashamed of feelings of hate? Should we not forgive those whom we find our-selves tempted to hate?

And if you hated somebody, did that mean that you wanted the object of your hatred to suffer? There was no doubt in her mind but that she would feel pleasure if Oedipus were to encounter some sort of setback. That is exactly how one felt in the pantomime when a villain—the unpleasant ugly sister or the sinister Captain Hook—was dealt a blow. But she was not sure about being the person who delivered that blow. Even the wicked suffer, she thought, and their pain is no different from the pain felt by the innocent, other, of course, than in its aetiology.

And yet, Oedipus had to be stopped. So she reached into her bag, took out the copy of the letter and handed it to Tom. He read it and looked up at her.

"Is this genuine?"

"Yes."

He looked down at the piece of paper. Then he lifted it to his lips and kissed it. "Lovely," he said.

37. Barbara Ragg Speaks to Hugh

IT WAS DONE. Tom had taken the copy of the letter, tucked it into an inside pocket and winked at his informant.

Barbara looked at him anxiously. "He won't find out where you got it, will he?"

Tom touched her arm. "Heavens no! We don't reveal our sources. I'd go to prison before doing that."

That was reassuring. "Good."

"But don't talk to anybody about this," Tom went on. "Often it's the sources who reveal themselves. You'd be surprised."

They finished their coffee and said goodbye, Tom going off to his interview at the Dorchester and Barbara making her way back to the flat. She was meeting Hugh for dinner, as he was travelling down to London that day. She felt slightly dirtied by handing over the letter, and seeing Hugh was just what she needed to take her mind off what had happened.

He was early, and she was still getting ready when he rang the doorbell.

"I know I said seven," he said, looking at his watch. "But I really couldn't wait until seven to see you."

They embraced on the doorstep. "I'm glad you're early," she said. "It gives us more time together."

He stroked her hair. "My lovely fiancée . . ."

They kissed. He does not smell of London, she thought; he smells of the Highlands. And then she thought: What an odd idea to entertain, that people should smell of the place they came from. But they did; each of us smells of our particular prison.

They went into the flat, and while Barbara finished getting ready Hugh poured them each a glass from the chilled bottle of white wine he had brought with him. She joined him in the kitchen, and they toasted one another.

"You," he said, lifting his glass.

"And you," she responded.

"Your day?" he asked. "Busy?"

She nodded. "I had a few meetings. Lots of telephone calls."

"Meetings with whom?"

She took a sip of her wine. Hugh liked white Burgundy, and that was what he had brought. "Well, I saw a journalist. We talked about . . ."

She stopped. She had been on the point of telling him what she and Tom had discussed, but then she realised that it would mean she had to reveal her affair with Oedipus Snark.

"About what?" Hugh prompted.

"About a politician." It was a stalling answer.

"Which one?"

Barbara walked over to the window. She was uncertain what to do. She did not want to keep anything from him—there should be no secrets in an engagement—but did one have to reveal everything about former affairs? Should a veil of tact not be drawn over at least some parts of one's history?

"Oedipus Snark." She had no alternative but to admit that, at least.

Hugh raised an eyebrow. "Snark? The one you sometimes see on the telly . . . That one . . . ?"

She nodded. "Yes."

"But surely you don't actually *know* him," said Hugh. "How would you know somebody like that?"

She avoided meeting his eyes. This had rapidly become far worse than she had imagined. If she told him that she and Oedipus had been lovers, then surely she would go down in his estimation; and yet, if she did not tell him and he were subsequently to find out—as was perfectly possible—he would be hurt by the fact that she had effectively lied to him. No, she would have to make a clean breast of it.

She turned to face him. "Hugh, I didn't want to talk about this, but . . . Well, you have to know that Oedipus Snark and I were together." She immediately realised the archness of her expression. "By which I mean we were lovers."

His face was impassive. "You?"

"Yes. We were together for four years. It was pretty one-sided, I'm afraid."

He looked relieved. "Oh, so he was keen on you, and you drifted into it. Oh, well—"

She stopped him. "No. Not at all. It was the other way round. I was keen on him, and he took me for granted. He didn't love me. I don't think he knew what the word meant. Eventually I left him, but way, way too late."

She drew in her breath. "And there's another thing I need to tell you," she said. "I've just found out something about myself—something I had no idea about."

He put down his glass. "I don't know . . ."

"Let me tell you," she said. "I'm a gypsy. Actually, part gypsy. My grandfather was a gypsy, you see, and I didn't know about it."

He was staring at her. "Is there anything else I should know?" And then, almost immediately, his face cracked into a wide smile. "These are little things, Barbara. They're . . . they're nothing at all. So what if you fell for Oedipus Snark? Nice women fall for dreadful men all the time. And the fact that you have gypsy blood in you is completely irrelevant to anything. All blood looks the same under the microscope, you know."

"It's red," she said.

"Precisely," said Hugh.

"I must say I'm relieved. I was worried that you would think differently about me." She reached out to take his hand. "I know it's stupid of me, but I did think that. I'm sorry."

"No, you don't need to apologise. There's nothing to be sorry about." He hesitated. "And it makes me realise that there's something I need to tell you. You've told me things about yourself. Now it's my turn."

She did not want this, and told him so. "I don't need to know everything about you, Hugh. I don't care if you did something awful. I really don't care."

"But I have to," he said. "I want to share my life with you—really share it—and that means there's something you need to know."

She sat down. "Well, if you must."

"I must."

"Go on, then."

He reached for the wine bottle and filled his glass; Barbara did not want a top-up.

"You remember how I told you about my trip to South America after I left school? Remember?"

She did. "You took a job as an English teacher. Colombia, wasn't it?"

"Yes. And then I went to spend some time as tutor to one of the boys from the school. The family was very wealthy and had that place in the country."

"With the swimming pool carved out of the rock?"

"Yes. But I didn't tell you about what happened to me there, did I?"

"No, I don't think you did. You said there was something you didn't want to talk about."

"Well, I want to talk about it now."

38. In the Cupboard

"I KNEW THAT things in that house weren't quite right," said Hugh. "It was difficult to put one's finger on it—atmospheres are like that, aren't they? One picks up on them, one senses them, but it's often rather hard, if not impossible, to put them into words."

Barbara nodded. She had no idea what Hugh's disclosure would be and, while she was steeling herself for the worst, she was uncertain what she would do if he were to confess that he had committed some terrible crime. But she thought it highly improbable: Hugh simply did not have it in him to do anything cruel or thoughtless— she was sure of that. An act of cowardice, then, a failure to do something that he should perhaps have done—that was far more likely.

"You may remember," Hugh continued, "my telling you about that boy's mother. She was typical of those rich South American women one sees from time to time—very elegantly dressed, expensively slim; large emeralds in strategic places. I suppose the emeralds are to be expected, given that Colombia produces them, but I hadn't imagined that people would wear jewels like that at *breakfast*.

"She was always criticising her son. He wasn't too bad, as those pampered rich kids go, and there were times when I itched to intervene on his behalf. I wanted to say to her, 'Look, why do you always run him down? Say something nice to him for a change— a word of praise, maybe.' But I didn't, of course. I felt insecure: I was far from home, I was their guest and, frankly, there was a whiff of danger about the whole set-up. Where did the money come from, I wondered? And why did the father spend so much time in Miami?

"She was a great socialite. Because her husband was away so much, I think she was bored. She held dinner parties every other night, her guests coming from the other large houses in the district. They drove over in those big four-wheel drives they liked so much. Tinted windows, armed drivers, that sort of thing.

"I was on duty for these dinner parties. I was put on show, so to speak; a trophy guest. I think she talked me up with these people, telling them that I was the son of a Scottish earl or something of the sort. One of them actually came up to me and said, 'I hear that you're a descendant of Macbeth. I'd like you to know I really enjoyed that play.'

"I did my best. A lot of the conversation passed me by. They loved dissecting friends who weren't there, and some of the stories were pretty uncharitable. Bored, rich people can be like that, you know—extremely malicious. I sat and listened to their exchanges and thought of how much I wanted to be home again.

"It was at one of these dinner parties that I found myself seated next to an extremely attractive woman who was distantly related, I had been told, to my hostess. Her husband, a sinister-looking man in a white dinner jacket, said little but listened very attentively whenever his wife spoke, nodding his agreement.

"She seemed very interested in what I was doing and what my plans were. She quizzed me about my interests and wanted to know whether I could dance. I told her that I had gone to ballroom-dancing lessons when I was at school, and this seemed to please her. She looked across at her husband and repeated what I had said about dancing lessons. He flashed a smile at me and nodded to his wife.

"After dinner we all went out onto the terrace, where coffee was served. My hostess drew me aside and whispered that I had been a great success with her cousin. 'She likes you,' she said. 'They are very influential people.'

"'She seems very interesting,' I replied.

"'Yes. And they wish to offer you a job for a couple of months. They own several cruise liners. It would be a job on one of the liners.'

"I told her that I was happy enough with what I was doing. I wasn't sure that I wanted to work at sea.

"She did not take this well. 'I wouldn't refuse, if I were you,' she said. 'When I said they are influential, what I meant is that they are *very* influential, if you get my drift. I don't think it would be *wise* to decline.'

"I found myself resenting this. Again it struck home as typical of rich people that they should feel they could tell others what to do. I said that, as far as I was concerned, there was simply no prospect of my working on one of the cruise liners. That was that, and there was no point in discussing it further.

"She gave me a very strange look and shrugged. Then she went off to talk to her cousin and the cousin's husband. They looked in my direction as she spoke, and I did not like the expression on the man's face. I put down my coffee cup and left the terrace to go back up to my room.

"The boy was there, hanging about outside my door. He put a finger to his lips to signal that we should not talk, and then he led me down the corridor to a large linen cupboard. He gestured that I should follow him into the cupboard and I did so. If somebody asks you to go into a cupboard, there is usually a good reason for it.

"There was no light inside and I found myself in pitch darkness. 'Be very careful,' he whispered. 'My mother is a very dangerous woman. And that cousin of hers is even more deadly. You must run away. You must not stay here any longer. You should go tonight—immediately. I can get one of the servants to take you to a place where there is a bus just after dawn. That will take you into Bogotá. Once you reach there, get out of the country. Don't wait—just get out.'

"I told him that I couldn't leave that night. I would think about it and decide what to do the following morning.

"He told me that this was a very bad decision. 'I know those people,' he said. 'They will stop at nothing.'

"'Tomorrow,' I said. 'I'll let you know what I decide to do.'

"He accepted this, but only reluctantly. 'Careful,' he whispered. 'And lock your door.'"

39. *Burundanga*

"THE PROBLEM, HOWEVER," Hugh continued, "was that my door did not have a lock. There was a keyhole, but when I inspected it closely I saw it was full of cobwebs. I'd noticed there were numerous spiders about the house, and I felt I had discovered their headquarters. It was clear that no key had been inserted in the lock for a very long time, and if I wanted to secure my room, I would have to move furniture up against the door.

"I felt vaguely ridiculous shifting the chest of drawers across the floor and positioning it against the door. It was comic, really, rather like hiding under the bedclothes as a child: if anybody wanted to get in, he would simply have to push hard against the door and the chest would yield. It would be a noisy business, though, and it would give me time to raise the alarm.

"Feeling slightly more secure, I went to bed and turned out the light. My mind was now made up: the following day I would speak to my hostess and tell her that I had decided to get back to Barranquilla. I could invent a reason for this, or could just tell her that it was what I wanted to do. After all, I was not beholden to this woman. I had not asked to be invited, and surely the whole point about being a guest was that one could go home when one wanted.

"It took me some time to fall asleep, and when I did it was one of those fitful sleeps that one has when something is preying on one's mind. I kept imagining that I was hearing the chest being shifted and would struggle back into consciousness and turn on the light, only to see that everything was exactly as I had left it. Eventually dawn came and I got up, still tired, and went to open the curtains and let in the morning light.

"My room was off a small terrace at the side of the house. Behind the curtain was a set of French doors that gave out onto this terrace. They afforded a good view of the hills and the canopy of uninterrupted green between the house and the slopes in the distance.

"My heart stopped. On the terrace in front of the door were two men, and as I drew the curtain one of them pushed the unlocked door open and seized me. I saw that one of them had a cloth of some sort in his hand, a red handkerchief perhaps, and he brought this up to my face as he moved forwards. I shouted out, but the cloth soon muffled my cries. And then there was oblivion—complete oblivion—and I knew nothing more until I woke up in another room, a small, stuffy room in which the loud hum of an air conditioner or fan reverberated.

"I had a splitting headache, but my vision was fine, and I felt no other pain. I stood up, rubbing my temples to ease the throbbing, and looked about me. The noise that I had thought was an air conditioner now changed note, and at the same time I felt vibration in the floor. At that moment, I realised that I was in a ship's cabin, and that the vibration came from the engine.

"I sat down again, hoping that this might ease my headache. It helped a bit, as did the rubbing of my temples. Now I was able to think, to try to grasp what had happened to me. I had been in my room and I had seen men on the terrace and then . . . The realisation came swiftly, and it was a frightening one. *Burundanga*. I had become a victim of *burundanga*. It all fitted: the man with the cloth, the amnesia, the waking with a headache.

"I knew about *burundanga* because I had been told about it by one of the young assistants at the school in Barranquilla. It had not happened to him—these stories rarely happened to the person who told them—but it had befallen a cousin in Medellín, a city noted for its lawlessness. This cousin had accepted a lift in a car—a rash thing to do in Colombia—and been offered a piece of cake by the driver. He began to eat the cake, and then passed out. The next thing he knew, he was lying at the roadside more than fifty miles away, clad only in his underpants. Everything had been stolen, including his clothes. He was picked up by a passing police car, and was told by the policemen that finding somebody in his state by the side of the road was nothing unusual. They explained how the drug known as *burundanga*—or scopolamine, to give it its scientific name—was a boon to thieves. It could be administered orally or by simply throwing a powder in the victim's face so that it would be breathed in. Once under its influence, one became completely compliant. That young man by the roadside would not have had to be stripped; he would have undressed without protest and handed over all his possessions with the same obliging meekness. And then came sleep and complete amnesia.

"I had listened to this explanation with fascinated horror. I had heard some disturbing things since coming to Colombia. I had heard of the ease with which one could arrange for the disposal of another—the price of a drive-by shooting in most places was little more than the cost of a night's stay in a modest hotel, or of a meal in a good restaurant. And such things could be arranged with virtual impunity. The police could not cope with the burden of looking into every homicide, and how could they possibly work out which youth on which motorcycle had pulled the trigger? That had appalled me, but somehow this drugging struck me as particularly sinister. I was struck, I suppose, by the overcoming of the personality that it involved. There was something especially disturbing about the idea that the victim could be made to comply so absolutely, could be led like a lamb to slaughter. And now it had happened to me, although I was fully clothed. They must have dressed me, I thought. I looked down: the clothes were mine, as were the shoes. I had been wearing pyjamas when they struck, and so I had been dressed as one might dress a mannequin, or I had dressed myself on their orders, like an automaton, a puppet."

40. Hugh's Confession

HUGH TOLD HIS extraordinary story without interruption, while Barbara listened wide-eyed. Had this narrative been delivered by an actor in a studio, dictated with all the dramatic emphasis required for a noir offering from some breathless writer of thrillers, it would have been difficult enough to believe; but here it was being told by somebody Barbara Ragg knew and trusted, delivered with a straight-faced sobriety and lack of embellishment that only enhanced its credibility. Hugh, though, sought reassurance that he was being believed.

"I'm not making this up," he said. "I promise you. This really happened."

She reached out to take his hand. "Of course you're not, my darling. And I believe you."

"It's just that you look . . . well, rather astounded."

She let go of his hand. "Astounded? Yes, well, who can blame me? It's quite astounding. It's like listening to David Balfour."

He took the reference. "*Kidnapped* was one of my favourite books when I was a boy. I had a copy that had belonged to my father when he was a boy. I loved it because David goes through our part of the world on his way back to Edinburgh. I used to think that perhaps he walked across our farm. I *played* at being David Balfour."

"Yes," she said. "I had *Anne of Green Gables*, and I longed to be Anne. More girly."

"You were, of course, a girl."

"I was. But please carry on. You found yourself in a ship's cabin. You said that those people owned cruise liners. It was . . ."

He took over. "Yes, it was one of their ships. Or so I imagined— I didn't see them, the cousins themselves, but it didn't take long

149

to put two and two together. In fact, by the time the door of the cabin opened—I had discovered I was locked in—I had more or less worked out what had happened to me. They had offered me a job of some sort on the boat and I'd refused. But what I had forgotten was that this was Colombia, and these people were, as I had been told, *very* influential. In Colombia that means one thing—they were Colombian mafia, big-time *narcotraficantes*. And what I didn't take account of, in my naivety, was that you simply did not decline an invitation from people like that. My hostess had tried to spell it out to me, and her son had underlined it, but I thought I knew better. Big mistake.

"You know, Barbara, because we live in a country like this, where the law is respected and even the most powerful can be called to account, we have no real idea of what it must be like to live in a place where you can't make the assumption, where there are people who consider themselves above the law and can do exactly what they want. It's a very strange feeling, you know—a feeling of being utterly and completely helpless. You feel powerless; you feel very much alone. And remember that I was only experiencing a little bit of it. I was in many ways a privileged outsider—I possessed a passport, even if I didn't have it on me; there was an embassy in Bogotá that could make enquiries as to my whereabouts, that would kick up a fuss if one of its citizens was in trouble—all of that. But imagine what it's like if you're a landless peasant in such a place, or a little person eking out a living in a stinking *barrio*, or a servant whose job depends on the whim of some heartless employer who cares nothing for you? Think of what that's like. Just think of what it's like to be nobody, and to realise that people can do whatever they like to you and you'll have no recourse, none at all. Not pretty, is it? But that's been people's lot for most of history, because human rights are a pretty recent invention, aren't they?"

Barbara did not think he wanted an answer, but he paused and

looked at her expectantly. She considered the question. When
were human rights invented? During the French Revolution? Or
was the idea as old as the idea of democracy?

"I'm not sure," she said. And then, rather wildly, she offered,
"The Enlightenment?"

Hugh shrugged; having asked the question, he now seemed
to have lost interest in it. "Of course, people had the consolation
of their beliefs, didn't they? In the past it might have been a little
easier to bear one's suffering because one thought that the people
who made one suffer would be called to account in the afterlife.
There might be no justice in this world but there was a pretty
strong measure of it in the next. So the torturer got away with it
for the time being, yet would regret every turn of the screw when
he faced his maker. But destroy all belief in eternal justice—as we
have more or less done—and all you have is the earthly variety,
which is pretty unreliable. So no consolation—just emptiness."

She wanted to say something now. "But what's the point of false
hope? What's the point of telling ourselves that something will happen when we know it won't? I'd like to believe in fairies but does it
help me to delude myself as to their existence?"

He looked away, and she wondered whether she had offended
him with a lightweight remark; she had not intended to be flippant.

"We don't need fairies," he said. "Because a belief in fairies
would make no difference to the way we behave towards one another. But a belief in some inherent justice in this world—a justice to which we're all subject—would make a big difference to
the way we act towards others here and now."

Barbara looked dubious. She was thinking about how escha-
tology might blunt the desire to do something about the here and
now. "So we *need* to believe in eternal justice—even if we know it
doesn't exist?"

Hugh made a gesture of resignation. "I know it sounds ridiculous—

believing something you don't believe. But it's a serious point, Barbara. It's the same in the debate on free will and determinism. Determinists argue that everything we do is caused by something else—by what's happened to us, by our genes, even by the dictates of geography. There's a lot to be said for that, but try living your life on a basis of determinism: no blame, no responsibility; passive acceptance is about the only position you could hold. So even if we think that determinism is true, *we still have to act as if free will exists—we really do.*"

"Oh," she said. And then, contemplating what he had said, she said, "Oh," again.

"So," Hugh went on, "there I was, effectively a prisoner. And then . . ."

He faltered, and she looked at him with concern. "Hugh, darling Hugh, if this is painful . . ."

He shook his head. "No, I'll tell you, Barbara—I have to tell you now. And I want to. You see, what happened was that I had been kidnapped and I was now about to be told why. They were going to make me a gigolo—a gigolo on their cruise liner."

Barbara gasped. She had not expected this.

She suddenly felt dizzy, almost vertiginous. Her breath came in shallow gasps. She tried to clear her head by shaking it; she stood up; she fell down.

41. On Board Ship

"MY DARLING!"

Hugh rushed to help Barbara to her feet. He thought at first that she had fainted, but she had not: her eyes had remained open, fixed on Hugh in an expression that combined astonishment with disbelief. And there was something else there too, he felt: disgust.

He took her hand, and for a moment it seemed that she flinched at his touch, as one might recoil from one who has confessed to contagiousness.

"Are you all right?"

His own question struck him as trite and inappropriate. Of course she was not all right: her legs had buckled under her, and she had narrowly avoided banging her head. But what else could one say in the circumstances?

Barbara nodded. She was back on her feet now, helped by Hugh. "Yes, I'm fine. Sorry about that. I think I must have slipped . . ."

"No," he said. "You didn't slip. You reacted to what I told you. I shocked you, didn't I? You almost fainted from shock."

She dusted down her jeans. "I didn't faint."

"Fine, you didn't faint. I'm sorry, though—I really am. Maybe I shouldn't have told you."

She was about to say that she was glad he had told her, but she realised that she was not. She would have much preferred him to say nothing, to keep it to himself. So she replied, "Maybe not. But you've started the story, and so I think you should tell me what happened afterwards."

"I'm not sure—"

She brushed aside his objection. "No, you have to, Hugh. You have to."

He sighed. "It's not very edifying."

"Tell me. Come on."

"All right," he began. "The door opened suddenly, and a man in uniform came in. He gestured to me to sit down on the bed while he took the sole chair in the cabin. He was a rather tough-looking man, with a prominent forehead. His uniform made it clear that he was one of the ship's officers—quite a senior one, judging by the gold bands circling the sleeves of his jacket.

"'You've been brought here because you were uncooperative,' he said to me. 'Well, now you cooperate, see, or . . .' He drew a finger across his neck in a slitting gesture.

"'You have no right to detain me,' I said. 'I shall . . .'

"He waited for me to articulate my threat but I could not think what I could do; if they kept me locked up in this cabin, then my powerlessness would be complete. I really was in no position to threaten anything.

"After a few moments, he spoke again. 'Let me make it quite clear,' he said. 'You are on this ship to perform certain duties. If you refuse to do these, or if you show any sign of distress to the passengers, then we shall simply dispose of you and bury you at sea. Do you understand? You will be watched on this ship and dealt with if you try anything untoward. Understand?'

"I had very little alternative, at least for the moment, and so I reluctantly nodded. 'And what are these duties?'

"He relaxed. 'Social, purely social. You are, if I may say so without being misunderstood, a very handsome young man. We have a few such young men on board to entertain our many lady guests. To dance with them. To talk to them. Many of these ladies are widows, and they very much appreciate the attentions of handsome young men—that will be confirmed by many widows to whom you speak. So you, my young friend, shall be given a badge which says *Official Gentleman*. You shall wear this at all times, and you shall make yourself available at each afternoon tea dance and in the evenings for the dinner dances. Understand?'

"I asked him if that was all, and he smiled enigmatically. 'There may be other things,' he said. 'But we do not need to talk about those. You'll find out soon enough.'

"I asked him whether I was expected to remain in the cabin, and he replied that this would be necessary only for the next half hour or so. 'By that time we will have put out to sea,' he said. 'Naturally, we expect you to attempt to escape. That would be futile in harbour, but on the high seas it would be even more so.'

"He left, and the door was locked from the other side. Just as he promised, half an hour or so later, he returned and invited me to see the ship. He explained that I would receive instructions from the officer in charge of the social programme, and he would introduce me to this person in the course of our tour of the vessel.

"I discovered that the ship was sizeable but not as large as many of the cruise ships I had seen off Barranquilla or Cartagena. The passengers, I think, were a cut above the average: there were very few loud, Hawaiian-print shirts and pant-suits—the passengers here were dressed more soberly and expensively. And they were international too: French, British—with a smattering of Argentinians and Brazilians. Most of them, I observed, were women.

"After I had been shown round I was left to my own devices. For a while I was unsure what to do: the ship was now some distance off the coast, but there was a fishing boat not too far away, and I toyed with the idea of jumping off and attracting their attention. Fortunately, I did not. The drop from the deck to the sea was considerable, and there was no certainty that the crew of the fishing boat would see me.

"The officer in charge of the social programme, a thin Venezuelan with a Zapata moustache, came to find me on deck. He was a man of few words, who communicated largely through quick, dismissive gestures. I made it clear to him that I was fluent in Spanish, but he simply responded that in that case I should save my breath to speak to the passengers. 'That's why you're here,' he said, handing me a badge. 'You dance every day—OK? A lady says

"You dance with me," you dance with big smile on your face—OK? You do what the lady want—OK?' At this point he made a dramatic, puzzling gesture, the meaning of which I was unable to fathom.

"The first dance was that evening. They brought me a dinner suit and a pair of black patent leather shoes. I put these on and went to stand in front of the mirror. But I couldn't look into that mirror, Barbara—I was far too ashamed."

42. Freddie's Rescuer

THE WOMAN WHO picked up Freddie de la Hay on that quiet Suffolk road was called Jane. She was, as chance would have it, a dog lover: as a girl she had been the owner of a matched pair of Jack Russells, and she had later owned, in succession, a short-lived bull terrier, who had died—valiantly, in a fight with another dog—and a yellow mongrel whom she had loved with all her heart but who had one day disappeared without trace. Jane's husband, a graphic designer, was largely indifferent to dogs but indulged his wife's need for canine company. They were a childless couple: two ectopic pregnancies had closed one door for them, and attempts to adopt had been frustrated by strains inflicted upon them by social workers. Jane found questioning by these people difficult to take and reacted testily. This raised suspicions in the minds of the social workers, and a spiral of distrust had been created. The final insult had come when one social worker had suggested that her husband, Phillip, lose weight before the question of adoption could be taken any further.

"But I am a fat man," said Phillip, who was always disarmingly honest. "That is what I am. I cannot help what I am. And, frankly, what has it got to do with you? What bearing has it on our wish to adopt?"

The social worker smiled. "You *can* help what you are, Phillip. If you didn't eat too much, you would not be overweight. And it *does* matter that you are carrying too much weight around. It will affect your health, and an adopted child has a right to a healthy parent."

This was followed by silence. Then Phillip replied. He spoke slowly, aware as he did so that every word would count against him in some assessment; every word he uttered would diminish their chances. But he could take it no more.

"A right to a healthy parent, you say? A *right* to a healthy parent? When exactly did you invent that right, may I ask? Children have parents given to them by chance. You may be lucky and get a great set of parents, or you may get people who don't love you, or who drink, or who end up in prison. But they are your parents and you have no right to anybody else. You just *have* parents. That's what parents are—they're the people you *get*."

The social worker merely smiled—a thin, tolerant smile of the sort one gives to those who say something naive or ridiculous. "I'm sorry," she said, "but I have to disagree." And she added: "Phillip."

This irritated Phillip even more. He had never invited her to use his first name; he was, as far as she was concerned, Mr. Stevens. He addressed her as Ms. Hebden, but she had gone straight to Phillip.

"You disagree, do you?" he said. "You would, wouldn't you?"

She sighed. "It doesn't help either of us to resort to aggressive language, Phillip. I'm only trying to help you."

"That surprises me," he said. "I would have said quite the opposite."

"Well, you're wrong, Phillip."

"Listen," he said. "I understand that you have to make sure that people are serious about adoption. I understand that you can't give a child to people who are going to change their minds two weeks later. I understand that. But you should accept that we know what we're doing. You should make precisely the same assumption that society makes about people who produce children themselves. They're left to get on with it, by and large—unless they run into people like you."

The social worker sighed again. "We have a duty, Phillip. We have a duty to ensure that things go well—and remember, when something goes wrong, *we* get the blame, don't we? Oh, don't look away, Phillip: you will have seen those reports in the newspapers where social workers are crucified because somebody failed to spot a violent parent, or the risk assessment wasn't carried out properly. They blame us—and they blame us with all the certainty of hindsight. Of course it should have been spotted. Of course it was possible to see that the brute of a father was going to do what he did. And so on. Us. They blame us. So turn on me, Phillip, and accuse me of being too intrusive."

They had stared at one another in silence, and then the social worker had remembered an appointment and taken her leave. Jane, who had listened to the exchange but not participated, went to her husband and put her arms about him to comfort him. "It doesn't matter, dear. It really doesn't. I'm happy enough—I've got you, and you're the nicest, gentlest person in the world."

"No," he said. "That's you."

This took place only a few months after the yellow dog had gone missing. "Perhaps somebody will send us a dog," Jane remarked a little later.

"What an odd thing to say! You aren't sent dogs, Jane dearest. You buy them, or you get them from the pound."

"Some dogs are sent," said Jane. "They are sent in the way in which prophets are sent. They are . . ."

He smiled, and kissed her. "Gentlest, most imaginative one. Yes, perhaps, we shall be sent a dog."

And here was Freddie de la Hay, sitting in the front seat of Jane's car, conducting himself with all his usual courtesy and consideration.

Freddie felt quite pleased with himself. The adventure down the rabbit hole had been traumatic, and he would not repeat it in future. It had produced, though, at least one good outcome, which was that he had retained some very interesting scents; these he was now savouring. The wetness on a dog's nose has a purpose beyond that of leaving imprints on windows or surprising a human leg under a table with an unexpected cold nuzzle: to this moist bulb small particles attach, allowing smells to be conducted to a dog's olfactory centres further up the snout. Freddie's excursion into the rabbit burrow had resulted in a whole library of scents being deposited on his nose, and he was now enjoying these, recognising some, interrogating others, filing them all away for future use. He was quite happy for this drive to continue indefinitely: he was warm and comfortable; he had all those scents; this woman who was driving him seemed kind and, most importantly, smelled good to dogs. Freddie saw no reason to be anxious.

Nor was he anxious when they reached their destination, a house set back from a village lane—a house with a small studio in its grounds in which Phillip worked.

Jane led Freddie into the studio. Phillip was working over the weekend because he had a job to finish by lunchtime on Monday.

"A dog," he remarked, barely looking up from his drawing board.

"Sent to us," said Jane.

43. Loving What You Can't Have

FREDDIE WAS PLEASED with his new surroundings. After their
brief visit to the studio, during which he was patted and spoken
to kindly by a man at a desk, Freddie accompanied Jane into the
kitchen in the main house. There, he immediately walked round the
room, sniffing at corners and investigating under tables and chairs.
He smelled food: crumbs and fragments on the floor; a smear of
something interesting on the hanging edge of a tablecloth (Mar-
mite, he realised, which made him remember, even if only briefly,
William, who liked to eat it at breakfast); a mélange of scents from
scraps inside a metal bin. It was a good room, Freddie thought; a
room that would keep one's nose twitching.

This initial exploration complete, Freddie then trotted down
the corridor that led from the kitchen into the downstairs living
room. From the olfactory point of view this room was less interesting than the kitchen, but there were still challenging scents to be
identified—the smell of a pile of old newspapers used to light fires;
a slightly fusty odour from a vase of wilting flowers; a sharp tang
from a patch of carpet on which traces of mud had been deposited
by somebody's shoes. There was enough here to keep Freddie busy
for several minutes before he pushed open a door that led from this
room to a narrow, sharply ascending staircase.

"All in good time," said a voice from behind him. "Time for a
snack, I think, Freddie."

Jane took Freddie by the collar and guided him back towards
the kitchen. He looked up at her slightly reproachfully; he did not
need to be dragged in this way—all that was required was a clear
indication of where to go and he would go there. But he did not

hold it against her, and he noted, with satisfaction, that the pressure around his neck eased as they entered the kitchen.

There was a plate of food on the floor, and Freddie set upon it with enthusiasm. The food was delicious—a warmed-up helping of stew extracted from the fridge—and Freddie glanced up gratefully as he wolfed it down. He had forgotten how hungry he was after his exertions in the rabbit burrow, but now his stomach felt comfortably full.

"You were ravenous, weren't you, Freddie de la Hay?"

Freddie looked up at Jane. He was not sure what she wanted of him; people always wanted something of a dog, and dogs by and large were prepared to give it. But now, feeling pleasantly drowsy after his meal, Freddie was uncertain what was expected of him. He lay down. The kitchen was warm and he was safe. He closed his eyes.

Phillip came in. "He seems to have settled in rather quickly," he said, looking down at Freddie.

"He's a lovely dog," said Jane. "Look at him."

"What breed do you think he is?"

Jane shrugged. "They have all these new breeds," she said. "Maybe he's one of those. You know, those crosses between Labradors and poodles and so on."

"Labradoodles? He's not one of those. No poodle in there. No Lab either, I'd say."

"No," mused Jane. "Maybe not. What was that ridiculous dog those people had? The people we met in the village the other day?"

"It was a cross between a chihuahua and a poodle. Wasn't it called a Poowawa?"

Jane nodded. "Something of the sort."

Phillip sat down at the table. "We can't keep him," he said gently. "You know that?"

Jane moved over to the window and gazed out into the night. "I know." She paused. "But what if . . ."

"Don't clutch at straws, darling. He won't have strayed far. Somebody will be looking for him."

She turned round. "But it was in the middle of nowhere, Phil. There weren't any houses in sight. It was right out at the edge of Hog's Farm. There's nothing there. He could have come from miles away."

Phillip thought about this. He was a compassionate person and he wanted his wife to be happy. She loved dogs, and this dog seemed to like her well enough. But one could not pursue one's own happiness at the cost of that of another. Somewhere out there in the night, this dog's owner would be fretting about getting him back; they could not ignore that.

He was about to point this out when Jane spoke. "But you're right. Of course, you're right." She looked at him. "What do we do? Go to the police?"

"Yes," he said. "They'll know what to do. Presumably there's a pound somewhere. They must have somewhere to take strays."

"They put them down," said Jane.

"Not immediately. They must try to find their owners."

Jane looked doubtful. "And how do they do that?"

Phillip did not know how. "They must have ways. Advertisements, maybe."

Jane did not think this likely. "I've never seen any advertisements like that."

"Well . . . well, look, darling, you really can't. You really can't take somebody else's dog, just like that. It's . . . well, it's stealing. You might as well go out in the street and snatch a dog. Same thing."

She turned away. "I know. You're right. Of course you're right . . . It's just that there's something special about this dog. Look at him. He communicates. It's like having a person in the room with you."

Like a child, thought Phillip, bitterly. It's like having a child. He knew how his wife felt, and he would have given anything to rid her of that pain, that sense of having lost something. Those ectopic pregnancies had not gone far, but they were the children they had lost, and nothing he could do or say seemed capable of easing the pain within her.

"My darling, we'll get another dog. We'll contact the breeder your mother told us about. We'll book a puppy. I promise."

Jane stared at the floor. "Yes. Thanks. Yes, we'll do that." She looked over at Freddie. "And this little chap?"

"The pound, I suppose."

They had dinner—a mushroom quiche which Jane had made earlier that day. Freddie, half asleep on the floor, smelled the mushrooms and looked up with interest. He had found something like that, he remembered, when he had been in the woods somewhere. He had found mushrooms and tried to eat them. But he had not liked the taste, and spat them out.

He watched. The people were eating those things and not spitting them out. Strange.

"Look at him," said Jane. "Just look at his eyes."

"Darling . . ."

"Oh, I know. But how can we? How can we just hand him over to the police? They won't love him. We do. We love him."

He sighed. "There's no point in loving what you can't have."

She responded with spirit. "Isn't there?" she asked. "Isn't that exactly what we do? All of us do it all the time, don't we?"

44. The Dreams of Freddie de la Hay

THAT NIGHT THE three of them slept in the same room—Jane, Phillip and, at the foot of the bed in an old cardboard box, Freddie de la Hay; Freddie, who had been trapped underground, where he had faced slow death by asphyxiation. The bedroom, which was under the eaves of the house, had a combed ceiling that lent a welcoming snugness to it. Floral wallpaper and ancient oak furniture— a Charles II trunk and a Dutch dresser of the same period—gave the room that air of understated comfort that some English bedrooms so effortlessly command. On the dresser, amid bottles of perfume and a silver-backed brush set, photographs of family further added to the homeliness of the room.

Phillip had been uncertain about having Freddie de la Hay in the bedroom. "We know nothing about him," he said. "We don't even know if he's house-trained. And what if he whines during the night?"

"Of course he's house-trained," said Jane. "You can tell by looking at him. He's an intelligent dog."

"If you're sure."

"I am."

He hesitated. "And, Jane . . . he's not going to stay. You know that, don't you? There's no point in your getting attached to him."

She nodded.

For his part, Freddie felt content to be in the room with these two people who had suddenly come into his life. He did not ask himself what he was doing there, nor why his stay was being prolonged; if he was to stay here it must be, he thought, because some higher power wished it so. So once he was settled in the box, he drifted into the sleep he had begun in the kitchen but which had been interrupted by the arrival of Phillip.

He dreamed. It was not a linear dream, but one that consisted of vague moments of excitement and fear. He was somewhere in a field, and the scent of rabbits was strong in his nostrils. He turned his head; the scent led to a thicket of trees bisected by a path. Freddie lifted his head up and quickly, effortlessly, he was at the edge of the thicket. This was a rabbit place: there could be no doubt about that. He dived into the undergrowth—it was easy in the dream: there was nothing to detain him, no thorns or obstructive branches, just soft leaves underfoot. It was dark, though, and it was hard to tell where the rabbits were, even if he knew they were nearby.

Then he found them, in the middle of the thicket, and they were not rabbits but ducks of the sort he had seen in London. He was momentarily nonplussed. The ducks looked at him with disdain; as well they might, for each time that he lunged at them, they rose up in a flutter of impunity, hovered briefly above his head, and then settled down again, just out of reach.

Suddenly the ducks were gone, and Freddie de la Hay turned round. His mouth, it seemed, was full of feathers, though he had not managed to catch any of the birds. Now, as he sought to clear the feathery obstruction, he found himself faced by the rabbits themselves. They were immense, a whole tribe of them, giant rabbits several times the size of Freddie and equipped, every one of them, with powerful legs and claws. One of them appeared to be the leader, and it was he who looked at Freddie most sternly. There was punishment in this rabbit's eyes; punishment and revenge.

Freddie de la Hay turned tail to run away, but his legs would not obey him. He whimpered; he looked back over his shoulder at the advancing Nemesis. He was sorry for what he had done to the rabbits. He was abject. He begged. And then, quite suddenly, he was awake, and he was in the bedroom with the two sleeping people. There were no ducks, no rabbits. They had been there, he was sure of it, but now they were no longer. He relaxed and lay down again; fear had driven him to his feet.

Jane was conscious that Freddie had woken up. Slipping out of bed, she knelt beside his sleeping-box.

"A bad dream?" she whispered.

Freddie looked up at her; grateful for the calming hand on his flank. He turned his head and licked her gently. She felt the rasp of his tongue, but let him continue.

"Don't worry," she whispered. "You won't have to go, if you don't want to. And you don't, do you?"

Freddie de la Hay made a snuffling sound, which Jane took as assent.

"Well, that's settled then."

She patted him and returned to bed. Freddie de la Hay drifted off to sleep again, as did Jane. Freddie's sleep now was dreamless, but Jane dreamed that she was in the village, with Freddie de la Hay. He was walking beside her, yet walking on two legs, like a child, and she was aware of the fact that he could talk. She was not sure what he was saying, but she felt proud of him and was keen for others to hear what he had to tell them.

And suddenly she was pushing a pram, and Freddie was in the pram, wrapped in a brightly coloured quilt. A woman came up to her—the woman from the post office, she thought—and shook a finger at her. "That's a wolf you have in there. You shouldn't have a wolf in a pram."

She reacted with indignation. "Not a wolf!" she shouted. "He's not a wolf, he's a baby."

The woman laughed, and called other women to join her. "That's definitely a wolf," somebody yelled. "Watch out, Red Riding Hood!"

She felt hot and ashamed. She began to run. "Not a wolf," she called out. "It's not a wolf."

She felt herself being shaken and the dream came to an abrupt end.

"My darling, my darling." It was Phillip's voice, and his hand upon her shoulder. "A bad dream. You were calling out."

She lay quite still. "Calling out?"

"Yes."

"What was I calling out?"

He hesitated. "Nothing important."

She pressed him. "Please tell me."

He hesitated still, but then he said, "You shouted, 'Not a baby, it's not a baby.'"

45. More Risotto

CAROLINE SLEPT MUCH more soundly that night. She usually remembered very few dreams—a couple of scenes, at the most, hopelessly jumbled up, were all that she could summon in the mornings, and even these recollected scraps soon faded. This was fortunate, perhaps, because it meant that in none of her dreams was she the subject of reproach, as well she might have been had she dreamed that night of James, her friend to whom she had lied about not going out and whom she had then encountered in the Greek restaurant. His look of betrayal had haunted her—for at least half an hour, until Ronald's conversation and charismatic presence made her forget her perfidy.

When she awoke, her first thought was of Ronald. He had slept in Jo's room, which had a made-up bed. She wondered what time he would have to be at work, and whether he would want any breakfast.

She got up, donned a dressing gown and went into the kitchen. Ronald was sitting at the table, a bowl of cereal before him.

"Hi," he said. "I hope you don't mind: I helped myself to muesli."

Caroline said she did not mind. "It's Jenny's, actually. But we all help ourselves to it. As long as we replace it from time to time."

"Would you like me to cook for you tonight?" asked Ronald.

Caroline smiled. "You don't have to."

"I know, but I want to."

"All right," she said. "What will you make?"

Ronald thought for a moment. "Risotto?"

She could not help herself smiling. "Oh . . ."

He looked concerned. "You don't like it? I can do something else if you want. I can make pizza—as long as I buy the base somewhere, I'll do the topping."

She assured him that risotto would be fine. "I had a friend who made risotto for me," she explained. She blushed as she realised that she had said she *had* a friend. She had lost James because she lied.

"I can pick up everything on the way back from the office," he said. "You could show me where things are in the kitchen."

Ronald went off to work, and Caroline followed shortly afterwards. Throughout the early part of the day, though, she found herself thinking of him, glancing at her watch to see what time it was and how long it would be before they met again. It was a familiar feeling, even if she had not experienced it for some time. It was, she realised, the feeling that attends falling for somebody; not just becoming mildly interested in somebody, but falling for him completely.

She tried to take command of the situation. I barely know him, she told herself; I have no idea what he's like. It would be rational to get to know him better before becoming involved; after all, one never knew whether closer acquaintanceship would lead to a dislike of a person's mannerisms, or their views for that matter. She would find out about Ronald in due course, and it would be so much more *sensible* if she were to wait a while. But then that was not how these things worked. Love came upon one; one did not plan its arrival. It arrived in its own time and with an agenda all of its own devising.

Caroline's employer, Tim Something, noticed that she was distracted.

"Something biting you?" he asked, as they made their way in his car to a late-morning photo shoot.

She was deliberately disingenuous. "What do you mean, *biting me?*"

He lit a cigarette, holding the wheel with one hand while he did so.

Caroline said, "I wish you'd be more careful. You shouldn't light a cigarette while you drive."

He sent a cloud of smoke up to the roof of the car; her nose tickled and she felt the urge to sneeze.

"Oh, listen to you," said Tim Something. "Little Miss Health and Safety."

"You may laugh," she said. "But accidents are caused that way. You can't drive and do other things. It's irresponsible."

"Oh yeah?" sneered Tim Something. "You may not be able to multitask, darling, but some of us can."

She sighed and looked away.

"Big date?" asked Tim Something. "That what's on your mind?"

It was none of his business, she thought. "Maybe," she said.

He sniggered. "Who is he?"

"A rather nice architect," she said. "You won't know him."

"Try me," said Tim Something.

"I don't know why you're being so poisonous today," said Caroline. There was something worrying her employer; normally he was perfectly civil. He liked her, she thought, or at least he gave every outward sign of being well disposed; she could not understand why he appeared to have turned against her. Unless . . . unless he was jealous.

The shoot was in Richmond. The traffic was slow and they were moving at a snail's pace when Tim Something opened his window to toss out the butt of his cigarette.

"Don't throw it out," said Caroline. "There's an ashtray."

"Oh, yes," said Tim Something. "Well, this is my car, as I recall, and I can do what—"

He did not finish the sentence. A van turned out of a side road and swung a wide arc across two lanes. Although Tim Something was not driving fast, the car's speed was enough for a considerable impact. Caroline screamed as the other vehicle thudded into them, and she screamed again as she saw Tim Something, who was not wearing a seatbelt, pushed forwards into the windscreen as if by a giant hand. There was the sound of shattering glass and rending metal. Then, in the silence that followed, the hiss of steam as liquid of some sort fell on a warm engine block.

Caroline, who had been wearing a belt, felt a sharp restraining tug and then, in her left leg, a searing pain. For a moment or two she was confused; everything happened so fast and with such attendant noise that it was difficult for her to take it all in. But then, as she slumped back in her seat, her mind became perfectly clear. They had collided with another vehicle, and Tim Something had been propelled through the windscreen. He was somewhere outside, and she was inside the crumpled shell of the car.

She stretched to feel the painful leg. It was wet to the touch, and she realised that what she felt was blood. She closed her eyes. She was alive. But what had become of Tim?

Her belt was not stuck and a quick movement released it. She leaned sideways and used her shoulder to push at the door of the car. Some obstruction seemed to be preventing it from opening, but with a further bit of pressure, it swung open.

She shifted in her seat and began to slide her legs out of the car. She could move, she discovered, but when she lowered her feet to the ground a searing pain shot up her leg. It was as painful as when the dentist touches a dental nerve: a sensation not unlike a bolt of electricity.

She gasped.

Tim Something was standing on the edge of the road, looking at his ruined car with anger. His face was scratched from the impact with the glass, but only mildly so. Caroline was astonished that her employer should be uninjured.

"Look what you made me do," he said peevishly.

Caroline closed her eyes. Ex-employer, she thought. As from now—right now: ex-employer.

46. In Helping Hands

THE DRIVER OF the van with which they had collided was shaken, but, like Tim Something, unhurt. It was he who telephoned for an ambulance, and it was he, too, who helped Caroline limp to the side of the road. Once there, she lay down on the coat that he placed on the pavement, while he held her hand and comforted her. Tim Something, still glowering, walked about his car, inspecting the damage and muttering to himself. From time to time he looked at his watch, obviously irate about being delayed.

"We're going to lose this job," he spat out as he came over to Caroline. "The client is going to find someone else."

Caroline said nothing, but at her side the van driver stared up at Tim.

"Are you blind, mate?" he asked. "Can't you see this young lady's hurt?"

Tim Something, who appeared not to have noticed him until now, looked at him scornfully. "Mind your own business. What do you know?"

This brought a spirited response. Standing up, the driver shouted, "I know that she's hurt, and all you seem to be concerned about is your precious—"

Tim did not let him finish. Swinging round, he brought his clenched fist up towards the man's chin. He muttered something as he did so, but his words were unclear. The driver saw what was coming and ducked, at the same time jabbing with his own fist at Tim's abdomen. His attack was more successful: with a sound like wind being knocked out of a bag, Tim doubled up, lost his footing and fell to the pavement.

Had he fallen a few inches to the right, Tim Something might have escaped injury. As it was, he fell in such a way that his head hit a metal bollard at the side of the road. Blood appeared remarkably quickly, running down Tim's face from a gash across his forehead. He groaned, and held a hand to the wound.

It was not a major wound, and the application of a handkerchief, passed to Tim by Caroline, soon stemmed the flow of blood.

"Did you see that?" Tim spluttered. "You're my witness, Caroline. You saw that?"

Caroline shook her head. "I saw you attack him," she said quietly. "I saw him defend himself. That's what I saw."

Tim glared at her in astonishment. "You're fired," he shouted.

"You can't fire somebody who's resigned," said Caroline. "And I resigned five minutes ago."

Any further exchange was prevented by the arrival of the ambulance. The two ambulance men, clad in green outfits, attended to Caroline first, placing her on a stretcher which they slid gently into the back of the vehicle. Then they inspected Tim Something's wound and offered to take him to hospital too. He had risen to his feet by now, though, and said that he needed no help.

"You take that to your GP then," said one of the ambulance men. "Get it dressed, sir."

The ambulance set off. Inside, Caroline lay on the stretcher and remembered a little rhyme from her childhood. It was for use when one saw an ambulance, and involved reciting the words "Touch your collar. Touch your toes. Hope you never go in one of those!" She used to say it religiously whenever she saw an ambulance speeding past, and had believed, as children do—and adults as well—that the words could protect us. And they sometimes did, of course, when uttered with such a degree of conviction as to rally the spirits. But now she was in an ambulance, heading to hospital; any protection the shibboleth might have given must have worn off.

"You'll be all right," said the ambulance man who was riding in the back with her, taking her hand gently in his. "A small laceration, I think, on your leg. Bruises too. But it doesn't look broken to me."

"It's sore," said Caroline.

He squeezed her hand. "Won't be long, love. Five, ten minutes."

They made their way through the traffic. Caroline stared up at the ceiling of the ambulance and thought of how, for some, it might be the last thing they saw in this world. Somewhere, for each of us, was a last ceiling, a last sky, before the end. She started to cry.

The ambulance man touched her cheek with the back of his hand. She was grateful for the sign of human comfort, even if the thought occurred to her that it was probably against the rules. No doubt these paramedics, these specialists in human suffering, were cautioned not to touch their passengers unnecessarily, for fear of all sorts of accusations. It was the same with teachers, who were warned against comforting children lest similar accusations arise. Caroline reflected: how strange, how completely bizarre that we should seek to prohibit the normal human responses to pain and distress. Of course we should embrace people who need embracing; of course we should hold their hands and seek to comfort them; of course we should.

She looked at the ambulance man. He had a kind face, she thought. There was a hint of the Caribbean in his accent.

"Thank you," she said. "Thank you for coming to collect me."

He smiled at her. "That's our job. We can't let people lie around on pavements all day, can we?"

Caroline laughed. "I feel so stupid. All helpless and stupid."

"Nobody's stupid, love," said the ambulance man. "None of God's children are stupid. You, me. Everyone."

She nodded. Her eyes were once again filling with tears. I am not crying for me, she thought; I'm crying because of . . . well, because of everything. Because there are people in the world who help other people. Because there are people who believe that we are God's children, as this man puts it. There are those who would mock an expression like that, who would condescend to this man, but he knew better than they; he knew one hundred times better, with his experience of pain and disaster.

The ambulance man glanced through the back window. "We'll be there in less than a minute. Then we'll pop this stretcher out and get you inside." He paused. "Would you like me to phone anybody? A friend? It would be good if somebody knew you were here. Your people, maybe."

My people. Who were they? Her mother and father, of course; they were her people, but who else was there? There was James: too late for that. And then she thought: Ronald. She had entered his mobile number into her own mobile and she had that on her, in the pocket of her jacket.

She gestured towards the pocket and the ambulance man took the phone out for her. "Go to the address book," she said. "Look up Ronald. Please phone him."

The ambulance man nodded and made the call. They were entering the hospital grounds, and Caroline was distracted by the flashing of a light as they approached the building.

The ambulance man handed the phone back to her. "I've told him," he said. "He's coming straight here."

She took the phone and thanked him.

"You don't need to thank me," he said. "You just go in there and get better quickly. Understand?"

47. Ronald Shows What He's Made of

CAROLINE FELT HERSELF being wheeled out of the ambulance and up a short ramp through the busy door of the Accident and Emergency department. It was an odd sensation, and she found herself wondering when she had last been wheeled by anybody; it must have been as a small child, she thought, when she was pushed in a pushchair, but naturally one remembered nothing of it. After that, wheeling happened only on occasions of misfortune—such as this undoubtedly was—until the time came to be wheeled on one's final journey, while people sang, perhaps, and one was surmounted by flowers. But enough of such thoughts; one should not think about final journeys on entering a hospital, and she put them out of her mind and thought instead of . . . of Ronald, who was coming to the hospital. She would ask him to phone her parents and tell them, although she did not want them making a great fuss and rushing up from Cheltenham when all she had was a sore leg.

And it was very sore, making her wince when her trolley went over a bump. The porter at her head bent down and said, "Sorry, love, the roads are in a terrible state."

Caroline managed to smile, if not to laugh. "Your driving's pretty good so far. Don't worry."

"You tell my missus that."

They continued along a corridor, and then stopped in what seemed to be a sort of lay-by for stretchers and trolleys. A nurse appeared and took Caroline's name and address, and asked her what medicines she was on. Then the nurse went away, to be replaced by another person who looked at her leg and said, "Not too bad. Seen worse." Then somebody else arrived and said, "X-Ray," to a person standing behind her, and that person said, "X-Ray," too.

Half an hour passed before somebody came to take her down the corridor. Caroline said, "X-Ray?" more in an attempt to make conversation than anything, and the person pushing the trolley nodded and said, "X-Ray."

They turned a corner. "X-Ray," the porter said again. And then added, "So long."

"So long," said Caroline.

A man in a blue outfit now arrived, and peered at her. She looked up. He smiled and consulted a piece of paper that somebody had placed on her lap. She stared at his badge. The print was smudged for some reason and she could not read what it said.

"I'm Ray," he said. "And we won't keep you long here. I just want to pop you over here and then you can go back. Take a quick holiday snap."

Caroline was helped onto a table. A machine hovered above her and the lights were bright. She closed her eyes.

"Stay still for a moment," said Ray from behind a screen. "That's it."

An assistant helped her back onto her trolley, and the porter who had first wheeled her in appeared. "Me again," he said, and then to the radiographer, "Thanks, Ray."

"Yes, thanks," said Caroline. And then added, "Do you think it's broken?"

Ray shrugged. "I won't be reading the scan, but it doesn't look like it to me. But you can get little fractures. Wait and see."

Ronald arrived another half an hour later. He had spent some time trying to locate Caroline, having been given conflicting directions, before he found her in the corridor. He came up to the trolley, running the last few paces, and took her hand in his.

"Oh my God, Caroline, what a terrible thing . . ."

She sought to calm him. "Not really. I don't think I'm badly hurt. It's just a bit sore."

"They said your leg was crushed. Somebody down there said—"

"It isn't. It's been cut, I think. I haven't really looked, but that's what it feels like."

Ronald squeezed her hand. "That's awful, just awful." He paused. "You're being pretty brave. I'd be terrified if it were me."

She smiled. "I'm sure you wouldn't."

He straightened her sheet—a useless, thoughtful gesture. "There," he said. "I'm going to stay with you until everything's sorted out. Then I can take you back. I borrowed a car from somebody at the office. I've left it down the road. I'll get a ticket, but it doesn't matter." He stroked her hand gently. "Poor you," he said.

Caroline considered the words "poor you." It was the best, most sympathetic thing you could say to anybody. There did not have to be an accident; you could say "poor you" in any circumstances and it would help. It was much better than saying good morning or uttering any other greeting; "poor you" could be used at any time and with anybody—everybody, but everybody, felt hard done by in at least some respect and would appreciate the sympathy.

"No, poor *you*," replied Caroline.

Ronald looked puzzled. "Why poor me?"

"Having to hang about in this hospital," said Caroline.

"I don't care about that at all," said Ronald. "The important thing is you. Poor you."

It was at this moment that something profound and changing happened to Caroline. She was not sure whether it involved a decision taken consciously and deliberately, or whether one did not take a decision to fall in love. But whichever it was, something that happened to her or something that she willed to happen, there was no doubt in her mind: five minutes ago she had not been in love; now she was.

She closed her eyes and then, opening them again, looked straight at Ronald. He smiled at her, and she thought: *His smile is very beautiful.*

She remembered her parents. "Could you phone my folks?"

His smile broadened. "I've done it already. I let them know you were going to be all right."

She felt a flood of gratitude for his thoughtfulness. James would have panicked; he would not have thought things through, as Ronald had. James would not have borrowed a car; James would not have— She stopped herself. It was disloyal to think in that way about James, and she should not compare the two of them anyway. James had been kind to her, and she had repaid him by lying to him.

A doctor appeared. "I need to take a look at this leg of yours," she said. "We can do it in the treatment room down there. Your boyfriend can wait here if he likes."

"That's fine," said Ronald. "I'll wait."

As the doctor said the word "boyfriend," Caroline noticed that Ronald gave her hand an extra squeeze: a squeeze of affirmation, of possession.

48. The Effects of Gravity

BARBARA WAS NOT unconscious at any stage: she had not fainted, but simply collapsed. It was a curious feeling, one for which she could not find exactly the right words.

"My limbs just seemed to lose their strength," she later said to a friend. "I was standing there, listening to Hugh, and suddenly my legs felt as if they had . . . well, as if the bit in the middle, the bone, had lost all its firmness. Very peculiar. It was as if my body was saying, 'There's no point in standing up any more.' Very curious."

"I fell down once after being in the gym," said the friend. "I'd spent fifty-five minutes on the cross-trainer and when I got off, my legs just didn't work. They went on strike."

"Yes, it's odd, isn't it?" mused Barbara. "Here we all are, standing up, when the natural position for all of us is really on the ground. If we gave up our daily fight against gravity, then that's where we'd be."

HER RECOVERY HAD been quick, and she had insisted that Hugh continue his story.

"They threatened you?" she asked.

"Yes, and I think they meant it," he continued. "If it had been anywhere else, I would have been prepared to chance things, but not Colombia. I really had no alternative but to do what they ordered."

"Of course you didn't," said Barbara. "But go on—what happened?"

"Well, there I was, in my dinner jacket," said Hugh. "I must say, it was a nice fit. And good material too—silk. The patent leather shoes were the real thing—and there was a starched white dress shirt. I had to put on my badge, which said *Official Gentleman* in English rather than Spanish. I didn't like that badge, but they told me I had to wear it.

"Well, as I said, I felt awful, but I was also quite hungry by now. My headache had worn off and I seemed none the worse for the drug they had used on me, so I set off for the dining room, which was at the back of the ship—the stern, I suppose. I picked up quite a few nautical terms over the next few days. Forward and aft, and things like that.

"When I went into the dining room, the head steward came over to me and winked. It was a horrible wink—a sort of leer, almost—as if he was party to some awful knowledge about me. Which I suppose he was, really. He said, 'I've got just the table for you, my friend. Over there by the window—you see it? Seven ladies—and you! Lucky fellow. Ha, ha! Trade you jobs any day of the week!'

"He took me over and introduced me to the women. 'Look who's coming to sit at your table, ladies,' he announced, in a horrible smarmy voice. 'Just for you and your entertainment!'

"Some of the ladies giggled. 'He speaks perfect Spanish, by the way,' said the steward. 'So none of you ladies say anything rude—he'll understand it!' Then he winked at the women, more or less one by one. It was awful. He told them that my name was Hugo—they could never pronounce Hugh—and so that was what I was known as.

"I sat between two ladies in their forties. They were dressed up to the nines, dripping with jewels, and one of them had already been to the cosmetic surgeon. You can always tell, you know—and it really doesn't help, does it? They had that slightly pinched look which comes when your skin is too tight. It's the same look that people have when they're wearing clothes that are too tight. They look as though they might pop out of their outfits if they move the wrong way. It's the same with cosmetic surgery. These people look as though their faces will fall off if they laugh.

"They asked me about myself. Had I been working on the ship for long? Where was I from? And so on. I realised that I could not tell them the truth about how I'd ended up there, since the officer had specifically warned me not to. So I made up something about having come to Colombia to teach English and then decided that dancing on a cruise liner was my true vocation.

"They thought this very interesting. 'If you have to dance, you have to dance,' said one. And the others all nodded their heads at this pearl of wisdom.

"Then one of them asked me whether I'd brought my girlfriend with me. There was a silence, with all the ladies at the table staring at me. I suppose I blushed. I told them that I didn't have a girlfriend at the moment. That, as it happened, was true.

"A couple of the women muttered something I didn't hear, and one of them laughed. But the woman sitting right next to me, who had introduced herself as Irma, whispered, 'I understand. You mustn't worry about it. I like sensitive men . . .' I didn't know what she meant at first, and then suddenly I realised. And that was when I had my brilliant idea: I would dance with the ladies—as ordered—but while we were dancing I would let drop a remark that they would interpret as meaning . . . well, that I wasn't interested.

"I turned to Irma and said, 'Well, there we are. But I really like dancing.' She nodded and said something about how what was most important was how one felt inside. At that moment the waiters brought the food and everybody started eating.

"At the end of the meal, after they had served coffee, the band struck up. I took Irma's hand, and she got up, looking triumphantly at her friends. We took to the floor and started to dance. She was quite a good dancer, and I rather liked her. She told me that she was from Buenos Aires and that her husband owned an aeronautical engineering firm. 'He only thinks of aeroplanes,' she said. 'Never of me.' I said, 'That's very bad luck,' and she nodded. 'You're very *simpático*,' she said. 'And you can dance so well, for one who speaks English.'

"I could see that we were going to get on. And then my second brilliant idea occurred: it was risky, but I thought it worth a try. 'Irma,' I whispered as we moved about the dance floor, 'could I stay with you in your cabin? I don't mean anything more than that—I mean just stay. I'm so lonely. Just for company—I can sleep on the sofa, if you've got one. Or on the floor. That's all, I promise.'

"She looked at me quizzically. 'Are you sure you're really . . . ?' She left the sentence unfinished. I nodded. 'Well, why not?' she said. 'Cruises are full of lonely people, aren't they? And I like you, Hugo. So yes, you move in with me. I've got a stateroom actually, so you can have your own cabin.'

"I felt immensely relieved. 'One thing, though,' I said. 'Will you tell one of the officers about this? I need permission, you see. But he won't object. It's that officer over there, by the door.'

"She nodded, and we danced over towards the door. It was the social officer, and he was watching me. She went up to him and spoke to him briefly before coming back. 'All fine,' she said. 'He just nodded discreetly and said that the company was happy to oblige.'

"As we left, the officer drew me aside. 'Well done,' he said, forcing a smile. 'Quick work there. She's a very important customer.'

"'I also like to oblige,' I said. 'And we Britons can teach you Latins a thing or two about these matters, you know.'

"I said the last bit in English, though, and he didn't understand. Which was just as well, I suppose."

49. Vertical Take-off

"IRMA HAD WHAT was probably the best accommodation on the ship—a set of staterooms. When I moved in with her that evening, I was astonished by the splendour of the appointments; my own tiny cabin, stuffy and claustrophobic, gave one barely enough room to turn round while getting dressed. I suppose that is how ships' cabins usually are, but it seemed to me that the naval architect who had designed mine must have taken perverse pleasure in stipulating such cramped and awkward dimensions.

"By contrast, when he sat down to design the staterooms he must have been filled with the spirit of Versailles. The door from the corridor outside admitted one immediately to a large sitting room that was filled with natural light. The light came through a pair of French doors of toughened glass giving out onto a private veranda deck outside. There were chintz-covered chairs and sofas and, on the tables behind the sofas, large bowls of flowers. I remember being struck by the scent of the roses and wondering how one could keep flowers fresh after days out at sea. Presumably there were cold rooms down in the bowels of the ship for this purpose. Perhaps the flowers were stacked there, surrounded by sides of beef and other foods—an extraordinary juxtaposition of beauty and simple human necessity.

"Beyond the sitting room, there were two further cabins. One was the principal bedroom and the other a dressing room of the sort that you find in grand houses—a small room with a single bed and a table to lay out your clothes. Irma directed me to this dressing room, which had its own small bathroom. Then she went to a fridge in the corner of the sitting room and extracted a bottle of champagne.

"I stored my stuff in my cabin, and joined her on the sofa. It was very chaste and respectable: she sat at one end and I at the other. She handed me a large flute of champagne, and we toasted each other in our new-found domesticity.

"She wanted to talk, and I sat there and listened. I had the impression that she was a very lonely woman and yearned for conversation. She told me straight out how old she was—forty-one—and she was pleased when I expressed surprise. 'I have a very conscientious beautician in Buenos Aires,' she said. 'She leaves nothing to chance. There are many creams.'

"Her husband, she explained, was a workaholic and took absolutely no interest in her feelings or in what she did. 'Sometimes,' she said, 'I believe that he doesn't notice whether I'm there or not. Last year I went to Italy for two months—we have a house on Lake Maggiore—and I think that he didn't even notice. I told him I was going, but when I returned, he expressed surprise when I began to talk about having been in Italy. Really, it is most deflating to discover that one's own husband should be so unaware of one's whereabouts.'

"I asked her if he knew that she was on this cruise. 'I told him,' she said, 'but I'm not sure if the information was absorbed. So I'd say that he probably doesn't.' She paused, and looked at me in an amused way. 'You must not worry, by the way. My husband is not remotely interested in the people whom I see. I have had *friends* before, and he has never expressed any views at all. I think he's quite relieved that I don't bother him in that respect. It's the planes, you see.'

"I asked her to tell me more. She had told me while we were dancing that he was the owner of an aeronautical engineering firm, and now she spoke a little bit more about this. 'He is really the only person in South America who knows about making planes. Those Venezuelans and Brazilians think they can make planes but, *pouf-là*, their planes barely get off the ground. You certainly

184

wouldn't catch me flying in any of those. Nor in a Russian plane. You should hear what my husband has to say about Russian aircraft—it's unprintable.

"'My husband made the GH-56. Have you heard of that one? It's marvellous for flying over the Andes because it's very easy to handle in those tricky air currents. And it takes very little to learn how to fly it: my husband says that he could train a complete novice—that's you or me—to fly one of those planes in under a week. Of course, he never had time to teach me how to fly—he's always been far too busy.

"'But it's not the GH-56 that takes up all his time. He's been working for years on a plane that he calls the Bi-directional, or Bi-D. It's a real obsession for him, I'm afraid. He had the idea when he started to study the causes of many of the light-aircraft crashes that take place up in the mountains. Apparently what happens is that pilots who are disoriented or not paying enough attention find themselves flying straight into slopes. By the time they see the ground ahead they often don't have enough time to turn round, and so they crash. My husband asked himself: what if they could simply stop, as if in a car, and then reverse?

"'Of course there's a good reason why they can't—in most planes, if you lose forward momentum, you stall and go down. Simple—even I know that. But that's forgetting that we already have vertical take-off and landing planes. So why not design one that could go into reverse and fly backwards, thus taking everybody out of danger?

"'So that's what he's been working on these past few years—a plane that can go in reverse. He's got close to it, but isn't quite there yet. So I never see him—he's always away at the factory, or going off to meet engineers in places like Houston. He does not love me, Hugo—he does not love me at all. He loves his planes. He loves the Bi-D most of all; he also loves the GH-56. There is no love left for me—none at all.'"

50. Just a Gigolo

IT WAS A sad story, said Hugh, even if it was told without self-pity.

"There was something about her that appealed to me," he continued. "She was a very attractive woman, of course, but her allure was broader than that. Perhaps it was the way she talked to me—she was one of those people who draw you in, so to speak, who make you feel that they're sharing some tremendous confidence with you. You know the type? When you analyse what they've said, it doesn't necessarily amount to much, but you don't feel that at the time. It seems as though what they're saying is terribly, terribly important.

"So there I was, spending my first night on board in the best accommodation on the ship. We finished our champagne, and she went off to her room and I to mine. I must say that I was rather pleased with myself: what had started as a bleak prospect now seemed much more palatable. Spending time in Irma's company was not going to be a chore at all—in fact, I rather looked forward to it—and being her companion meant that I would be protected from the attentions of other ladies. It was also clear that with Irma protecting me, there was little the sinister entertainments officer could do to harm me.

"Did I think of escape? Well, yes, I did, but I realised that I could bide my time. I knew the cruise was going to be calling at a number of places; now that I was with Irma, I would no doubt be able to go ashore with her, and then lose myself in a crowd. We were due to go to Jamaica, I'd heard, and it would be easy to seek refuge in Kingston or Port Antonio. If it was Kingston, I could claim the protection of the British High Commission there, and I would no doubt be on a flight home within days. So, for the time being, I decided that I might as well just enjoy myself.

"The next morning we had breakfast together on the veranda deck of the stateroom. Irma ordered a couple of trays to be brought up, and we sat there enjoying the best that the kitchens could produce. Then we went for a walk along the main deck. Irma took my arm, and we looked, I imagine, like any other couple on the boat. She stopped to talk to a few of her acquaintances, and I saw them glancing at me and then at her knowingly. It was clear what they thought, and I knew that my plan was working well. I think she took a certain pleasure in showing me off.

"And so it continued over the next few days. We played deck quoits, went swimming in the first-class pool and played a weird South American card game which she taught me. We went to see films too, and entered the ship's fancy-dress competition. I went as a pirate and Irma as a female aviator; she had obtained flying glasses from somewhere or other, and one of those strange leather caps pilots and racing drivers used to wear. She looked very glamorous and dashing . . . I suppose it would have continued like that had it not been for . . ."

Hugh hesitated, and Barbara, who had been listening to him intently, urged him on.

"Something went wrong?"

He did not answer immediately.

"Oh Hugh," Barbara said, "you can't keep me in suspense."

He swallowed hard. "I'm ashamed of the next bit, Barbara. I'm afraid that . . . Oh well, here goes. It was quite hard sharing a stateroom with her, if you see what I mean. She was very attractive, and she had these marvellous silk pyjamas and . . . Well, I'm afraid that one thing led to another."

He paused, watching for the effect of his words. Barbara did not flinch. "One thing often leads to another, I've found," she said quietly.

Hugh looked miserable. "Are you going to think the less of me?

Please don't. You see, I had no intention of starting anything with her, but I'm afraid I just couldn't help it. And she . . . Well, she was a bit surprised and said, 'What does this mean, Hugo? Have you decided to *change*? Or are you like that aircraft my husband keeps building—the one that goes backwards and forwards? The Bi-D.'

"I didn't answer her, and so she said, 'Well, actions speak louder than words, don't they?' And that was the beginning of our affair. There, I've said it. I had thought I was going to avoid being a gigolo, but that was exactly what I had become. I was a kept man too—"

Barbara raised a hand to stop him. "Please don't say that, Hugh! You were *not* a gigolo, neither were you a kept man. You were a *captive*. And that's absolutely different. There's an ocean of difference between the two. And anyway, it was only until you could escape— only until you reached Jamaica."

Hugh shook his head. "I wish that were true, but it isn't, I'm afraid. You see, when we reached Jamaica, I went ashore with Irma. We went on a tour and saw the sights, and then we went to lunch at a restaurant just outside town. I could very easily have run away at that point—there was only one officer from the ship with our party and he didn't seem to be watching me very closely. I could have escaped but, you know what, Barbara? I went back to the ship entirely voluntarily."

Barbara stared at him. "Why?" she asked.

Hugh looked down at the floor. "I was enjoying myself," he said. He raised his eyes and met her gaze. "So you see, Barbara, I was a gigolo in every sense of the word. I was signed up. Committed. Call it what you like."

51. In the Bag

WILLIAM'S WEEKEND WITH his friends, Geoffrey and Maggie, was turning out to be neither restful nor enjoyable. Things could have been worse, of course: there must be weekends during which the hosts' house burns to the ground, one of the guests murders another, the hostess is arrested in extradition proceedings or the guests are all poisoned by the inclusion of death's cap mushrooms in the stew. Such weekends must be very difficult indeed, not least because of the wording of the thank-you letters that one would have to write. The disaster, whatever it was, could hardly be ignored, but must be referred to tactfully in the letter, and always set in proper perspective. Thus, in the case of mushroom poisoning, one would comment on how the other courses of the meal were delicious; in the case of the hostess's arrest, one would say something comforting about the ability of defence lawyers in the jurisdiction to which she was being extradited—and so on, *mutatis mutandis*, trying at all times to be as positive as possible.

In William's case, the weekend got off to an egregiously bad start with Maggie's extraordinary confession that for years she had nurtured a secret passion for him. Such declarations can be unsettling, especially when they come from the wife of one of one's oldest friends. So it was hardly conducive to the spirit of relaxed and tolerant friendship that is the hallmark of a good weekend visit; and how badly it was to go further downhill with the subsequent realisation that Freddie de la Hay was lost, possibly permanently. This realisation dawned shortly before dinner, when Freddie had still not returned, and, in the fading light, William began to walk through the neighbouring fields, calling his dog's name but getting no response: no bark or whimper, no howl, just silence as the descending night swallowed his calls.

Those who had been invited for dinner—specifically to meet William—came and went with scarcely a glimpse of their fellow guest. They were disappointed but understanding; being country people themselves, they knew the importance of animals and could sympathise with the distress that follows upon the disappearance of a much-loved dog. A couple of them spotted William as they drove home—a figure outlined against the night sky, stumbling across a field, in danger, they thought, of suffering the fate of Freddie de la Hay himself—of losing his way, of falling into a ditch or breaking an ankle in a rabbit hole.

But none of this happened to William, and he returned to the house shortly before midnight, dirty and dispirited. Geoffrey tried to cheer him up, pronouncing optimistically on the likelihood that Freddie would suddenly show up the next morning none the worse for his escapade. "They follow an interesting scent," he said, "and then they suddenly realise that they've gone too far. They find their own way back, though, as often as not."

William was not in the least bit consoled by this, and when he awoke the next morning he did so with the sinking feeling that there would be no sign of Freddie that day. And he was to be proved right: though he covered even more ground in his searches, when evening came Freddie was still lost. Even Geoffrey seemed less optimistic, and dinner on Saturday was an affair of long faces and very little conversation.

Freddie was reported as missing to the local police on Sunday. Then, once that was done and William had made a final drive around the network of local lanes, stopping every so often to call for Freddie, he said goodbye to Geoffrey and Maggie, before heading home. There was nothing in his leave-taking with Maggie to give any indication that what was happening was more than one good friend saying goodbye to another; but William sensed that something was changed between them. Maggie embraced him, avoiding his eyes, and that confirmed his fears that things were not and could never again be the same.

The drive home was melancholy. He switched on the car radio for distraction, but thoughts of Freddie de la Hay kept intruding. Was he still alive, or had he died some awful, suffocating death in a rabbit hole? Had he been run over and bundled guiltily into a ditch by a driver too cowardly to make enquiry or too selfish to take him to a vet? Both of these were possibilities, William thought, and both were very hard for him to accept.

William wondered whether he should have stayed a little longer with Geoffrey and Maggie in order to widen the search. The difficulty with that, though, was that somebody had to open the shop the next morning, and his assistant was on a week's holiday. And it would not make any difference, he decided, because Freddie was dead—he was sure of it.

He parked the car in its lockup and made his way back to Corduroy Mansions. It was now late on Sunday afternoon, an emotionally flat time for many people, and for none more than William that day. Letting himself into the flat, he put on some music in an attempt to cheer himself up. He chose the Penguin Café Orchestra, a lively band that could normally lift any depressed spirit—but not his at that particular moment. And then he remembered why: this was Freddie de la Hay's favourite music. He turned off the CD player and switched on the television. It was a banal game show, but at least it amounted to light and noise.

He went into his bedroom and began to unpack his bag. He had bought a new pair of Belgian shoes, but he had barely worn them that weekend; he replaced them on the shoe rack next to his wardrobe. Then he took out his dirty washing and bundled it into the washing basket for his cleaner to tackle the following day. Then his spare pair of socks and . . . He stopped. Somebody had slipped an envelope into his bag, a white envelope on which these words were written: *William—you must read this.*

He opened the envelope and took out a folded sheet of paper.

"Dearest William," he read. "Since I spoke to you on Friday I have been unable to think of anything but you. I have tried to fight my feelings, and I have failed. I cannot conquer them. I have to see you, my darling, I really do. If there was ever any doubt in my mind as to the rightness of our getting together, now there is none. And so, I am coming to see you in London. I'll arrive at the end of the week and shall stay in Islington with my cousin. Please keep Friday night for me—I'll come to Corduroy Mansions and we can go out for dinner, my treat. Thank you, and keep safe, my darling— Maggie."

52. Cosmo Bartonette Arrives

IF WILLIAM WAS inclined to self-doubt, the same cannot be said for his son, Eddie. While his father wrestled with the anxiety stemming from his increasingly complicated life, Eddie was cheerfully embarking on the next stage of the plan that he and Merle had hatched to convert the house in the Windward Islands into a hotel. They had travelled there a week or so earlier, and were now waiting at the local airport—a modest affair—for the arrival of the aircraft that was bringing the celebrated interior designer Cosmo Bartonette, to put into effect his themed conversion of the house.

Cosmo appeared to be not in the least tired by the long journey from London, via a change of plane at Kingston.

"My dears!" he said. "Here I am, completely *un-wilted*, thanks to the ministrations of British Airways first class. Bumped up from mere business class into first because somebody somewhere—and God bless him—recognised who I was! Honestly, my dears, I had no intention of trading on my name but I could hardly prevent them in their eagerness!"

"Nice bit of luck," said Eddie, taking Cosmo's suitcase from him.

"Indeed," said Cosmo, kissing Merle on the cheek. "Perhaps I'm *hedged about* by the protection of the saint who looks after interior designers—and there must be one, though who knows what he's called; I don't. One thing's for certain, though: he must have had *tremendously* good taste, both in this life and in the next. Perhaps he met his saintly end while rearranging furniture, or *refusing* to hand over to some *beastly* pagans the plans for the decoration of his bishop's palace."

They left the airport and set off on the hour-long journey to the house. Cosmo spoke more or less without interruption. "I must say," he began, gazing out of the window at the passing countryside, "I must say that I'm getting a strong impression of *green*. That is undoubtedly the *key* of this *delightful* landscape. I believe in keys, you know, in the same way as musicians believe in them. The predominant shade provides the *key* in which we experience our surroundings. There are some places that are blue, and some places that are white. Finland is white. Have you been to Helsinki? It has a strong feeling of white: white steel, white glass, white snow-covered fields.

"This place is very green. This is a green, green place. See over there, see those trees? That verdant, brilliant green. It's all so green.

"Have you been to Cape Town? I did some designs for one of those new hotels they have down there, near the waterfront. Its key is blue, not the dark blue that the sea tends to be but an attenuated blue, a hazy blue. I simply *must* tell you, I've never seen blue like that before—never, except once, in Western Australia. You know, where Australia turns a corner and goes on and on, all the way to the next corner, down near Melbourne? Well, that bit, that corner just below Perth, has the same blue. Remarkable."

By the time they reached the house, Merle had become grimly silent. While Cosmo unpacked in his room, she drew Eddie aside.

"He's a gas-bag, Eddie," she whispered. "I wish he'd just shut up, or take a deep breath or something."

Eddie smiled, and pressed a silencing finger to her lips. "He's the talent, Merlie. He's the real thing. These guys are like that. There's a direct link between their very creative minds and their tongues. They can't help it."

Merle was not convinced. "And do you know what this is going to cost, Ed? Did you look at the figures in the letter he sent?"

"Worth every penny, Merlie," said Eddie. "You can't get quality for nothing. My old man always says: you get what you pay for. And he's right. Stands to reason, doesn't it?"

Cosmo reappeared and insisted that Eddie show him round the house. The building work had now been done, and the rooms were ready for Cosmo to supervise the installation of what he called the *accoutrements*. These had arrived from London a few days earlier and were waiting in a crate behind the main building.

"We must start with the bar," said Cosmo. "I've been *dreaming* about that bar, Eddie. Positively salivating at the thought of what we're going to do there. The Hemingway Rum Bar. Ernest's place. Eddie, it's going to be seriously *hot*."

Eddie took him into the bar, which had been created by knocking together two large rooms at the front of the house. As they entered, Cosmo stopped just inside and let out a low whistle. "*Magnifico!* Oh, this is *just* right. Great big fishing trophies over there on the wall above the bar—perfect space—marlin, tuna, I've got both in the crate, you know. Not in formaldehyde, like Damien's smelly old shark, but stuffed and mounted on *gorgeous* hardwood boards. Beautiful. And perhaps you could pay a few

convincing *fishermen* to perch on the bar stools and *thrill* visitors
with their fishing stories."

He moved further into the room. "I'm getting a very authentic
feeling, Eddie. You know how it is when you realise that your vision is absolutely spot-on for the space? It's all very well doing it
on paper, Eddie—it can be so different from actually confronting
the virgin space. Fortunately it hasn't happened to me too often,
but I have occasionally found myself working with a space that just
refused to give itself up to the plan—like a Sabine woman *resisting*
abduction by a *pushy* Roman! Well, perhaps not quite, but something not too dissimilar.

"Not here, though. Everything is going to work perfectly—it really is. Fabrics, wall colours, surface textures. Everything. But let's
not just stand here and talk. I'm positively *rolling up* my sleeves,
Eddie. Let's get your boys in, and they too can roll up their sleeves
and get down to work. *Aux armes, citoyens!*"

Eddie had hired a team of local decorators to assist Cosmo, and
this firm's men duly arrived in a green van.

"Green," said Cosmo as he watched the van draw up. "You see
what I mean, Eddie? Green is the key here. That is the *leitmotiv*.
Green, with mere touches of blue to remind us that *el mar* is out
there—*el mar* in which the great fish swim and *cavort* in all their
Hemingwayesque strength and beauty!"

"Sure," said Eddie.

53. The Real Man Within

OVER THE NEXT few days, Eddie and Cosmo Bartonette worked feverishly to finish the decoration of the Hemingway Bar. Eddie was surprised by the energy of the celebrated interior decorator: he had imagined that Cosmo would direct operations but do little physical labour himself. The contrary proved to be true, with Cosmo lifting and shifting furniture and other items with as much gusto—and effect—as the crew of cheerful mesomorphs hired by Eddie.

The transformation of the empty room was largely completed by the end of the third day. The walls had been painted dark green—a choice of colour about which Eddie had been unenthusiastic at the beginning but now fully accepted—and they had been hung with the fishing trophies that Cosmo had sent over from London. A large stuffed marlin, its colours accentuated by varnish, now dominated the space behind the bar, and here and there on the other walls there were tuna, barracuda and one or two unidentifiable fish, all mounted on trophy boards, on which the details of their capture—probably apocryphal—had been inscribed in black lettering.

Then there were numerous framed photographs that were to occupy almost all the remaining wall space.

"I feel very proud of these," said Cosmo, as he began to unpack the pictures from their crates. "Look at this one, Ed. This is absolutely *gen*, apart from the signature, which I did and I'm frankly rather proud of. It's Hemingway standing outside Sloppy Joe's bar, his local, you know—*quel nom!* And that's Scott Fitzgerald, or his friend, Bill Bird. Who knows? So I signed Fitzgerald's name—because who on earth knows how Bill Bird signed his name? *Pas moi.*

"And this one here—what a frame, Ed! See? That's Hemingway—you can tell by now, of course, I don't need to explain to you. But that's him in Africa, on safari. The elephant's dead, by the way—its eyes are open but our bearded friend has dispatched him, I'm afraid. He dispatched rather a lot of things, I regret to say, but let's not go there. I expect the people who come to this bar will not be exactly *sensitive*."

And so it continued until, at the end of the third day, Cosmo sank into a copious leather armchair—one which he had designated as Papa's Chair.

"Well!" he exclaimed. "Here I *sink*. Papa himself—that's what old Hem was called, Ed—Papa himself could have sat here and ended the day with a whisky. I've worked far harder today than he ever did—old fraud. Oops, not the thing to say in the Hemingway Bar, but I feel I deserve a little bit of *truth* after working like a Trojan all day. Did the Trojans work, Ed? You bet yours they did! Whoever they were!"

"Yeah," said Eddie. "They worked all right. Always working."

"Quite so. But listen, Eddie boy, would you be kind enough to fix old Cosmo a large G and T? None of your smelly old rum, if you don't mind. Gordon's and Shh-you-know-who, and not too much of the latter. Ta terrifically."

They sat at the open window, sipping their drinks, the glasses cold and moist against their hands.

Cosmo looked thoughtful. "You know something?" he suddenly asked.

"Maybe," said Ed. "Depends what."

"You know, I don't think I *like* this Hemingway character."

Eddie shrugged. "He seemed all right to me."

"He was fighting against something, you know," Cosmo went on. "There he was trying so terribly hard to be tough. All the time. Woke up in the morning and presumably had to remind himself to be tough. And they aren't, you know, Eddie. Men like that aren't really tough."

Eddie shrugged again. "Depends. Some are."

Cosmo shook his head. "No, I don't think they are. And I'm saying that because . . . Well, I may as well let you into a little secret: what you see with me isn't really what you get."

Eddie glanced at Cosmo over the rim of his glass. He was not sure where this conversation was leading and felt slightly uncomfortable.

"No, don't worry," said Cosmo. "I'm not going to embarrass you. Let me tell you right now, Ed, I'm straight. There, I've said it. I'm straight. I've got a partner in London—a woman. We've been together for eleven years."

Eddie could not conceal his surprise, and Cosmo smiled at the reaction.

"Yes, I knew that would make you raise an eyebrow. You see, in order to get on in the interior design business, you have to camp it up a bit. Which is what I've been doing all along. I do it so well that it's become second nature."

"Oh," said Eddie.

"When I started in the business," Cosmo continued, "I was just myself, and it didn't work. I was treated with condescension because people thought, how could somebody as straight and boring as this have a good eye? That's what they thought—you could just see it. And so I decided it would be better for business if I acted up a bit, and that's what I did. Business went through the roof. I was a really good actor." ·

Eddie smiled. "You certainly fooled me."

"There you have it," said Cosmo. "The pretence works."

Eddie smiled. "So what now?"

"I drop it with you," said Cosmo. "I finish the job here and go back to London. And start to camp it up again."

"Not easy," said Eddie.

"No, you're wrong. Very easy." Cosmo sighed. "You know something else, Ed?"

"Yes?"

There was a moment's hesitation. Then Cosmo said, "Do you think we could go fishing?"

Eddie stood up and looked out of the window. The evening sun was on the water—a shimmer of red. "I'd love to. There's Captain Banks—he does stuff for us in the marina. He's got a boat. He'll take us out tomorrow, if you like. He says that there are marlin running . . ."

"Great," said Cosmo. "I love fishing."

Eddie looked out at the sea again. He loved fishing too, but he was thinking of something else. He realised that he had rather enjoyed the past few days of interior decorating.

54. Out of Left Field

FOR A SHORT while after reading the letter Maggie had slipped into his weekend bag, William paced about his flat like a caged lion. His feelings were in turmoil but the predominant emotion brought about by her letter was one of panic. It seemed to him that he had very little room for manoeuvre: Maggie had not suggested a visit to London; she had *announced* it. There had been no enquiry as to whether he thought it a good idea, or whether it suited him; she simply said that she was coming to see him and that he was to keep Friday evening free.

And she had gone further. She had repeated—in quite unequivocal terms—her declaration of love for him. Such a declaration can be emotionally taxing at the best of times, even when it comes from one in whose breast one hopes such sentiments might be harboured; but when it comes from out of left field, as he thought of it, it can be completely destabilising.

The metaphor that crossed his mind—from out of left field—was unexpected, and for a few moments he was distracted from thoughts of Maggie and her impending visit. Coming out of left field was, he assumed, a baseball expression. William had very little notion of the rules of baseball; it seemed to him that it was rather like the game of rounders, which he had played as a child, and that left field must be the section of the field on the batter's left. Or was it batsman? That was cricket—another obscure game, but at least one which made perfect sense to him, and to all rational, unexcitable people.

But speculation on metaphors provides at best temporary relief from dread of the sort William was now experiencing. He felt trapped. If he did nothing, Maggie would arrive, and he would be faced with the embarrassment of spelling out to her that they had to avoid seeing one another. In other words, he would have to tell her that their friendship, which went back many years, was over. It would not be an easy task. And if he sought to forestall or prevent her visit, either he would have to come up with some excuse as to why he was not able to see her, or he would have to give her the same brush-off by telephone—which would be excruciatingly difficult—or by letter, which would be heartless. And yet, she had chosen to declare herself in writing, and so he was surely within his rights to reply in the same coin. But was it a matter of rights . . . ?

He sighed. There were occasions in life when the only course of action open to one was to disappear. That was how the late Lord Lucan must have felt, he thought, when he realised that he had made a terrible mistake and that his options were somewhat restricted. Or those other people he had read about who left their clothes on the beach and departed, under false identities, for South America. It was strange how South America was the preferred destination for people in flight. Was it because there were few questions asked in South American countries, or was their attitude towards fugitives particularly welcoming? If it was the latter, perhaps the immigration forms at their airports had a special box you could tick: where it asked for the reason for travel, alongside *business* and *tourism* there would be a box which said *flight*.

He stopped pacing. His situation was not as bad as Lord Lucan's. He had done nothing wrong. He had broken no laws, and had not even encouraged Maggie in any way. He had behaved with complete propriety throughout and had nothing to reproach himself for. So what he should do, he decided, was to take a deep breath and do what the British always do in the face of crisis: put the kettle on for tea. That was what they did when they heard the Spanish Armada was heading their way: they had tea. That was what they did when they realised that the Luftwaffe was droning towards them; those pictures of the pilots sitting on the grass in front of their Spitfires—what were they doing? They were drinking tea.

He went through to the kitchen and filled the kettle. A few minutes later, he was sitting in a chair, a cup of tea in his hand, and feeling much calmer. It was then that Marcia arrived.

William was not expecting his friend, but when the door buzzer sounded and he heard her familiar voice through the intercom, he felt a sudden surge of relief. Marcia was *safe*. She was just the person he needed to talk to; indeed she was just the person to take the whole matter off his hands. He would confide in her, ask her advice and then simply get her to sort out the situation for him. How fortunate he was to have such a friend.

Marcia arrived with a tray of sardine canapés.

"The Portuguese embassy again," she explained airily. "They

were having a small reception for a terribly dull professor who's here to lecture on some poet or other. Nobody came. Almost as bad as the party at the Icelandic embassy for that person who wrote sagas, or read them or whatever."

Marcia, whose business Marcia's Table specialised in catering for diplomatic receptions, often brought William leftovers from these occasions. He had had sardine canapés from the Portuguese embassy before, and rather enjoyed them.

"You're a real honey," he said, taking the tray from her and putting it down on the table. He kissed her lightly on each cheek before picking up a canapé; in general it is better to kiss people before you eat sardines, he thought, rather than afterwards.

She was slightly surprised by the warmth of his greeting; she often found William distracted, as if thinking of something else altogether.

"Where's Freddie de la Hay?" she asked, looking around the room. "He usually greets me."

In his distress over Maggie's letter, William had momentarily forgotten about Freddie's disappearance, and Marcia's question brought it back to him.

"Oh Marcia, I've had an absolutely terrible weekend. Really awful!"

She reached out to touch him gently on the forearm. "Terrible? What's happened?"

He told her about Freddie de la Hay, and she gripped his arm in sympathy. "William, darling, how . . ."

"Yes, it's awful, just awful. Freddie's dead—I'm sure of it. But it gets worse. I've . . ."

She put her arms about him. "Darling, you just tell me. Then I'll sort it out. Meantime, have another canapé."

55. Marcia's Idea

AMONG MARCIA'S MANY good points was an ability to listen sympathetically. As William helped himself to a surplus Portuguese sardine canapé, he told her of his fears for the safety of Freddie de la Hay. Marcia agreed that the situation was not encouraging but urged him not to give up on Freddie just yet.

"*Nil desperandum*, William," she said soothingly. "It's the only Latin I know, I'm afraid, but it's definitely true."

"Latin makes things sound weightier than they really are," said William. "But when you come to look at the situation, putting aside Latin expressions, it's not very good."

"But dogs are always wandering off," said Marcia. "Cats too. My sister Holly's Burmese cat went off for ten days last year and then suddenly turned up as if nothing had happened. There's every chance that Freddie will come back."

"Where?" asked William. "Here? London?"

"No, I wouldn't say that. I meant back to your friends' place."

William was silent. When he was a young boy, he had read a book called *Ginger's Adventures* about a dog that had fled his pampered life in London to return to a satisfactory existence in the country. William had been greatly influenced by this story, particularly Ginger's triumphant and adventurous journey through an idyllic English countryside of steam trains and duck ponds. He imagined Freddie attempting the journey now through a landscape of motorways and urban sprawl. As for the chances of his returning to Geoffrey and Maggie's house, it would have been more likely had Freddie spent any significant time there—which he had not. No, Freddie was lost, and William might as well accept the fact.

He stared bleakly at Marcia, who stroked his arm soothingly. "I know," she said. "I know how hard it must be." ,

William sighed. "But it's not just that. It's . . ." He hesitated, but knew that now was the moment to unburden himself.

"Yes?" said Marcia, pressing him to take another sardine canapé.

William swallowed. "My friends, Geoffrey and Maggie—I've spoken to you about them, haven't I?"

Marcia frowned. "I think so. They're the ones who had the garden centre?"

"Yes. And various other businesses. Now they have a pig farm."

"I love pigs," mused Marcia. "British Saddleback pigs in particular. They look so contented in their stripyness. Does Geoffrey have any Saddlebacks, do you know?"

William brushed aside her question. It was no time to be talking about rare-breed pigs. "I don't know, Marcia," he said peevishly. "And I really don't think it's important."

She could tell that he was upset, so said nothing and waited for him to continue.

"As you know, Geoffrey and I have been friends for ages," said William. "I suppose you could call him my oldest friend."

"No substitute for old friends," said Marcia, not knowing that this, indeed, was part of William's problem. "Do you know, I read in the paper recently that one quarter of the people in this country remain in touch with their best friend from primary school. One quarter! Can you imagine that? Do you still keep up with anybody from primary school?"

Again, the question was inadvertently tactless. "Yes," said William. "Geoffrey. We were in an organisation called the Woodcraft Folk. I was made to join it by my father."

"I've heard of them," said Marcia. "Didn't you dance around in the forests? Wear green and so on?"

"That's not the point, Marcia," said William. "And I do wish you'd stop interrupting me."

She bit her lip. "You can be rather abrupt at times, William," she said. "I'm just trying to help, you know."

He looked apologetic. "I'm sorry. I'm under stress."

"I know."

"You see, Maggie is also an old friend. Both of them are."

Marcia nodded. "Yes, I know that."

"But now Maggie's suddenly come out and told me that she's in love with me," William blurted out. "Just like that. We were on a walk together, and she suddenly told me that she's been in love with me for years. You can imagine how I felt."

Marcia was silenced by this disclosure, and for a few minutes neither spoke. Then Marcia said, "And?"

"And I didn't do anything to bring it on," said William miserably. "Nothing at all. She's the wife of my oldest friend, for heaven's sake."

Marcia shook her head gravely, like a tradesman surveying a do-it-yourself disaster. "Oh dear," she said. "Oh dear, oh dear."

"Indeed," said William. "Now what do I do? She's written to me and announced—announced, mind you, not asked—that she's coming to see me on Friday so that we can go out for dinner. What on earth can I do—tell her not to come? Not open the door to her?"

"No, you can hardly do that," said Marcia. "Just picture this . . . this *harridan* pounding on the front door of Corduroy Mansions. Think of the *gossip*."

"She's no harridan," said William. "She's an extremely attractive woman. She's not a harridan at all."

"Trollop, then," said Marcia.

William looked incensed. "And she's not that either!"

"Well," countered Marcia, "here she is, a married woman, trying to start an affair. How do you know that she hasn't tried it with any number of men?"

"Don't be ridiculous!" snapped William. "She's an expert on Iris Murdoch."

Marcia made a placatory gesture. "All right. But anyhow, you couldn't just refuse to let her in."

"No, maybe not," said William.

"So we must do something a little more subtle."

Marcia's use of *we* sometimes irritated William, especially when she claimed to be speaking for both of them. But now he welcomed it, as it suggested that she either already had or would shortly invent a plan.

"I take it that you told her it's not on?" Marcia asked.

"Not quite," said William, adding quickly: "But I didn't encourage her in any way."

"And do you think she'll take no for an answer?"

William thought for a moment before replying. "No," he said. "I don't think she will. Once she gets an idea, Maggie can be quite difficult to deflect. She's a bit like an ocean liner that takes some time to change course."

"Then we need to *show* her it's hopeless," said Marcia.

"And how do I do that?"

Marcia pointed to the third finger on her left hand. "You get me a ring," she said. "No, don't worry—just for a limited time. An engagement ring." She paused. "And you leave the rest to me."

56. Freddie de la Hay's New Life

FREDDIE DE LA HAY spent an untroubled night in his new home. When morning came, Jane took him out for a brief walk while Phillip prepared breakfast for the three of them: Freddie was to get a couple of lamb chops in gravy—a luxury, of course, but there was no dog food in the household. When Freddie came back in, his nose twitched with pleasure at the smell of the chops.

"I'll pick up some tins of dog food later this morning," said Jane. "They have it in the village shop—big tins of it."

Phillip shook his head. "Darling, we're not going to need dog food, are we? Freddie can't stay—and he'll be fed once he's in the pound."

She looked down at the floor. "But, dearest, we can't take him there—they'll put him down. That's what they do if a dog isn't claimed after a certain amount of time."

"We can't keep him, darling. He belongs to somebody."

She was ready with her retort. "To somebody who can't be bothered to look after him properly, you mean. Look, Phil, we're doing Freddie a favour here—and probably also the person who dumped him."

"How do you know he was dumped? What if Freddie was taking a walk with his owner, and just got carried away and got lost? How do you know that there isn't a person somewhere who's missing his companion, who's weeping for the loss of his dog? What's our duty to that person, whoever he is?"

Jane glanced away sullenly. "They should have chipped him then."

Phillip looked down at Freddie, who wagged his tail encouragingly. "Where do you find the chip?" he asked.

"Round about the neck, I think," said Jane. "Or that's where my aunt's dog had his chip. It turned septic and he had to have an operation to have the wound drained."

Bending down, Phillip felt gently around Freddie's neck. "There's a lump," he said. "Feel—just here, on the side."

Jane felt Freddie's neck. Phillip was right, though she was loath to admit it. "Yes, there is something. Perhaps it's just a scar. Or a wart maybe."

Phillip did not think so. "No, it feels square, or rectangular, per-haps. It's a chip if you ask me, and that means we can take him to the vet and have it read. Vets all keep the scanner thingy that enables them to read the animal's address."

Jane was downcast. "I suppose so," she said. She did not feel enthusiastic.

They discussed who would take Freddie to the vet, and it fell to Jane because Phillip had a deadline to meet on some artwork for an advertising agency. "Nice coincidence," he said. "It's a national ad for dog food. A very straightforward message in a very straight-forward ad: 'Happy Dogs Eat Beefies Dog Food.' Not a sophisticated pitch, but it's urgent apparently because the campaign launches in a couple of days."

"They don't give you much notice," said Jane. "They're always expecting you to produce work the day before yesterday."

"Nature of the business," said Phillip. "And as I said, it's a very simple ad—just the message and a picture of a dog who—" He broke off; he was looking down at Freddie with renewed interest. "A picture of a dog. Hmm."

"Use Freddie," suggested Jane. "I'll take a nice shot of him and you can see what you might do with it."

"Why not?" said Phillip. "I was going to get an image from an image bank. But they can charge hundreds of pounds for a single licence. If we had our own photograph, it would be our copyright. No fees. Clients love that."

Jane fetched her camera and an old hairbrush. A good brushing, much enjoyed by Freddie, who liked the sensation of the bristles upon his skin, made him look much more presentable. After that, Jane dropped to her knees and started to take eye-level photographs of Freddie, clicking her fingers loudly to attract his attention at the appropriate time. Several of her shots were very good—one exceptionally so.

"That's the dog!" exclaimed Phillip, when she showed him the results. "All we need is one photo: here we've got three or four that would do perfectly. Well done!"

He went out to his studio, Jane's camera in his hand, and downloaded the photographs. Then, selecting one, he pasted it into his design for the advertisement and began the task of cropping and enhancing it. Freddie de la Hay, it transpired, took a very good photograph, and his image was soon neatly framed within the text of the proud claims of Beefies. "Beefies: invented by dogs *for* dogs," the advertisement boasted.

He showed it to Jane, who agreed that it was both charming and direct. "Who'll be able to resist Freddie de la Hay?" she said.

"Dogs, I expect," said Phillip. "But the ad isn't directed at them." He paused. "Anyway, darling, you take him off to the vet and get that chip read. Then we can reunite him with his poor owner."

Jane led Freddie de la Hay to the car parked outside the house—the same car in which he had been rescued only the evening before. Freddie, who enjoyed any car journey, jumped into the passenger seat and fastened himself into his seatbelt, much to Jane's amused delight.

"You really are a wonderful creature, Freddie de la Hay," she said as she drove off. She was going to the local vet's surgery, which was a ten-minute drive away, between two nearby villages. But she interrupted her journey, pulling in to the side of the road and extracting from her pocket a large U-shaped magnet. Leaning over towards Freddie, she applied the magnet to the loose skin around his neck, rubbing it backwards and forwards over one area in particular. Backwards and forwards. Backwards and forwards.

57. Risotto at Last

THE DOCTOR WHO examined Caroline's damaged leg was reassuring. "No fracture, I'm happy to say," she said. "Or none that I can see from the scans. It looks fine to me. So we'll just give you a tetanus injection and put a dressing on, and you'll be free to go. Can your boyfriend take you home all right?"

Boyfriend! Caroline nodded. "He's so good," she said. "He came straight here."

The doctor smiled. "Lucky girl," she said. "Hold on to him. I wish . . ." She hesitated, and bit her lip.

Caroline looked at her. "You wish what?"

The doctor sighed. "I shouldn't burden you with my troubles. It's not right . . . It's just that I've been seeing somebody who . . . well, who wouldn't do for me what your boyfriend has done for you. Men can be selfish, I'm afraid."

Caroline reached out and touched the doctor gently on the sleeve of her jacket. "People can change," she said. "It happens." It was a trite thing to say, and she realised just how trite it was even as she spoke. But what else could she say?

"I hope so," said the doctor, dabbing carefully at the laceration on Caroline's leg. "Why do we fall in love with the wrong sort of men? What makes us do it?"

Caroline looked up at the ceiling. Had she ever fallen in love with James, or had she felt only friendship for him? They were two very different things, she thought.

"We go for looks sometimes," she said. "And looks, I think, are the weakest grounds for falling for anybody. And yet . . ."

The doctor looked up. "Yet what?"

"Yet we fall in love with beauty," Caroline went on. "I studied art history, you know, and we learned a lot about that. We had a whole series of lectures on the importance of beauty and how it moved us. There's an American professor of aesthetics called Elaine Scarry— have you heard of her? She wrote a book called *On Beauty and Being Just*, which is all about how beauty is tied up with our notions of the just. We love beauty because we love justice."

The doctor said, "This might hurt a bit," and it did, but only for a moment.

"I would have loved to study art," the doctor went on to say, extracting a dressing from a sterile packet. "I love going to the National Gallery and just wandering round. I used to do that when I was a student—when medicine and everything connected with it became too much. I wandered round the gallery. The Tate too, but not all of it. I don't go in for these installations, do you?"

Caroline was counting the tiles on the ceiling. "No, I don't like them. They're banal—completely banal."

"The Turner Prize," said the doctor. "The ultimate in banality."

"Banality beyond measure," agreed Caroline. She would never have believed it that morning if somebody had said to her: you'll be discussing the Turner Prize this evening on a hospital trolley. But she was.

When the doctor had finished with Caroline, she escorted her to where Ronald was waiting. "Here we are," she said, smiling at him. "Here's your girlfriend restored to you, as good as new, I hope."

Ronald was effusive in his thanks, and the doctor smiled as she shook hands with Caroline. "Don't overdo things just yet," she said. "And take a painkiller tonight to get some sleep. We can give you something if you like."

Caroline had some aspirin in the flat and said that she would take those. The doctor went off, leaving Caroline alone with Ronald. He leaned forward and kissed her. He did it naturally—as if they had been together for years; she returned the kiss.

He looked at his watch. "I'll take you home and phone in to the office. I'll tell them I'm not coming back to work."

"You shouldn't," she said. "Not just for me."

"No. I insist."

He walked with her to his borrowed car, giving her his arm. She felt curiously elated; not only had she been relatively undamaged by the accident—and was conscious of her good fortune in that respect—but also she felt exhilarated by her discovery of Ronald. For that was what it was—a discovery, every bit as thrilling as if she had found treasure, or a long-sought-after bargain. And there was a sense of novelty too, of things that had only just begun but were now opening up to her.

They drove back to Corduroy Mansions, where Ronald dropped her off before taking the car back to its owner. He would be back, he said, within an hour or so, and then he would go to the shops to get ingredients for their dinner.

"Risotto," he said.

She touched his cheek. "It's lovely having somebody to cook risotto for one. It really is." And then she burst out laughing. "How corny I sound."

"But it's true," he said, smiling and laying his hand gently against her cheek: the reciprocated gesture. "There's something very calming about risotto. You can eat it very slowly, if you like, grain by grain, cherishing each one. That's how we should approach life, I think. We should savour every little bit of it, every single grain."

He went off, to return more or less when he said he would, only a few minutes late. She had been on the sofa in the sitting room when she heard his key in the door, but she rose to her feet, wincing slightly at the pain as she put weight on her damaged leg.

"Are you all right?" he asked. "Are you sure you're all right?"

"Yes," she said. "It's a bit sore, that's all. I'll be fine."

He went into the kitchen, and there was a small explosion. For a moment Caroline thought, quite absurdly, *He's shot himself.* But of course he had not; it was a champagne cork.

He came back, holding the bottle of champagne, the vapour rising from its neck like the smoke of a tiny, languid volcano. He had two glasses in his other hand, and he set these on the table. Then he poured a liberal quantity of champagne into each.

The bubbles danced. She heard them, or thought she did.

58. Responsibility for What We Do

BARBARA RAGG WAS not sure whether Hugh had anything more to say. The story he had told had engaged her completely, and she had not questioned him on any aspect of it. But now she found herself desperate to know how the situation had resolved itself—*if* it had resolved itself: a novelist might tie up all remaining loose ends, but life did not necessarily do the same. The circumstances that came about often petered out in a lame way; characters who had been central to the narrative simply went away, sometimes without any explanation. They died at the wrong time, leaving things unsaid, things undone. Great hopes came to nothing; the wrong people won; the ship that was due to come home so gloriously never even made it to port, or was empty when it arrived.

Such was real life; the novelist, however, did not always accept it, and as often as not pandered to the reader's strong desire that things should work out in the end. Like William's friend Maggie, Barbara had read her Iris Murdoch, and remembered that in one of her novels, after some sort of resolution has come to all but one of the characters, the remaining person in the tale—an *echt* psychopath—has yet to be dealt with. He has to change: he has to become good. But how is this to be achieved? Let incredulity be strained, even to breaking point: he sees a flying saucer and is utterly transformed morally.

Barbara looked at Hugh. "So," she said. "So you had the chance to escape but didn't take it?"

There was undisguised misery in his voice as he answered. "I'm afraid I didn't."

She considered this. "You needn't reproach yourself, you know. It's a well-known phenomenon, I believe. The captive begins to identify with the captors. The psychological strain is just too much for some people, and they give in and join what appears to be the more powerful side."

In his misery, Hugh appeared not to have absorbed her message. "I should have taken the opportunity," he said. "There would have been no danger. I should have—"

She leaned forward. "Listen, Hugh. Just listen to me. You never blame somebody for what they do in conditions of constraint. You just don't. It's as simple as that."

She thought at first that he wanted to believe her—and would. He seemed to wrestle with the idea for a few moments, and then for a brief while to cheer up. But the downcast, abnegating look returned, the expression which seemed to deny the possibility of release that an excuse might entail; the look of guilt which she found strangely unattractive. Guilt does not endear; it may provoke sympathy, but it does not endear.

"I'm afraid it doesn't work, Barbara."

"What doesn't work?"

"The idea that I let myself off the hook because I was not free to do otherwise. I was free."

She shook her head vigorously. "No, you weren't. You weren't, Hugh." She marshalled her thoughts. "Look, if somebody does something because he is in a certain position, then the fact that he is in that position at all becomes relevant." She paused. "Do I make myself clear?"

He answered quickly. "No."

She tried again. "Take the case of a soldier—a conscript. He has no choice about going into the army—if he refuses, let's say he'll be put into prison or shot or whatever. Now, once he's in the army, he's not exactly a free agent, is he? He has to obey orders, and he knows that if he doesn't he'll be punished severely—maybe even put in front of a firing squad. Can we blame him for what he does in those circumstances?"

Hugh frowned. "But we do, don't we? A soldier has no defence if he obeys a manifestly illegal order. Wasn't that what Nuremberg was all about?"

Barbara thought about this. Hugh was right: soldiers were generally not allowed to claim a defence of superior orders when they had carried out an atrocity. But did that apply to the rest of us?

"I suppose we do blame soldiers," she said. "But I must admit I feel rather uncomfortable about it. Blame the men at the top—the colonels, the generals, or whatever—but not the men lower down."

"You can't do that. The whole point of the principle is that it deters people. If the men at the bottom won't do the dirty work, then the dirty work won't be done."

Barbara felt frustrated. She wanted to give Hugh some psychological absolution, and he was resolutely arguing his way out of it. Did he *want* to feel guilty? Some people, she reminded herself, need guilt. It was a form of masochism, perhaps; feeling guilty also made one feel more important, it defined one.

"Hugh," she began again, "you really mustn't blame yourself. This whole discussion about soldiers is off the point. There are reasons why we hold soldiers responsible—it's different with ordinary people. The world isn't going to change one iota if we say that somebody who becomes a gigolo because he's kidnapped has no choice. It's absurd to blame yourself for something you didn't start."

"A gigolo," he said morosely. "I was a gigolo."

Barbara's irritation now showed. "Oh for heaven's sake, Hugh, get a grip."

He looked at her reproachfully. "Get a grip? Get a grip? Is that how you think one deals with something like this? Is it, Barbara? Because if it is, I think you're being seriously unsympathetic."

"Oh shut up, Hugh. This is getting ridiculous. You're wallowing in self-pity, and I'm afraid I don't find it very attractive. Especially in a man."

He stiffened. "Especially in a man? So you think there's one rule for men and another for women? We have to be all tough and self-controlled. We're not allowed to cry. We're not allowed to dwell on our hurt. Is that what you think, Barbara?"

"Well, since you mention it, I think men shouldn't use expressions like 'dwell on our hurt.' Men shouldn't say things like that. Sorry, but that's my view."

He became silent, and she thought, with utter clarity: *I've lost him*.

59. *Et Tu,* Rupert

BARBARA SET OFF for the Ragg Porter Literary Agency the next day in a state of confusion. Her argument with Hugh the previous evening appeared to have changed everything in their relationship. They had parted without saying goodbye, he standing up and walking out, she tight-lipped but inwardly aghast at the fact that she had, in one or two sentences, destroyed all tender feeling between them. Could words be so powerful? It seemed that they could.

Of course, there were lovers' tiffs. People argued with one another and most arguments were more prolonged and intense than theirs had been. Neither had thrown anything at the other. Neither had said anything completely unforgivable. What had Barbara done? She had simply said that men shouldn't use certain expressions. That was not particularly significant. Or was it? If you said to a man that he was using an expression that men shouldn't use, were you casting aspersions on his masculinity? Possibly. But should a man be sensitive about something like that? Probably not. Though many were.

Taking her normal route across the park gave her time to order her thoughts. She had fallen out with Hugh over his revelation of having been a gigolo. When she first heard the story, she took the view that it had not been his fault, and she argued the case for that. But now, as she followed a diagonal path across an awakening park, she started to wonder whether Hugh's self-blame might have substance. He was right: he could have run away and yet he had stayed and enjoyed being a kept man on the cruise liner; he had shared the bed of that South American aircraft manufacturer's wife not because anybody was forcing him to do so, but because he wanted to. If he had remained with her as a willing lover, then surely that made him no longer a gigolo? Does a slave cease to be a slave when he stops serving because he is forced to and instead serves out of love for his master or mistress?

She wrestled with this and other thoughts as to the moral implications of the situation, but they all seemed to lead her back to the question of her feelings for Hugh. Had they changed at all? Did she still love him? She stopped walking and stood still where she was on the path. It was a moment of insight—one of those mystical experiences that people have at unexpected times, vouchsafing a vision of what really is. She did not truly love Hugh, she realised; she only thought she loved him because he made her feel better about herself. He was something that had *happened to her*. He was not a person whom she cherished for himself. That was different; quite different.

The realisation that she had had such a narrow escape from making the wrong decision made her feel quite heady. She looked up at the sky. Dizzy. But don't worry, Barbara. You've survived. You're free again. You're yourself. Don't worry.

She continued her journey. Now she felt guilty too. She had misled Hugh; she had made him think he was loved, and yet she had been unable to give him that love. She looked about her at the people walking through the park. She saw a woman throw a stick for a dog to catch. She saw a young man and woman walking hand in hand. She saw a man immobile in a t'ai chi pose. All of these people were pursuing their self-interest in whatever way seemed right for them. She was no different. She was no ogress, who had devoured Hugh and then spat him out. She had really believed that she loved him; she had acted in good faith. But still she felt guilty.

By the time she arrived at work, she was in a better frame of mind. She felt raw, as one always does after an argument, but at least she would be able to work, and the mundane tasks of the day would take her mind off her personal circumstances, would take the edge off her discomfort.

"Mr. Porter was hoping to see you," said the receptionist.

"Oh yes?"

"I think it's important."

She shrugged, and made her way down the corridor to her office. Rupert Porter could not summon her to his office like some employee; they were fellow directors of the company and of equal status. In fact, if Barbara wanted to argue the point, she could draw attention to the fact that Ragg came before Porter in the name of the firm. This reflected the undeniable historical truth that her father was the senior partner to Fatty Porter when the firm had been a partnership rather than a company. In so far as she had stepped into her father's shoes, and Rupert had stepped into Fatty's, that made her the senior director.

Her secretary had opened the mail and laid the letters out on a tray on her desk. There was nothing of any great significance, she noted, though there were several attractive offers which she would take pleasure in passing on to her clients later that morning. One was for a manuscript that had proved virtually unsaleable: a novel about a medieval monk who discovers that the abbot is possessed. A ridiculous notion, but the manuscript had now found a publisher who said he believed in it. The author, a rather dusty man who lived in an old rectory in Rutland, would be pleased, no doubt.

There was a perfunctory knock on the door, followed by the appearance of Rupert.

"Barbara, I need to talk to you."

She looked up. "Certainly. Take a seat, Rupert."

He shook his head. "No need to prolong this. It's about Errol Greatorex—the autobiography of the yeti."

"Oh, yes. I'm expecting a couple of new chapters soon. He said he'd send them. Do you want to read them?"

Rupert smiled. "No need. He'll be sending them to me, in fact. I'm taking him over."

Barbara put down the letter she was holding. "You? He's my client, Rupert."

"Was, Barbara. *Was* your client. He's come over to me, along with the yeti."

"The yeti? The yeti is *my* client, Rupert. You can't just *take* these people."

"They asked, Barbara. It wasn't me."

She rose to her feet. "You're saying that the yeti asked? You don't even believe in the yeti, Rupert. You said so."

"I do, now that I've met him."

"And he asked to go over to you?"

"Yes."

60. Oedipus Encounters the New Rules

OEDIPUS SNARK WAS extremely pleased to be a government minister, even one so lowly as to be left off just about every list of who did what. His position was vague: so much so that the post in question was sometimes described as being "The Undersecretary for This and That." Oedipus himself had used this name for it in the past—at the expense of the then occupant, a political rival—but upon his own appointment had dropped the joke.

"It's a relatively minor appointment, as these things go," he said to friends. "But it is influential, you know. Part of it is to do with science, and investment in training. We need more scientists, you see, and that's where I come in."

He also liked to point out that the post in question had been occupied by a politician who subsequently became extremely influential. "Not quite prime minister," he said, "but close enough. Had he not been defeated in an election, he would have been PM pretty soon. No doubt about that. And he was where I am now for at least three months. It's a bit of a springboard, this post. Rising stars, you know."

The perks that went with the post were small enough, yet Oedipus guarded them jealously. He had a shared government car, which he used rather more than the other minister to whom it had been allocated; he had a full-time secretary; and he was entitled to two tickets to the Garden Party. That was not quite all: as a government minister, he was also entitled to hang in his office one painting from the government collection. Ministers, of course, are aware of the interest that journalists take in their choice of art, and most choose with one eye to how their selection will reflect on them. For this reason, the best paintings—those of some artistic significance and aesthetic quality—are frequently ignored in favour of paintings by contemporary artists whose work is deemed to be progressive, forward-looking or indeed at the cutting edge. Most of these works are not ones that anybody would wish to have on a wall in circumstances other than at night or in a darkened room, and the ministers in question are obliged to spend an uncomfortable time averting their eyes from the visual disasters they have favoured. Eventually those paintings are returned to the collection and something more pleasing—even if unfashionable—is put on the wall; or they are inadvertently mistaken for rubbish by the cleaners and sent off to the dump alongside all the waste paper generated in such heroic quantities by these sorts of offices.

But Oedipus did not choose anything like that. When asked to select a painting for his office, he had requested Titian's *Diana and Actaeon*, only to be told that this painting was currently in the collection of the national galleries and not available for ministerial use. A subsequent request for Bronzino's *Allegory with Venus and Cupid* was also turned down—on the same grounds—and Oedipus eventually settled for a small watercolour sketch by Sir Stanley Spencer.

Now ensconced in his Whitehall fastness, Oedipus set about his ministerial tasks, enjoying his power to order civil servants to troop into his office and brief him not only on the subject of his portfolio but also on the portfolios of other, more senior ministers, whose positions he envied and would like to obtain in some way or other. In this way, he received detailed briefings on subjects as diverse as the European Union's policy on barge traffic on inland rivers, the attitude of the United Kingdom to the issue of international sale of goods treaties and the development of offshore resources in the South China Sea.

Ideally, Oedipus would have liked to be Foreign Secretary, a post he recognised as having considerable options for foreign travel, which he enjoyed. He watched with envy the peregrinations of the current incumbent, and studied in detail the issue of access to the VIP suites at Heathrow airport. Oedipus had been outraged to discover that he was not on the list of those entitled to use these suites, and had demanded an explanation from the civil servant with whom he had raised the matter.

"Well, frankly, sir," said the official, "you aren't actually a *very* important person. You are undoubtedly an *important* person—and I would be the first to acknowledge that, I do assure you—but in terms of the eligibility requirements agreed between HMG and BAA, you are not a VIP."

Oedipus had glowered. "So I must go about government business mixing with the public? Is that what you're saying?"

"More or less, sir. In fact, yes, I think I can commit to that position. Yes, that's what I might be considered to be saying."

Oedipus laughed sneeringly. "And I suppose I have to go economy class. I suppose you expect me to sit at the rear of the plane with the screaming babies and the students and whatnot?"

He intended it as a joke—a *reductio ad absurdum*—and did not expect the civil servant's reply.

"Yes."

"You're not serious," said Oedipus.

"Yes, I'm afraid I am. Under the new rules, the austerity provisions, all *junior* government ministers—and I'm afraid, sir, you're not considered *senior*, which I suppose, on one view of the matter, implies that you're junior—under the new austerity provisions, junior ministers are required to travel in economy class, and I wouldn't wish to labour this point, but I feel I must inform you: you are also required to get an advance-purchase economy ticket where possible. On a cheap airline too."

Oedipus could barely speak, but he did manage to say, "What's the point, may I ask? What's the point of being in office if these indignities . . ."

The civil servant answered, "Well, with respect, sir, I would have thought that the point of being in office was to serve the public. I know it's a terribly old-fashioned view—and not one which all of our political masters are *entirely* enthusiastic about—but it is, I think, a view which finds acceptance, and indeed, one would go so far as to say, full endorsement, by at least ninety-nine point nine per cent of the population of this country, that is, in a manner of speaking, by that body of persons sometimes vulgarly referred to as *the people*."

Oedipus was silent. He would see about that.

The civil servant coughed discreetly. "Of course," he added, "when I say ninety-nine point nine per cent of the people, I am merely hazarding a guess. It's possible that the correct figure is even higher, perhaps so close to one hundred per cent as to make the opinion to all intents and purposes unanimous. To put it crudely, one might even use an expression such as 'everybody thinks.'"

"Do they?" said Oedipus, his voice heavy with sarcasm.

"Yes," said the civil servant. "They do."

61. Big Science Calls

THE INDIGNITIES OF economy-class travel were inflicted on Oedipus Snark and other junior ministers by what he saw as an excessively penny-pinching government. The fact that he was himself a member of that government was, he felt, beside the point.

"Show me one mention, just one single mention," he expostulated, "in the manifestos of either my party or that of our coalition partners of anything—*anything*—to do with making Ministers of the Crown travel in the back of the plane. Found it? No, you wouldn't, would you, because it isn't there. So on what authority do they cut a well-established and necessary arrangement for the maintenance of high standards of government? Now, it's not just comfort, it's security as well—in fact, it's mostly about security. We have to deal with confidential papers when we travel, and how can things remain confidential when you have some oaf leaning over your shoulder looking at your working papers?"

That was the essence of his position, but there were further arguments to be advanced. "Frankly," Oedipus said, "I don't see why they don't make a distinction between travel arrangements for us and for members of the former government. When we go on these House of Commons committee trips, I think they should make business class available to our people and not to the opposition. Why? Well, it's their fault, isn't it? They're the ones who caused the crisis by overspending with reckless abandon for the last *n* years. So let them suffer the consequences of economising. Yes, why not? Your mess—you clean it up. The polluter pays—or, in this context, the spender saves. Ha! That would teach them a thing or two.

"And there's another thing," he continued. "On our side of the House we believe in individual effort and in letting people enjoy the benefits of their hard work. The other side doesn't—not really; they may say they do, but have you noticed how they cross their fingers when they talk about rewarding effort? Have you noticed that? So I think we should recognise their strong anti-elitist senti-ments and save them the embarrassment of travelling business class by forbidding it—for them at least. Ha!"

Of course, these arguments—like most of the views expressed by Oedipus Snark—got him nowhere, and he found himself con-strained to accept an economy-class ticket to Geneva when he and twelve other MPs on the All-Party Committee on Pure Scientific Research were invited to visit the Large Hadron Collider. This project was funded in part by the British government, which gave over seventy million pounds a year as part of its support of scien-tific endeavour. The Collider authorities were always keen to en-thuse politicians over the research they undertook, and so a regular stream of members of parliament paid a visit each year to the vast tunnel under the Alps where particles were accelerated towards one another at speeds close to the speed of light. The resultant events promised to show us just what conditions were like a fraction of a second after the Big Bang—information that the government of the United Kingdom was keen to obtain for some reason.

Oedipus rapidly cleared his diary for the three days that the trip would require. There was to have been a meeting with his constituency party committee—it was easily set aside on the grounds of absence "on government business." There was an invi-tation to visit a new school, which he had already put off once before; it could be postponed again—in fact, cancelled altogether. After all, it was just a school. And there was a meeting which had been set up by a conservation pressure group—they could be strung along indefinitely, irritating people that they were, going on about voles or whatever it was. There were no voles in his constituency, he was sure of it, and yet they had targeted him for some reason. Cancelled.

Big science called, and science did not get any bigger than the Large Hadron Collider. Oedipus was a bit hazy about what exactly it did and how it did it, but he had seen pictures of it and it was certainly large: Los Alamos stuff, this. They were looking for something, he had read, and when they found it they would know how it all started: the slime, the human race, the Liberal Democrat party—the lot! It had some bearing on evolution, of course, and Lib Dems, as everybody knew, were the most evolved of the available political species! He might try that joke on some of his colleagues; he was building up a reputation for being a bit of a wag, and these sorts of *bons mots* always helped.

The day before the departure for Geneva, Oedipus received a telephone call from a journalist. He was always happy to speak to journalists, and he enjoyed nothing more than profile features about the decor of his flat or the three best books he had read in the last year. Favourite restaurants too—he liked those features; the Notting Hill Bistro had been a recent haunt, as had Semplice, off Blenheim Street. This journalist presumably wanted something along those lines, and he would try to oblige. A good newspaper article, he had once been told, was worth at least eighty votes, while a television interview—a successful one—was worth two hundred and fifty.

The journalist was quick to come to the point. He had come into possession of papers relating to a transaction between Oedipus and a certain businessman which suggested that influence had been used to secure a contract: money had changed hands. The documents appeared genuine. Did Mr. Snark have any comment to make?

Oedipus issued an immediate denial. Any such documents, he said, were certainly fakes, and if any mention were made of them in the press he would instruct his solicitors to start proceedings for libel. Would the journalist please inform his editor of this immediately. And goodbye.

He put the receiver down. The back of his neck felt hot, and his heart was thumping within him. He had a good idea of what those documents were, and he knew that the most likely person to have had access to them was Barbara Ragg, his lover at the time. Barbara! So this was her revenge, was it? Well, she was in for an unpleasant surprise—an extremely unpleasant surprise indeed. But for the time being he would put the whole thing out of his mind. CERN beckoned, with its hadron collider and its accelerated particles. Perhaps they would find the Higgs Boson at last, or another particle. It would be wonderful to have a particle named after one. The Snark Particle. It sounded very appropriate. If he mentioned his role in continuing British financial support for the collider, the director might take the hint and choose that name for a particle. Not necessarily a big or important particle, but a particle nonetheless.

62. In the Collider

WHEN THE PARTY of British MPs arrived at CERN, they were met by one of the associate directors, the director himself being at a conference in Berlin. This associate director was one of the British appointments, a slight Ulsterman who had pursued a career in physics at Imperial College before transferring to the accelerator project. Dr. David Ferman was a softly spoken man who lived for the more abstruse, remote provinces of physics; if anybody knew how the universe started, it was said, he did. He met the MPs in one of the conference rooms, where coffee was served before the tour was due to begin.

"I'm not sure how much you know about this project, ladies and gentlemen," Dr. Ferman began. "As you know, we get a lot of press coverage, but we do not always find that the public grasps exactly what we're about. Not that anybody can blame them: our work is very much at the cutting edge of modern physics, and there are plenty of people with degrees in physics who might be quite hazy on what it's all about. So please don't hesitate to ask questions."

There then followed a half-hour presentation on electroweak forces, the discovery of the W and Z bosons and the hunt for Higgs. Some of the MPs followed the lecture, but most quickly became lost. Oedipus followed nothing at all, though he did recognise references to gravity, with which he, like most of us, was familiar. References to antimatter intrigued him, and in the question time at the end he took up Dr. Ferman's comment about the explosive potential of a pound of antimatter.

"It would be a substantial bang," said Dr. Ferman. "The equivalent of about several thousand atomic bombs. But I wouldn't worry about it too much if I were you."

Oedipus assumed a severe expression. "You've heard of the precautionary principle, Dr. Ferman," he said. "It's our job as politicians— and especially those of us who happen to be government ministers—to be prepared for all eventualities. I don't think we should make light of the threat that antimatter could represent to democracies if it got into irresponsible hands."

Dr. Ferman said nothing for a moment, which make Oedipus look about him with a slightly superior smile. The other MPs waited for the physicist's reaction.

"By all means, take precautions," said Dr. Ferman. "I would never encourage anybody to be foolhardy in these areas."

"Exactly," said Oedipus. "I'm glad that you take my point."

"Of course, it would be a long-term threat," continued Dr. Ferman. "It's not short-term."

"Ah, but that's what we need to guard against," Oedipus crowed. "Short-termism. We need to take the long view."

Dr. Ferman shrugged. "By all means," he said. "But it would take all our collider resources about sixty billion years to produce enough antimatter to make one bomb. I assume that even your planning horizons, Mr. Snark, do not extend that far into the future. Or am I doing you an injustice? I am aware, of course, that you are a member of a government that is deliberately taking the longer view. Perhaps, therefore, you're correct, and we should plan for the next sixty billion years."

There was a snigger from one or two of the MPs, and Oedipus turned red.

"So," Dr. Ferman went on, "are there any other questions—short-term or long-term?"

The jibe brought another burst of laughter. "It's going to take your party at least sixty billion years to get into power on your own," said a sharp-faced MP, pointing a bony finger at Oedipus. This brought even greater laughter from everybody present, except from Dr. Ferman, who clearly wanted to laugh too but decided that tact precluded it.

They now left the conference room and moved towards a large metal door marked *Hadron Collider: No Admittance.*

"I'm happy to say that this sign doesn't apply to us," said Dr. Ferman. "We don't want just anybody wandering around the collider, but the director and I are allowed to take groups in. Please put on this protective gear, though—these plastic hats and shoe covers. We don't want the wrong sort of particle getting in there!"

Dressed in their special outfits, the MPs followed Dr. Ferman through the door and into a high tunnel stretching into the distance on either side. There were great magnets on the side of the tunnel and a bewildering array of scientific hardware—wires, switches, large metal boxes.

"We can take a brief walk down the collider," said Dr. Ferman. "If you see anything that interests you, just ask. Not even I know what everything does in this box of tricks, but I have a general idea."

They walked down the collider, speechless at the size and majesty of the great instrument. Then the party returned to the door by which they had entered and were led off to the control room. Standing in front of a bank of screens and switchboards, Dr. Ferman explained that it was very fortunate that the visit coincided with an experiment being conducted that day.

"We're actually going to be switching the thing on," he said. "Then we're going to accelerate two streams of particles and bring them into collision. This will release an extraordinary amount of energy, but only for a very short time."

"What about the danger of black holes?" asked one of the MPs. "Couldn't they swallow us all up?"

"There's no real danger of that," said Dr. Ferman. "If we create any, they'll be terribly small and short-lived. Please don't worry."

Dr. Ferman went over to confer with a small group of scientists. He nodded and one of the scientists flicked a switch. There was a humming sound, and rows of instruments began to blink red and green. "Any moment now," said Dr. Ferman. "There we are. Here they come. You're witnessing something significant here, ladies and gentlemen. Here they are. Whoosh! Bang!"

"Technical terms of physics," whispered one MP.

There were further reactions from the instruments. Then Dr. Ferman turned to face his guests. "Any questions about what you've just seen? Are you reasonably clear on this, Mr. Snark? Mr. Snark . . . Has anybody seen Mr. Snark?"

"I saw him in the tunnel," volunteered one of the MPs. "But that was about fifteen minutes ago."

Dr. Ferman gasped. "Oh no!" he wailed. "He will have been atomised."

"Excuse me, Dr. Ferman," interrupted one of the scientists. "We have a rather curious burst of particle activity on this screen here. Look, just about junction forty-six in the accelerator. All these quarks and stuff here flying off in every direction, quite an explosion. Look at that. Very unusual."

"His final photograph," muttered Dr. Ferman, staring at the screen, at the delicate dancing lines of sub-atomic activity, like a burst of miniature fireworks against a small square of velvet sky.

"Oh dear," muttered an MP. "Bye-election."

63. Mariology, Etc.

BASIL WICKRAMSINGHE WAS a man of private and scholarly pursuits. He occupied the ground-floor flat in Corduroy Mansions, a fact which meant that all the other residents had to walk past his front door on their way in or out. For the most part, he kept to himself, although on the rare occasions when there was what William called a "house party," he came along and appeared to enjoy himself. For the rest of the time, he was hardly to be seen, slipping out of the house in the morning rather earlier than anybody else and returning in the late afternoon, shortly before everybody else came back from work.

Basil was a High Anglican, a member of the congregation of a nearby church where mass was said, incense used and devotees of the Blessed Virgin Mary exchanged their arcane messages. Basil approved of incense, the smell of which he liked and had sought to emulate in his choice of aftershave lotion, and he had no objection to the use of the term "mass." He was less enthusiastic about the cult of Mary, which made him feel somewhat uneasy, but, being of a tolerant disposition, he accepted that those who found something in such areas of interest *needed* whatever it was that their practices gave them, and it was not for him to pass judgement. In particular, he remained silent when two middle-aged ladies claimed to have seen the Virgin Mary *and* St. Anne on Ebury Street. Their claim was taken seriously by other mariologists on the vestry committee, but Basil had his doubts. These were based on the patent unlikelihood of the Virgin Mary, and indeed St. Anne, feeling the need to manifest, on a Tuesday of all days—in Pimlico of all places—and on the fact that the visitation was supposed to have taken place on the pavement directly outside the ladies' small—and struggling—gift shop. If the sighting were to be confirmed, of course, it would undoubtedly be good for business. This consideration had not escaped other traders in the area, who had been quick to report that they had themselves seen two unusually dressed women on the street early on the morning in question, one of them, significantly, wearing a long blue robe.

But where Basil did have strong views was on the subject of liturgical language. Basil believed in the English language, and its ability to express spirituality in a particularly effective register. He knew all about James VI and I, and about his sponsorship of the Authorised Version. He had read and appreciated Adam Nicolson's *Power and Glory*, which was all about the process of translation. Somehow the language had been just right, encapsulating the full beauty of the English of the time—a language both majestic and poetic. As a boy in Sri Lanka, a third-generation Anglican, he had read a copy of the King James Bible given to him by an uncle and thrilled at the language. When he first encountered the *New English Bible*, he could not believe the contrast: the poetry had gone, completely, to be replaced by the language of the call centre, the morning bulletin from the meteorological office or the assembly manual accompanying an item of do-it-yourself furniture. Why had they done this? he asked himself. Why had they rooted out all sense of mystery, of immanence, of solemnity, when everybody had been capable of understanding it? The answer was depressingly clear: this was done precisely to get rid of mystery, immanence and solemnity. And the same thing had been done to the *Book of Common Prayer*—with its echoing, resonant Cranmerian prose; the enemies of linguistic beauty had had a field day there, thought Basil.

Basil was an important member of the James VI and I Society, which he had helped to found, and which met every two months in his flat in Corduroy Mansions. The society's purpose was to preserve the memory of that unusual monarch, celebrating his writings and achievements. Their annual party took place on the anniversary of the death of Elizabeth I, whom the Society did not like because of her role in the death of James's mother. One might have thought that the elapse of a considerable number of centuries would be sufficient to allow forgiveness to take root, but not in this case. Elizabeth I had a lot to answer for, and the James VI and I Society was not going to let her off the hook so easily.

Basil had a sweet tooth, and one of his favourite ports of call was William Curley's chocolate shop, not far from the shop where William had bought his ill-fated Belgian shoes. Mr. Curley's creations existed for the temptation of the likes of Basil, and virtually every day he called in there on his way back from work to buy a small selection of handmade chocolates. From time to time he would take a seat at one of the tables and order a cup of chocolate, which he would consume while reading the newspaper or correcting the proofs of the *James VI and I News*, of which he was the editor.

On this occasion, though, Basil had neither newspaper nor proofs with him when he went into Curley's. He had left his newspaper in the office, having lent it to one of the trainee accountants who had yet to return it, and there would not be another issue of the James newsletter for another three months. Nursing his cup of freshly made hot chocolate, he looked around the shop. There were a couple of young women gossiping at a nearby table, but their conversation was discreet and he could not hear what they were talking about. Basil liked women—and women liked him—and there was nothing he enjoyed more than being invited to participate in a conversation with women. But it rarely happened; the human world, he reflected, was divided into little clusters of people—tiny tribes, small groups of friends, families—and if you belonged to only a few of these, then your life was circumscribed. He would love to have a gossipy conversation with people he simply bumped into, but he lived in the wrong world for that.

Noticing that somebody had left a magazine on the chair beside him, he picked it up and read the title: *The World of Dogs*. Basil smiled. There was a magazine for every interest, he thought; the other day he had paused in front of a newsagent at Victoria station and seen the bewildering array of magazines. He had been amused by the newsagent's shelf categories: Women's Interests; Lifestyle; Men's Interests. The magazines under Men's Interests were all about cars, motorbikes and DIY. Limited, he thought, but probably commercially astute. Other categories might be just as descriptive, but risked offending the customer. Computer magazines, for example, could be filed in a section labelled Geeks, and some of the more esoteric titles—were people really interested in *that*?—could be filed under Freaks. Mountaineering magazines, of which he noticed there were several, would of course go under Peaks, and ornithology magazines—again there was more than one of these—would be best placed under Beaks. The magazine for DIY plumbers, *Home Plumber Today*, would naturally be placed under Leaks . . . He stopped himself. The anarchic, inventive excursus was his weakness and could go on for hours, if he allowed it.

He began to page through *The World of Dogs*. There was an editorial on obedience issues and an article on the economics of setting up a grooming parlour. There was "A Vet Writes," a column of queries about canine complaints, all answered in measured, sensible terms. And then there was a double-page advertisement for a dog food. It featured, not surprisingly, a dog. The surprise came, though, in the face of the dog staring out at the reader.

Basil recognised him.

64. Dogs, Models, Familiarity

BASIL STARED AT the glossy photograph of Freddie de la Hay. The dog looked familiar, but it took him a while to establish why this should be. Dogs of the same breed were all very much alike, in his view; how would one tell one Labrador from another? he wondered. And yet presumably owners of Labradors could pick out their own dog in a crowd of other Labradors. He thought that this might be on the basis of facial expression, or something to do with the eyes, but he was not sure.

A dog, of course, could identify its owner in a large group of humans. Basil knew that there had been a lot of research into how people recognised one another, but he doubted whether anybody had been able to understand how it worked for dogs. They probably used the sense of smell more than visual clues; that, he had read, was how they remembered—the smells were filed away in a massive olfactory memory. How weak was our own memory of smells,

Basil reflected. What did he remember? Incense, truffle oil, vanilla, cardamom, thyme, freshly ground pepper.

The thought of pepper reminded him that he needed to buy some more. Basil refused to accept the black pepper sold in super-markets. "Dust," he said. "Like the tea they put in teabags. Dust." How different were the fresh peppercorns he sent off for from a mail-order spice business in Sussex. This company imported pep-per directly from Kerala and bagged it up for their clients in small linen sacks. These peppercorns, when put in the grinder and bro-ken into fragments, released an aroma that tickled the nose and delighted the palate. It was a proper spice—a delicious, layered taste that bore little relation to the bland sneezing-powder sold as pepper to an unsuspecting public.

Basil's attention returned to the photograph of the dog. Yes, it was very familiar . . . He smiled as he placed it. It was that dog upstairs—Freddie de la Hay—William French's dog. Basil had al-ways rather liked him, and on the relatively infrequent occasions on which he had met him, he had bent down and let Freddie lick the back of his hand appreciatively.

Of course, this would just be a dog who looked rather like Fred-die—it was unlikely to be the same dog. Basil found that he never actually knew the people whose picture appeared in papers or mag-azines, and the same would apply *a fortiori*, perhaps, to pictures of dogs. Presumably people who featured in advertisements were rec-ognised by their friends, who might say things like "Oh, there she is eating chocolate *again*," or "Oh, there's a picture of Bill shaving." The male models were the funniest; they all sucked in their cheeks so assiduously. Perhaps the marketing experts had worked out that we were impressed by men who sucked in their cheeks when they faced the camera; that we trusted them and would therefore want whatever product they were advertising.

Basil's eye ran across the advertisement. There was a tiny credit printed along the side, and he strained to read it. *Photo: East An-glia Graphic Arts; model: FDLH.* He reread it, just to make sure. *FDLH:* Freddie de la Hay. It had to be him; most dogs did not have initials, or just had one, such as R. It was highly unlikely—indeed impossible—that there could be another dog with those initials. No, this was his friend, Freddie.

Basil wondered whether William had seen the advertisement. He had presumably lent his dog to the photographer for this pur-pose but he might not have seen the published photograph. If this were so, then he should perhaps take the magazine home and show it to him. It would be a neighbourly thing to do, decided Basil.

He opened his briefcase and was about to slip the magazine in-side when a thought occurred to him. Was this magazine his now, or did it still belong to somebody else? Basil was scrupulously hon-est; so honest, indeed, that the tax authorities had asked him not to submit quite so many receipts when preparing his own tax returns. "We like to see the paper record, Mr. Wickramsinghe," a tax inspec-tor had said, "but a receipt for seven pence is probably taking things a bit far. And as for declaring a five-pound note that you found in the street and picked up—well, we're not quite sure that that counts as income. Anyway, it's not yours, you know."

It was an interesting point that had sent Basil off to telephone a lawyer friend and ask him for a ruling.

"He's right," said the lawyer. "Lost property still belongs to the person who lost it. That fiver belongs to the poor chap out of whose pocket it dropped."

"But what do I do if I don't know who he is?"

"You hand it in to the police or a lost property department. They try to trace the owner—theoretically. I can't imagine them making much effort with a five-pound note. But something big would be different."

"And if the owner doesn't come forward?" asked Basil.

"Then you get it as the finder," said the lawyer. "Or I think that's the rule."

"Who owns rubbish?" asked Basil. "The things in the bin in the park? Who owns them?"

"I don't think one would want to stick one's hand in there. That's abandoned property, I think—or it's been made over to the council. The general rule is that if property is abandoned, it belongs to the person who finds it."

Basil looked at the magazine. If it had been abandoned, then he could become the owner and it would be perfectly permissible to put it in his briefcase. He glanced around him. The two young women at the nearby table were certainly not the owners of *The World of Dogs*; had it been a copy of *Harper's Bazaar*, then they might have been—but not this. What about the shop itself? No, he had never known them to leave magazines about the place.

With the magazine tucked away in his briefcase, Basil left the chocolatier's shop and walked the short distance back to Corduroy Mansions. That evening, after he had eaten his solitary dinner in front of the television, he retrieved the magazine from his briefcase and went upstairs to knock at William's door.

65. A Generous Gesture

WILLIAM CONSIDERED BASIL Wickramsinghe to be the ideal neighbour: quiet, courteous and helpful. In fact, the only respect in which the domestic arrangements in Corduroy Mansions could be improved upon, he thought, would be if Basil Wickramsinghe were to move from the ground-floor flat to the flat immediately below his own, and if Caroline and the girls—there was a boy now too, he noticed—were to move into the ground-floor flat in place of Basil. This view was not formed by any antipathy to Caroline or her flatmates; it was just that there were occasions, and not many at that, when he heard a bit of noise coming from the flat below. Basil, by contrast, was as quiet as a church mouse.

"Mr. Wickramsinghe!" William exclaimed when he answered the door that evening. "Do come in, please. This is a rare honour!"

"I do not like to disturb you," said Basil. "I hope that this isn't inconvenient."

"Of course it's not inconvenient. Come in, come in. May I offer you something? A glass of something?"

"Last time I was here you gave me an extremely delicious glass of wine," said Basil. "It had a nutty flavour, as I recall."

"That will have been Madeira," said William. "Very suitable to be taken by the glass. That particular Madeira, I think, was recommended by my friend, Will Lyons. I don't know whether you've read his column at all, but he knows what he's talking about in my view. That was quite an old Blandy's. None left, I'm afraid, but I can offer—"

"Please don't open anything special for me," said Basil.

It was typical of his neighbour's self-effacing modesty, thought William; others would have no compunction in sampling the best thing on offer when visiting the flat of a wine-dealer.

"But I do have another Madeira, as it happens," said William. "I'll find it and we can sample it."

William went to fetch the Madeira, returning with two generous glasses of an iodine-coloured liquid. Handing one to Basil, he raised his glass in a toast, which Basil reciprocated.

They sat together in the drawing room. To begin with, the conversation was mostly small talk. William asked what had been happening in the James VI and I Society, and Basil replied that there was very little going on. "We're mostly reactive," he said. "We exist to protect the reputation of James. If anybody launches an attack, then we're ready to defend his memory. But at the moment, nobody seems to have it in for him."

"I know so little about him," mused William. "It's odd, isn't it, how you find so few people these days who mention James I. You get a bit of discussion down at the pub about Charles I, and Charles II too. But James—nothing really."

"Which pub?" asked Basil with interest. "Which pub do they discuss Charles I in?"

"Oh, I didn't mean any particular pub," said William. "I meant pubs in general."

Basil looked disappointed. "I would love to find a pub where these matters are debated," he said. "It's usually football. And I'm afraid I have no interest in that at all."

"I don't blame you," said William. "All these prima donnas prancing about the football field. I thought it was meant to be a team game."

"It's the same with everything," said Basil. "The cult of celebrity has infected everything." He paused. "And their wives. People keep going on about footballers' wives. Why not other wives? Mathematicians' wives, for example. How about taking an interest in them?"

William laughed. "The wives of mathematicians will surely be very different," he said. "But I suspect that they won't make such entertaining television."

Basil nodded. "Indeed," he said.

Then Basil glanced round the room. "Where's Freddie?" he asked.

William looked down into his glass; the feeling of loss was every bit as raw as it had been when he drove down to London on that melancholy evening. "Frankly," he confessed, "I don't know. He may be dead—in fact, I think he is."

Basil was aghast. "I'm terribly sorry. I didn't—"

William brushed the apology aside. "Nothing to apologise for," he said. "You weren't to know."

Basil asked what had happened and received a full account of Freddie's disappearance at the farm and the fruitless search that followed. "I phoned the RSPCA," William went on. "I put the word out, but no dogs answering his description have been handed in. So I fear that we've lost Freddie altogether—probably down a rabbit hole or something like that."

Basil reached into his briefcase, which he had brought upstairs with him. "Do you know this magazine?" he asked, extracting *The World of Dogs*.

William glanced at the magazine and shook his head sadly. "I can't say I've ever seen it." He paused. "Oh look, I'm not thinking of getting a replacement just yet. Freddie de la Hay is—or should I say *was*—the most wonderful dog. He will be a hard act for any dog to follow, I'm afraid."

"No, that's not why I've brought this along," said Basil.

"You're getting a dog yourself?"

"No. But look . . ." He paged through the magazine. "Here. Look at this."

"My goodness, that's a dead ringer for my Freddie. Look at it. He had a patch of colour right there, where this dog has. Perhaps they're related—I can imagine that Pimlico terriers are all related in one way or another."

"I think it's your dog," said Basil quietly. "In fact, I'm *sure* it's your dog."

"I don't see how you can say that," said William. "Just because he looks . . ."

He did not finish. Basil pointed to the side of the picture where the credits were set out, and William saw the initials: *FDLH*. "I just don't believe it," he said. "I just don't."

"But it must be him," said Basil. "Those are his initials, and I doubt that there is another dog in these islands who has the same combination of letters in his name. I think it's an open-and-shut case."

William looked at Basil, and smiled. "Thank God for you," he said.

"Would you like me to track him down?" said Basil. "I have a few days off, and I would love to play the amateur detective. Please let me recover him for you. I'll track down the photographer and get the name of the modelling agency or whatever. It'll be plain sailing after that."

William did not have to ponder this offer for long.

"I accept," he said. And he thought: You nice, nice man. You kind, helpful man. You generous, decent man.

66. Team Moongrove

THE NEXT DAY was perhaps one of the most eventful days of Terence Moongrove's life. That is not to say that his life over the last few years had been without incident. There had been his trip to Bulgaria—arranged by a few like-minded residents of Cheltenham—when he had first encountered the works of Peter Deunov and become involved in the sacred dance movement. That had been not only fascinating, but perilous as well: adherents of Deunov enjoy dancing on mountain tops—the better to communicate with Beings of Light—and Terence had very nearly slipped at an important stage in proceedings; very nearly, but had not, and had survived to found the ultimately highly successful Cheltenham Deunov Association. Then there had been the business with the Green Man, whom Terence had seen among the rhododendron bushes of his garden. It is given to few of us—in sobriety at least—to see an actual Green Man, and Terence was adamant that his had been no mere apparition. He was not to know, of course, that the Green Man in question was really Lennie Marchbanks bedecked in leaves, at the behest of his sister, Berthea Snark. And most recently there had been the purchase, with Monty Bismarck, of the 1932 Frazer Nash, which he and Monty were now planning to race.

Monty Bismarck had lost no time in collecting the expensive racing car from Richard Latcham, a gifted and generous restorer of such vehicles. Richard had not met Monty before and was concerned that the young man knew what he was doing.

"You will be careful," he warned. "These cars can be tricky, particularly on bends. Please drive it responsibly."

"Yeah, sure, sure," said Monty. "No probs."

"And you mentioned a co-driver," said Richard.

"Yeah," said Monty. "He's the geezer who's paying for it. Nice guy. Terence Moongrove. Lives over in Cheltenham, near my old man. Heard of him?"

Richard shook his head. "I can't say I have."

"Drives a Porsche," continued Monty. "Really keen on motoring. Great guy."

The Frazer Nash was brought back to Cheltenham, where it was much admired by Terence. Berthea, who was staying with her brother at the time, watched from an upstairs window as Monty and Terence examined the car on the front drive. She shook her head with a sense of foreboding.

"I've lined up our first race meeting," said Monty. "Tomorrow, in fact. There's a good racing circuit not too far away—I've entered us for a couple of races. Me first, then you. We each get a go."

"That's jolly exciting, Monty," said Terence. "And I've already bought one of those old leather thingies you wear when you race these vintage cars—you know the cap thingies with the goggles? I'll lend it to you, if you like."

"Cool," said Monty. Then he added, "Don't try to go fast, Mr. Moongrove. Not the first few times. Let the others get to the front; you just drive quietly behind them. Then you might have your chance to put your foot down at the end—who knows? But safety first, OK? Let's make that the motto of Team Bismarck."

Terence smiled, but only for a moment. "Why Team Bismarck?" he asked peevishly. "Why not Team Moongrove?"

Monty shrugged. "I just thought it sounded good. Team Bismarck—more cutting edge. That's all."

"Well, I don't see why we should use your name rather than mine when I paid for the car. I jolly well did, you know, Monty. It's my car, you know."

Monty pacified him. "That's cool with me, Mr. Moongrove. Team Moongrove it is. Sounds really cool."

On the day in question, they drove over to the racing circuit together in the Frazer Nash, with Monty at the wheel and Terence listening carefully as the issue of the gears was explained. When they arrived, there was already a large crowd milling about, and the Frazer Nash was much admired by those who considered themselves cognoscenti—which meant everybody present.

Monty drove in the first race, and the car performed well, resulting in a fourth place. Terence, watching from the pits, where he was wearing a set of old blue overalls which Monty had obtained for him from Lennie Marchbanks, applauded loudly and patted Monty on the back as he got out of the car.

"That's really good, Monty," he said.

"Yeah, wasn't bad," said Monty. "I had some pretty stiff competition. Brennan in an old Jag XK120, Mitchell in a Mitchell Supercharged Special, May in a Wingfield Special. Pretty good drivers, that lot."

"Well, I can hardly wait for my turn," said Terence.

"Yes," said Monty. "And have you noticed that the chap who sold it to you is in your race? Richard Latcham. Just keep behind him— he'll look after you."

"I will," said Terence. "Go, Team Moongrove!"

Monty smiled bravely. "Just remember, Mr. Moongrove—keep to the back. Best tactic. Don't go too fast. Easy does it."

Terence's race was announced. Pulling the goggles over his eyes, he climbed into the Frazer Nash and drove it hesitantly to the start line.

"Ladies and gents," said a voice over the loudspeakers. "Next race: the Tom Delaney Trophy. And a pretty impressive line-up we have too. Latcham in a Mitchell Special Mark 1, Conoley in a TR3, Catherwood in a Talbot-Darracq, Macpherson in a Supercharged Bristol 400 and Moongrove in a Frazer Nash."

At the mention of his name, Terence waved to the crowd and sounded his horn. None of the other drivers did this, and one or two of them looked at him in a curious way. Terence gave a further wave, especially directed at them.

The race began. Latcham, Conoley, Catherwood and Macpherson all shot forwards with roaring engines, in a cloud of blue smoke; Terence started, but somewhat slowly, and also slightly erratically. However, he soon got the hang of the accelerator and the Frazer Nash picked up speed. At the first bend, he tried to remember what he had been taught about the gears but could not, and the Frazer Nash, not having differentials in its rear axle, rocketed around the corner *completely sideways*. Strange, thought Terence, as he pulled the car back the right way. The next corner came rather too quickly, and again the Frazer Nash's lack of a differential resulted in an extraordinary sideways manoeuvre. This brought him past Latcham and Catherwood.

By the time the cars were on the final circuit, Terence was in the lead. Unfortunately, however, he chose to change gear, hoping to build up a bit more speed. This might have worked, but instead Terence found himself in neutral and coasting to a stop. The other cars, swerving sharply, shot past him. Terence struggled with the gears and managed to engage one, which was reverse. He began to go backwards.

When he arrived in the pits, Monty was there to greet him.

"Fantastic driving, Mr. Moongrove!" he shouted.

Terence beamed with delight. "I jolly well nearly won, Monty. Did you see me?"

"I did, Mr. Moongrove. But what happened at the end? Why did you go backwards?"

"The gears are jolly difficult, Monty. You warned me."

"Well, it didn't matter. You did really well. Team Moongrove is proud of you."

Terence took off the goggles. "Thanks, Monty. But, my goodness, I could do with a cup of camomile tea. Do you think they've got any camomile tea here, Monty? It's frightfully good for the stomach, you know."

67. A Phone Call from Switzerland

It was shortly after Terence had returned from the racing circuit that the telephone call came through. He was soaking in a hot bath, reflecting on his first experience driving the Frazer Nash, and so the phone was answered by Berthea. She did not like answering her brother's phone, as she found his callers were usually rather vague, mystical people who had no real idea why they had called in the first place. This call, as it happened, was for her.

"Dr. Snark?"

The voice had a foreign accent, and she wondered what she was going to be asked to buy. But it was Terence's phone and not hers . . .

"Yes."

"This is Millette Antoine calling from Geneva. From CERN."

"Lucerne?"

"No, CERN, the European Organisation for Nuclear Research."

Berthea was at a loss. "Oh . . ."

"Your son, Mr. Snark. He has been with us in a visiting group of politicians. I'm sorry to say there has been an accident."

Berthea sat down. Her breath came quickly. She closed her eyes, as we will sometimes close our eyes to shut out the unbearable. She felt a sudden, overwhelming regret. There was no other term for it. Pure regret. The son she had disliked so intensely. Her son.

"I'm happy to say that he appears to be fine," said the voice quickly. "He is very fortunate. The party was inside the particle accelerator and Mr. Snark was left behind by some terrible mistake, and we turned it on. We didn't know."

Berthea gasped. "With him in . . . in the . . . in the accelerator?"

"CERN very much regrets this, madam, I assure you. It has never happened before, and we shall ensure that it does not happen again. Procedures are already in place."

"How is he? You said that he was uninjured."

"He seems to be unaffected. But we have removed him to hospital for investigation, just to make sure. I don't think he will be in for more than a day or two. He asked me to telephone you and assure you that he was fine—he thought that it would be a good idea to do this in case the accident got into the news. He didn't want you to hear about it on the radio or some other way."

"How thoughtful of him," said Berthea. "I'm very relieved."

She meant it, but no sooner had she said this than it occurred to her that something was wrong: Oedipus had been thoughtful.

"May I ask you something?" Berthea said.

"Of course."

"What was his state of mind? Was he very upset?"

The answer came quickly. "Not at all. It's quite remarkable, Dr. Snark, but your son was very good about it. He did not complain—not once. He said that it was very foolish of him to wander off from the group. He went to look at some magnets, apparently, and when he turned round the others had gone. He couldn't find his way out."

Berthea's mouth dropped. "Very good about it?"

"Yes," continued Millette Antoine. "I was on the scene when they brought him out. He seemed slightly confused at first, and asked what dimension he was in. But it was just a joke, I think, and then he apologised for causing us anxiety and said how sorry he was to have affected the experiment. It was quite remarkable. I remember thinking, in fact, this man is very saintly. You must be very proud of him, Dr. Snark."

Berthea spoke faintly. "Proud? Well . . ."

"If I may say so, Dr. Snark, it's typical of you British. You're so understated. I am Swiss, and I can say that a Swiss person would be very angry to be trapped in a particle accelerator. We don't like that sort of thing. And put a French person in a particle accelerator and *oh là là!* Or a German—*mein Gott!* You British are very accepting—particularly your son."

The telephone call lasted a few minutes more. Then Switzerland rang off, and Berthea Snark sat for almost half an hour, staring at the ceiling of the room in which she had taken the call. She was immensely relieved that Oedipus had survived, but her relief was eclipsed by her astonishment at the account she had had of his behaviour. This was not her son at all—or not how her son *used* to be. Had the experience changed him in some extraordinary way, perhaps by rearranging his neurons in such a way as to effect a complete personality change? Was such a thing possible?

It was. In hospital in Geneva, Oedipus Snark, MP lay in bed, crisp white sheets pulled up to his chin. He felt physically fine—indeed he saw no reason to be in hospital at all, but they had asked him to go in and he wanted to be as obliging as possible. Yes, he felt well in a bodily sense, but he also felt strangely different. There was no anger; there was no ego—or at least the ego was not asserting itself; there was no sense of wanting anything. That was the curious thing, he did not *want*—at least not for himself. He wanted things for others. He wanted others to have what *they* needed. He did not need anything more himself.

He asked himself whether he had always felt like that. He thought he had not. But strangely enough, the memory of what he had been like before had faded. It was not him any more. He was a new man altogether.

He got out of bed and looked out of the window. The hospital was set in extensive grounds and had a large ornate fountain in front of it. From this fountain there played forth jets of water, rising and falling in delicate sprays. Beyond the fountain there was a road that stretched out across a small parkland—the road along which he had been driven when they brought him there. A road . . . Where did it lead? he wondered. And the curious thought occurred: this was a road to Damascus.

68. At the Drinks Party

TERENCE EVENTUALLY EMERGED from his hot bath.

"I feel much better for that," he said to Berthea. "It's a rather dirty business, motor racing. In fact, I don't think I'll do it again. There's an awful lot of grease, and the *noise*, Berthy! My poor ears were ringing."

"I've just had a telephone call, Terence—"

"Oh yes. Well, I've just had a hot bath, which was jolly refreshing. And now we're going for drinkies, aren't we? Those Jarvis people. What's his name? Rufus. And she's called something too, but I can't remember . . . She's Frances, isn't she?"

"My telephone call, Terence. It seems that Oedipus—"

"I thought I might mix us a martini, Berthy—before we go to those Jarvises. I need Dutch courage to face people like that. He's impossible, Berthy. No spirituality at all. Or none I can discern. I wonder why they even bother to ask us. Unless it's you, of course, Berthy. Remember how you used to get all those invitations to birthday parties, and I just tagged along? And I used to cry because you had all the fun."

"Terence, that was a long time ago; we must move on from childhood."

"Oh, I've moved on, Berthy. You don't need to lecture me about moving on."

"Good. Well, I wanted to tell you about this phone call I had."

"Not now, Berthy. I'm going to mix martinis. Very weak, even if we're going to walk to *Mon Repos* or whatever they call their house. Just a little finger of you-know-what topped up with a splash of the other stuff. You leave it to me, Berthy. We can celebrate my race today."

"But you told me you came last."

"I'm not ashamed of that, Berthy. Never be ashamed of being last. Last can be first, and first can be last."

After their martinis, which, as usual, Terence made far too strong, they walked the half mile to the house of Rufus and Frances Jarvis. Rufus was not an enthusiastic party-giver, but Frances was, and she had decided to throw this party when both Caroline and Ronald came home for the weekend.

"It's no coincidence," she had said to Rufus. "Caroline rings up and announces that she's coming home this weekend. Then, within hours, Ronald phones Peggy Warden and says he's also coming home. That can mean only one thing, in my view."

Rufus looked bored. He was used to his wife's scheming; this was nothing new. "Which is?"

"Which is that they are getting on well. I knew they would. I knew it."

"Oh, well. If they're sharing that flat, then I assume they're getting on well enough. But you can't read much else into it, I would have thought."

"Can't you? Well, I assure you that I can, Rufus. At long last, she's going for the right sort of boy. I'm very pleased, Rufus—very pleased indeed."

CAROLINE ARRIVED ONLY a couple of hours before the guests were due. She helped her mother in the kitchen, where she was preparing plates of canapés, small pieces of brown bread topped with smoked salmon and a large tray of boiled quails' eggs.

"So, here we are, darling," said Frances as she cut a lemon into thin slices. "How nice that Ronald has been able to come down this weekend too. We're so pleased about that."

Caroline said nothing.

"He's such a nice boy," Frances went on.

Caroline, tight-lipped, nodded.

"Not that we're at all interested in interfering, darling. You know that, don't you?"

Caroline tasted a piece of salmon. "Interfering in what?"

"In your private life, dear. You know what I mean."

"Good."

"But at the same time," Frances went on, "I must say that Ronald is exactly the sort of boy we would like to see you with. Just as long as you know. And I think that Peggy feels the same."

Caroline drew in her breath. "You've talked to her about it?"

"Not exactly *talked* about it. Not exactly."

"Then how have you communicated? Semaphore?"

"No need to be rude, darling."

The guests arrived, the Wardens first, bringing Ronald with them. Caroline led him into the kitchen and poured him a drink. When he took it from her, their fingers touched. He smiled at her.

"My mother," whispered Caroline. "She's driving me up the wall."

"Mine too," said Ronald.

Caroline hesitated. "Do you think we've been set up, Ronald?"

He took a sip of his drink. "I was wondering about that too."

Caroline seethed. "What do they want for us—this . . . ?" She turned in the direction of the drawing room, where further guests, including Terence and Berthea, were milling about. "Do they want us to live like this? To be like these people?"

Ronald shrugged. "I suppose all parents want that for their children. They want them to be clones of themselves. Think the same thoughts, like the same things—the whole deal."

Caroline sighed. "It makes me want to run away. Just to get away altogether."

"But we've already got out of it," said Ronald. "We've got as far as London."

"Let's run away together," said Caroline suddenly.

He laughed. "I've got a job. You've got . . . Well, you had a job. And where would we go?"

"Australia? I know some people in Melbourne. We could get one of those short working visas and . . . well, we could just see what happened."

"It's mad."

The idea, which had been so spontaneous and ill thought out, now seemed to her entirely reasonable. "Why not? Anyway,

I suppose we'd better go back in there and be sociable. Have you ever met Mr. Moongrove, by the way? You should meet him. He's a scream. And he's got that sister of his with him. She lives just round the corner from Corduroy Mansions—I bumped into her once in London. I didn't know she was Mr. Moongrove's sister then."

They went into the drawing room, where they became involved in conversation with the guests. Rufus was liberal with his wine, and the party was soon in full swing, the hubbub of conversation growing steadily louder. Caroline, separated from Ronald, who was on the other side of the room engaged in conversation with Rufus, found herself sitting on a sofa next to Berthea.

"That young man," said Berthea, "he's with you?"

Caroline nodded. "We share a flat. And yes, he's my boyfriend. A very new one, but a boyfriend."

Berthea smiled. "How lucky you are. Just to have somebody. And I suppose to have your life ahead of you."

"Do people who have their life ahead of them necessarily feel good about it?" Caroline asked.

Berthea looked at her thoughtfully. "If they think about it— which I suppose many don't. Do you think about it?"

Caroline reflected on her conversation in the kitchen with Ronald. "I've just been talking to Ronald about . . ." She suddenly wanted to confide in Berthea. "We were talking about dropping everything and going to Australia."

Berthea considered this for a moment. Then she said, "Follow your heart. It's the only thing to do." She took a sip of wine. "Do you know, Caroline—I've spent years and years in psychotherapeutic practice. I've helped people endlessly with problems of every complexion. But the only advice that I think should be taken seriously—taken as unconditionally *true*—is this: follow your heart. I know it sounds trite, but it's the only thing to do. Because at the end of the day your heart will stop beating, and it will be too late to regret that you didn't go where it prompted you to go."

Caroline glanced across the room to where Ronald was standing. He caught her eye, and smiled. She knew then what she had to do. She knew.

69. The Yeti on the Line

"La Ragg is going to regret her perfidy," said Rupert Porter to his wife, Gloria. "I would not like to be her—I really wouldn't."

"To think that we trusted her," said Gloria. "I had a sneaking feeling that things were not going to work out, you know. It seemed to be too good to be true that she should suddenly see the justice of your claim on her flat."

Rupert shook his head, as if to show disbelief that anybody could have acted so badly. "I really have no alternative but to force her out of the firm," he said. "But the other directors are so wishy-washy when it comes to these things."

"Spineless," said Gloria.

"Well, they may be that, but they know how many pence make sixpence. If they see Barbara losing clients and her contribution to the overall income of the firm going down, they'll be happier about my suggestion to vote her off the board and out the door."

It was in pursuance of this plan that Rupert had contacted Errol Greatorex, the famed American travel writer and author—in the sense of being an amanuensis—of *The Autobiography of a Yeti*. Rupert had told him that Barbara was having a nervous breakdown and he was taking on a number of her clients.

"She's become quite paranoid, by the way," he explained. "So don't, whatever you do, discuss this with her. Don't tell her what I said—it could drive her over the brink, I'm afraid. And anyway, she's in massive denial—she won't know what you're talking about."

"This is very sad," said Errol Greatorex. "The yeti will be disappointed. He's very loyal, you know, and likes to work with the same people as much as possible."

"Naturally," said Rupert. "I can well understand. It must be difficult when you're . . . when you're a yeti."

"It sure is," said Errol. "But fortunately I have his trust."

"I do hope that I can meet him some day," said Rupert. "Perhaps we could have lunch?"

"Yetis don't do lunch," said Errol.

"Ah."

"It's not that he's antisocial," Errol went on. "He's shy—and that's different from being antisocial. And he does go out for meals occasionally. He doesn't like it, though, when people stare at him. The other day we were in the Savoy Grill and a couple of people started to stare. The yeti became quite anxious. He's sensitive, you see; yetis are very sensitive."

"I see," said Rupert. "May I ask you: Does he speak good English?"

Errol became animated. "Good English? He certainly does. He learned it at that mission school he went to. Correct English—which they still speak in that part of the world, unlike the version that the BBC is pushing these days."

"I suppose that his own language has one hundred and twelve words for the different types of snow?"

"No," said Errol, unimaginatively. "There's only one word—*poradh'bisney*. It covers all sorts of snow."

Once the yeti's affairs had been transferred out of Barbara's care, Rupert set about arranging for other clients of Barbara's to move to him. In each case he told the same story: Barbara was seriously depressed—and they should not talk to her about the matter in any circumstances—and the simplest thing was to switch to his stable of authors. "Poor Barbara," he said to the authors. "She's simply worked too hard on your behalf, and now she's experiencing the consequences for her health. So sad. But please, whatever you do, don't discuss this with her. It could drive her over the edge, and then think how you'd feel."

For Barbara's part, she was at a loss to understand why Errol Greatorex should have suddenly gone off her. She had always worked very hard on his behalf, she felt, and had been responsible for his getting a number of lucrative contracts. Why should he suddenly take against her like this? It was all very puzzling.

She decided to telephone Errol and have it out with him. She made the call on Saturday, at nine-fifteen in the morning, when, in her experience, most people tended to be at home.

The phone rang for some time. Out shopping with the yeti, she thought. Perhaps yetis were early risers, the sun generally hitting the mountain peaks before it arrived in the valleys. But then the phone was picked up.

"Errol?"

Silence.

"It's Barbara Ragg."

She waited for something to be said. Nothing came.

"Errol?"

And then the thought occurred to her: *It was the yeti.*

"Is that you, yeti?" she asked. "Is it you?"

There was a strange sound at the other end—a sound not unlike a sack of loose coal being dragged across corrugated steel. Then a deep voice came down the line.

"Yeti." It was just one word, but it was uttered clearly and unambiguously. The yeti had answered the telephone!

Suddenly Barbara had an idea. "Barbara Ragg here," she said. "I was your agent. There's no need to be afraid of me."

"Yeti not frightened," came the deep voice. "Yeti very brave."

Barbara thought that his English did not sound as impressive as Errol had implied. The yeti might have verbs, of course, but might be leaving them out in order to appear cool. It was certainly fashionable to leave out verbs, along with adjectives, adverbs and all references to literature, art, history or the classics. Perhaps the yeti was just being fashionable.

"Poor yeti," said Barbara. "Many dangers for yeti here in London. Many bad people in London. Eat yetis. Bad people make big stew of poor yeti. Bad, bad."

The yeti gasped. "London not good place. Buses too red. People too fat—maybe from eating poor yetis. Very bad."

"All of that true," said Barbara. "Rupert Porter very bad man. Father of Rupert very greedy—called Fatty Porter for that reason. No coincidence. Very bad men. Grandfather of Rupert went to Nepal many moons ago. Shot a yeti. No reason. Very bad. Rupert same bad as daddy and daddy-daddy."

"Oo! Rupert no say he not like poor yeti. Yeti eat Rupert maybe sometime. Good restaurant in Notting Hill cook Rupert—put on menu for yetis. Yetis very happy."

"Good idea," said Barbara. "Meantime yeti go to dinner with Barbara Ragg. Sign new contract. All settled."

"Dinner with agent very good," said the yeti. "Eat contract if not good, but not eat agent. Not fault of agent—except Rupert. Rupert fault."

"Where yeti want to go for dinner?" asked Barbara.

"Yeti like Italian food," said the yeti.

Barbara mentioned a well-known Italian restaurant not far from her flat. "Yeti come for dinner tonight. Music in restaurant and maybe dancing afterwards. Never know."

"Yeti very pleased," said the yeti.

He thought: It's quite a strain leaving out auxiliary verbs, but that's apparently what she wants; strange people, the English. Very strange.

70. Shadows in the Cave

"It was remarkably easy," said Marcia. "Almost too easy, in fact. The poor woman—I felt rather sorry for her. She opened her mouth to say something and then she just burst into tears. I ended up comforting her. Personally, I blame Iris Murdoch."

She was sitting with William in his flat in Corduroy Mansions telling him about her encounter with Maggie, who, having confessed her love for William, had then peremptorily announced that she was coming down to London to see him—and presumably to take him away with her. Fortunately, Marcia had stepped in.

"Iris Murdoch?" said William. "Why blame her?"

"Well, you told me Maggie was doing a doctoral thesis on Iris Murdoch, didn't you? That means she must be up to here in the goings-on in those novels of hers. And I've read one or two of them, William. I know you think you're my intellectual superior, but I've read more than you might imagine."

William protested. "Of course I don't think I'm your intellectual superior. You're making me sound like some sort of intellectual snob. I'm not, you know."

She looked at him fondly. He was not a snob—of any sort; he was a good and kind man. "I'm sorry, William. I didn't mean it that way. It's just that sometimes you dismiss the things I say rather too readily. I think that you don't give me credit for . . . well, for knowing a thing or two."

Suddenly he felt intensely warm towards her. She was right: she did know a thing or two—she knew much more than he did, he suspected.

"And I have read my Iris Murdoch," Marcia continued. "I've read *Under the Net* and *The Red and the Green* and *The Philosopher's Pupil*. So I do know."

"All right," said William. "I can't remember her novels—they all merge into one for me—one big circle of rather clever people dealing with personal torment, that's what the books are to me."

"Well, that's why I think they've rather turned her head. There are so many affairs in Murdoch's novels, and I think Maggie failed to make a sharp distinction between the real world and the world of those characters. So you became one of the characters in her mind and she fell in love with you and then wondered what would a woman in an Iris Murdoch novel do in such circumstances. Answer—go to London, which is what she did."

"And you waylaid her as she was coming here?"

"Yes. I waited outside in my little van, and when I saw a woman going up to the downstairs door, I leaped out and said, 'You must be Maggie.' She was a bit surprised, but I managed to persuade her to join me for a cup of tea at Daylesford's, and that's where I told her."

William looked out of the window. He was not enjoying this.

"I told her that I understood how she might feel about you, but it's simply too late. And then I showed her my left hand and made a very obvious gesture. She saw the ring, and that's when she put two and two together and started to cry."

"I hate hearing this," said William. "I hate to think of people crying."

"I know you do," said Marcia. "But it worked out in the end. She pulled herself together and seemed just to go on to the next thing. She muttered something about having to go to the London Library, and then wiped the mascara off her cheeks and went away."

William sighed. "I wish she hadn't gone and fallen in love with me. I really wish that."

Marcia said, "I understand."

He thought: Understand *what*? Did she understand how people in general might fall in love, or how Maggie in particular might have fallen in love with him? He was about to ask her when the bell rang. He rose and went to answer the door.

A hurricane of energy entered the room. Freddie de la Hay, released from his leash by Basil Wickramsinghe, leaped across the threshold and threw himself at William. William gave a shout and went down on his knees, hugging Freddie de la Hay to him, receiving ample licks to brow, wrists, hands, chin.

Basil Wickramsinghe hung his head modestly as thanks were heaped upon him. "If it hadn't been for Basil," William said to Marcia, "I would never have got Freddie back."

"Oh, surely not," said Basil. "It would have worked out, I think."

Marcia smiled. "I think we should have a celebratory dinner," she said. "What have you got in the house?"

William spoke between Freddie's excited howls, "Some pasta. I believe there's a bit of chicken. Mushrooms."

"Ideal," she said.

"Five loaves and five fishes would be enough," said Basil.

William and Basil stayed in the sitting room while Marcia began to cook the dinner. "She won't let me in the kitchen when she's working," explained William. "She's a professional cook, you see, and they don't like amateurs cluttering the place up."

"She's a very fine woman," said Basil, who knew Marcia slightly and had always rather admired her. "And I couldn't help but notice that she's wearing a ring." He indicated his third finger discreetly.

Marcia, in the kitchen, heard what was being said, such were the acoustic properties of the flat. She paused in her labours, standing quite still. In the glass of the oven door she could make out the reflections of the two men sitting in the living room, across the corridor. She watched, as the prisoners in Plato's cave fixed their eyes on the moving shadows of the real world outside.

"Yes," said William. "An engagement ring."

There was brief silence. Then Basil Wickramsinghe said, "You're a lucky man, William. You really are."

William said, "Yes, I think I am."

Marcia leaned forwards and closed her eyes, such was her joy. Then she composed herself and continued to work on the meal as if nothing had happened, though she knew in her heart that everything had.

THE CORDUROY MANSIONS SERIES

> "A new cast of characters to love."
> —*Entertainment Weekly*

CORDUROY MANSIONS

In London's hip Pimlico neighborhood, Corduroy Mansions, a block of crumbling brickwork and dormer windows is home to a delightfully eccentric cast of residents including, but not limited to: a wine merchant who desperately hopes his son will move out; a boutique caterer who has designs on the oenophile down the hall; a snarky member of Parliament; and Freddie de la Hay, a vegetarian Pimlico terrier.

Volume 1

THE DOG WHO CAME IN FROM THE COLD

Freddie de la Hay has been recruited by MI6 to infiltrate a Russian spy ring. A pair of New Age operators wants to use Terence Moongrove's estate as a center for cosmological studies. Literary agent Barbara Ragg represents a man who hangs out with the Abominable Snowman, and the rest of the denizens of the housing block have issues of their own.

Volume 2

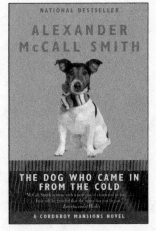

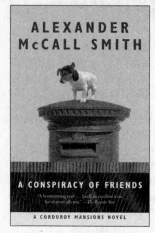

A CONSPIRACY OF FRIENDS

There's never a dull moment for the residents of Corduroy Mansions: Berthea Snark is still at work on her scathing biography of her own son; literary agents Rupert Porter and Barbara Ragg are still battling each other; fine-arts graduate Caroline Jarvis is busy blurring the line between friendship and romance; and William French is still worrying that his son, Eddie, may never leave home. But uppermost on everyone's mind is Freddie de la Hay— William's faithful terrier (and without a doubt the only dog clever enough to have been recruited by MI6)—who has disappeared while on a mystery tour around the Suffolk countryside.

Volume 3

THE NO. 1 LADIES' DETECTIVE AGENCY SERIES

Read them all....
"There is no end to the pleasure."
—*The New York Times Book Review*

The No. 1 Ladies' Detective Agency—Volume 1

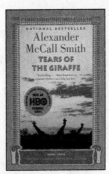

Tears of the Giraffe—Volume 2

Morality for Beautiful Girls—Volume 3

The Kalahari Typing School for Men—Volume 4

The Full Cupboard of Life—Volume 5

In the Company of Cheerful Ladies —Volume 6

Blue Shoes and Happiness —Volume 7

The Good Husband of Zebra Drive —Volume 8

The Miracle at Speedy Motors —Volume 9

Tea Time for the Traditionally Built —Volume 10

The Double Comfort Safari Club —Volume 11

The Saturday Big Tent Wedding Party —Volume 12

The Limpopo Academy of Private Detection —Volume 13

THE GREAT CAKE MYSTERY

"A detective is born! Lucky young readers will now be able to make the acquaintance of the one and only Precious—Alexander McCall Smith's beguiling and intrepid Botswanian sleuth, as she takes on her very first case."
—Mary Pope Osborne, bestselling author of *The Magic Tree House* series

THE MYSTERY OF MEERKAT HILL

Precious has a new mystery to solve! When her friend's family's most valuable cow vanishes, Precious must devise a plan to find the missing animal. But she needs the help of the family's pet meerkat to solve the case. Will she succeed and what obstacles will she face on her path?

Illustration © Iain McIntosh

THE ISABEL DALHOUSIE NOVELS

"The literary equivalent of herbal tea and a cozy fire. . . .
McCall Smith's Scotland [is] well worth future visits."
—*The New York Times*

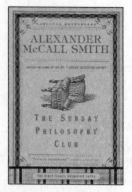

The Sunday Philosophy Club

Isabel Dalhousie is fond of problems, and sometimes she becomes interested in problems that are, quite frankly, none of her business—including some that are best left to the police. Filled with endearingly thorny characters and a Scottish atmosphere as thick as a highland mist, *The Sunday Philosophy Club* is an irresistible pleasure.

Volume 1

Friends, Lovers, Chocolate

While taking care of her niece Cat's deli, Isabel meets a heart transplant patient who has had some strange experiences in the wake of his surgery. Against the advice of her housekeeper, Isabel is intent on investigating. Matters are further complicated when Cat returns from vacation with a new boyfriend, and Isabel's fondness for him lands her in another muddle.

Volume 2

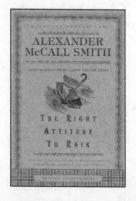

The Right Attitude to Rain

When Isabel's cousin from Dallas arrives in Edinburgh, she introduces Isabel to a bigwig Texan whose young fiancée may just be after his money. Then there's her niece, Cat, who's busy falling for a man whom Isabel suspects of being an incorrigible mama's boy. Isabel is advised to stay out of it all, but the philosophical issues of these matters of the heart prove too tempting for her to resist.

Volume 3

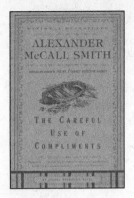

The Careful Use of Compliments

There's a new little Dalhousie on the scene, and while the arrival of Isabel's son presents her with the myriad wonders of life, it doesn't diminish her curiosity about other things. While attending an art auction, she discovers a mystery revealed in one of the paintings, launching her into yet another intriguing investigation.

Volume 4

The Comforts of a Muddy Saturday

A doctor's career has been ruined by allegations of medical fraud and Isabel cannot ignore what may be a miscarriage of justice. Meanwhile, there is her baby, Charlie, who needs looking after; her niece, Cat, who needs someone to mind her deli; and a mysterious composer who has latched on to Jamie, making Isabel decidedly uncomfortable.

Volume 5

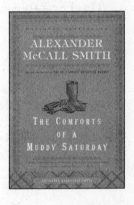

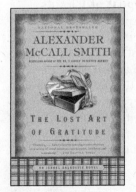

The Lost Art of Gratitude

When Minty Auchterlonie takes Isabel into her confidence about the complicated troubles at the investment bank she heads, Isabel finds herself going another round: Is Minty to be trusted? Or is she the perpetrator of an enormous financial fraud? As always, Isabel makes her way toward the heart of the problem.

Volume 6

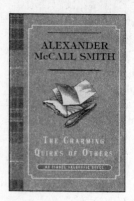

The Charming Quirks of Others

Old friends of Isabel's ask for her help in a rather tricky situation: A successor is being sought for the headmaster position at their alma mater and an anonymous letter has alleged that one of the candidates has a very serious skeleton in their closet. Could Isabel discreetly look into it?

Volume 7

The Forgotten Affairs of Youth

A visiting Australian philosopher asks Isabel's help to find her biological father. As usual, Isabel cannot help but oblige, even though she has concerns of her own. Her young son Charlie is now walking and talking, and her housekeeper Grace regularly attends a spiritualist who has taken to providing interesting advice. And could it finally be time for Jamie and Isabel to get married?

Volume 8

The Uncommon Appeal of Clouds

Isabel answers an unexpected appeal from a wealthy Scottish collector, Duncan Munrowe, who has been robbed of a valuable painting. Never one to refuse an appeal, she agrees, and discovers that the thieves may be closer to the owner than he ever would have expected. Isabel also copes with life's issues, large and small, and finds herself tested as a parent, a philosopher, and a friend.

Volume 9

THE 44 SCOTLAND STREET SERIES

**"Will make you feel as though you live in Edinburgh. . . .
Long live the folks on Scotland Street."**
—*The Times-Picayune* (New Orleans)

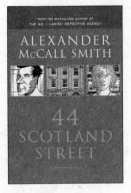

44 SCOTLAND STREET

All of Alexander McCall Smith's trademark
warmth and wit come into play in this novel
chronicling the lives of the residents of a
converted Georgian town house in Edinburgh.
Complete with colorful characters, love
triangles, and even a mysterious art caper,
this is an unforgettable portrait of Edinburgh
society.

Volume 1

ESPRESSO TALES

The eccentric residents of 44 Scotland Street
are back. From the talented six-year-old Bertie,
who is forced to arrive in pink overalls for his
first day of class, to the self-absorbed Bruce,
who contemplates a change of career in
between admiring glances in the mirror, there
is much in store as fall settles on Edinburgh.

Volume 2

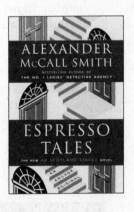

LOVE OVER SCOTLAND

From conducting perilous anthropological
studies of pirate households to being inadvertently left behind on a school trip to Paris, the
wonderful misadventures of the residents of
44 Scotland Street will charm and delight.

Volume 3

THE WORLD ACCORDING TO BERTIE

Pat is forced to deal with the reappearance of Bruce, which has her heart skipping—and not in the most pleasant way. Angus Lordie's dog, Cyril, has been taken away by the authorities, accused of being a serial biter, and Bertie, the beleaguered Italian-speaking prodigy and saxophonist, now has a little brother, Ulysses, who he hopes will distract his mother, Irene.

Volume 4

THE UNBEARABLE LIGHTNESS OF SCONES

The Unbearable Lightness of Scones finds Bertie still troubled by his rather overbearing mother, Irene, but seeking his escape in the cub scouts. Matthew is rising to the challenge of married life, while Domenica epitomizes the loneliness of the long-distance intellectual, and Cyril succumbs to the kind of romantic temptation that no dog can resist, creating a small problem, or rather six of them, for his friend and owner, Angus Lordie.

Volume 5

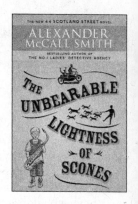

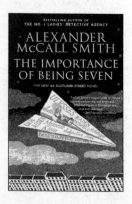

THE IMPORTANCE OF BEING SEVEN

Bertie is—finally!—about to turn seven. But one afternoon he mislays his meddling mother, Irene, and learns a valuable lesson. Angus and Domenica contemplate whether to give in to romance on holiday in Italy, and even usually down-to-earth Big Lou is overheard discussing cosmetic surgery.

Volume 6

THE PORTUGUESE IRREGULAR VERBS SERIES

"A deftly rendered trilogy . . . [with] endearingly eccentric characters."
—*Chicago Sun-Times*

Welcome to the insane and rarified world of Professor Dr Moritz-Maria von Igelfeld of the Institute of Romance Philology. Von Igelfeld is engaged in a never-ending quest to win the respect he feels certain he is due—a quest that has a way of going hilariously astray.

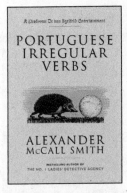

Portuguese Irregular Verbs

The Finer Points of Sausage Dogs

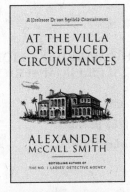

At the Villa of Reduced Circumstances

Unusual Uses for Olive Oil

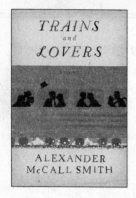

TRAINS AND LOVERS

A wonderful new novel that explores the nature of love—and trains—through a series of intertwined romantic tales told by four strangers who meet as they travel by rail from Edinburgh to London.

LA'S ORCHESTRA SAVES THE WORLD

A heartwarming novel about the life-affirming powers of music and companionship during a time of war.

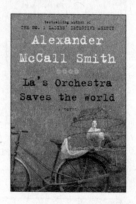

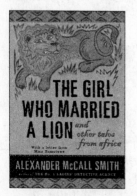

THE GIRL WHO MARRIED A LION AND OTHER TALES FROM AFRICA

"These are pithy, engaging tales, as habit-forming as peanuts."
—*Publishers Weekly*